RECKL

The stairway was poorly lit. The expression in her large eyes was unfathomable. I put my hands on her shoulders and kissed her again. There was a small wordless exclamation deep in her throat. A soft little tongue darted forward to meet my own.

My fingers unbuttoned the silk blouse, plunged inside the constriction of a bust bodice, touched smooth skin. The breasts fitted neatly into the palm of my hand, the nipples were large and very hard. I rolled them between forefinger and thumb.

A slight tremor passed through her body and suddenly her hands were at my waist, unbuckling my belt . . .

Also available from Headline Delta:

Amorous Liaisons
Lustful Liaisons
A Man With Three Maids
Venus In Paris
A Lady Of Quality
The Love Pagoda
The Education Of A Maiden
Maid's Night In
Lena's Story
The Lusts Of The Borgias
States Of Ecstasy
Wanton Pleasures
The Secret Diary Of Mata Hari
Sweet Sins
The Carefree Courtesan
Sweet Sensations
Hidden Rapture
Cremorne Gardens
The Temptations Of Cremorne
The Pleasures Of Women
The Secrets Of Women
The Delights Of Women
Love Italian Style
Ecstasy Italian Style
Eroticon Dreams
Eroticon Desires
Pathways Of Pleasure
A Slave To Love
The Girls' Boarding School

Reckless Liaisons

Anonymous

HEADLINE DELTA

Copyright © 1994 Meyrick Johnston

The right of Meyrick Johnston to be identified as the Author of
the Work has been asserted by him in accordance with the
Copyright, Designs and Patents Act 1988.

First published in 1994
by HEADLINE BOOK PUBLISHING

A HEADLINE DELTA paperback

10 9 8 7 6 5 4 3 2 1

All rights reserved. No part of this publication may be
reproduced, stored in a retrieval system, or transmitted,
in any form or by any means without the prior written
permission of the publisher, nor be otherwise circulated
in any form of binding or cover other than that in which
it is published and without a similar condition being
imposed on the subsequent purchaser.

All characters in this publication are fictitious
and any resemblance to real persons, living or dead,
is purely coincidental.

ISBN   0 7472 4246 1

Typeset by Avon Dataset Ltd, Bidford-on-Avon

Printed and bound in Great Britain by
HarperCollins Manufacturing, Glasgow

HEADLINE BOOK PUBLISHING
A division of Hodder Headline PLC
Headline House
79 Great Titchfield Street
London W1P 7FN

Reckless Liaisons

PART ONE

Paris, August 1922

Paul

Chapter One

There are people who count sheep when they cannot sleep: they visualise a flock leaping over a gate and mentally tick off each one as it lands. One, two, three, four . . . seventeen, eighteen, nineteen . . . thirty-three, thirty-four . . . and so on until they drift away.

Personally, I prefer to count women: I keep a tally of the ones I've been to bed with; and they're not jumping over a gate either.

Evelyn, Margot, Françoise, Claude . . . fat Frieda, Tamara, Heather with the limp . . . Christine, Monika — *Ah, Monika! Now there was a girl! Big, firm breasts and billowy hips, with a mouth that would make a blind man* . . . Never mind. Monika, Georgette, Fifi, Anne . . . Margery, Grace and — *what* was the name of that Viennese waitress at the Dome?

The supply of imaginary sheep of course is inexhaustible, but the number of real ladies who have — shall we say? — granted me their favours is limited. I run out of candidates after forty. Well, forty-one if you count Laurence. That's not a bad score for my age, I suppose — I was thirty-three last birthday — but if I'm still awake when I come to the end of the line, then I have to subdivide, as it were, and start again on a different tack.

Of the Famous Forty-One, which had splendid, I

mean really perfect, breasts? Evelyn and Margot are non-starters here. Françoise, certainly (a girl who could keep your hands full). Claude's had dropped. Frieda was too much of a good thing. Tamara and Christine would both qualify. And Heather's limp never affected the superb balance of her upperworks. Which brings us back to Monika. *Firm, resilient, a gorgeous shape — those twin peaks, so erotically out-thrust, still jutted upwards with formidable effect even when she was lying flat on her back. Which she usually was.*

And if I'm *still* awake after the breasts? Which of them has the flattest belly? Which the most slender legs?

The trouble is that by the time I get to the legs I'm likely to be wide awake again and wishing one of those girls was here in bed with me now . . .

Back to Monika then. Why ever did I let her go? Well, to be honest it was she who let *me* go: she found a type with a Hispano-Suiza . . . *Wait a minute! It's just come back to me: the waitress's name was Gloria. Gloria Sackhol* . . . But if Monika's no more than a memory, that memory is stronger than half the real things happening to me in real life today. Perhaps I'm growing old too young.

I met her at a fashion show at the House of Worth. That's not surprising in itself: I'm in the fashion business; I illustrate the creations of the top designers for the classier magazines. What was surprising was to find *her* there. For Monika didn't give a hoot for clothes: she only came into her own when she was *un*dressed; a fashion show was the last thing likely to interest her. But the girl was full of paradoxes. She was an intellectual, you see — and the sexiest, free-love, kicker-over-of-the-traces to hit Paris since the notorious *Grandes Cocottes* held court at Maxim's in the Belle Epoque. The contrast was even echoed in her appearance. That voluptuous, hourglass body with its tiny waist was surmounted by a small head with aquiline features, a chiselled mouth and man-short dark hair severely cut in what was known as an Eton crop. If the body matched the bed in which she spent so much of her time, the head went with the Sorbonne where she was preparing her Doctorate in Philosophy – and each of those elements underlined in an extraordinarily sensuous way its total opposition to the other.

My paradoxical paramour! In Shakespeare's time, I suppose I could have called her my Para-Doxy . . .

Long gone now, but my goodness – like Percy Bysshe Shelley's music when soft voices die – how the lady vibrates in my memory!

Sometimes, waking at night, I still imagine I can feel the warmth of her hot body beside me; sometimes I am haunted by the musky, almost feral smell of her flesh, that personal perfume overlaid and under-scored so discreetly with the application of Mme. Coco Chanel's latest numbered scent.

Indeed, so strong is the impact of emotional recall, I can fancy it surrounding me as I lie awake now.

Wait.

It was Chanel, always Chanel, never anything but Chanel with Monika. We used to joke about it.

What my imagination feeds to me now is a Worth perfume. The latest, only launched this month. Has the machinery of my recollection gone awry?

I take a deep breath. The scent is stronger than ever.

The machinery has not even been engaged — and, no, I am not dreaming. *The Worth perfume is real. And the musk. And the heat . . . especially that of the fingers laid across the inside of my thigh.*

A woman, a flesh and blood female person, is sharing my bed!

Perhaps, after all, I had dropped off to sleep. But even so! I struggle to sit up, throwing aside the covers. 'What the devil . . . ?'

The fingers tighten imperceptibly. I am sleeping without pyjamas, and I feel hot breath on my arm. A moist lip brushes my wrist.

'I didn't want to risk startling you,' a soft, quite deep but undeniably female voice murmurs, 'but, goodness, I thought you were *never* going to wake up!'

Chapter Two

I sat up straight, turned away from my mysterious companion, and reached across to switch on the bedside lamp. Fingers, surprisingly muscular now, gripped my shoulder, urging me back into the centre of the bed. 'No,' the voice murmured. 'Not now. Not yet. Please.'

I lay obediently back among the pillows. What the hell — in a situation like this it cost me nothing to play along. 'When, then?' I asked.

'Afterwards.'

'After what?'

I heard a melodious chuckle. The fingers were transferred back to my thigh. 'Guess.'

By this time the mind was racing a bit. I didn't recognise the voice; I had never knowingly slept with anyone using that particular Worth perfume; for the moment I had nothing else to go on. So . . . here is this complete stranger who has crawled into my bed while I slept. Why? And why doesn't she want the light on?

Because she is impossibly ugly? Disfigured? A harelip? Because she is old or fat? Because maybe I do know her, *by sight* — and she is somebody else's wife? Someone important, someone important to me?

If the chuckle implied what I thought it implied, the first question would be the easier to answer. Then, once my own hands were engaged, perhaps they would give me a clue to the second. I shifted my body slightly towards her – and was at once aware of the heat distilled from her flesh. My hip touched a thigh; my calf grazed the tapered smoothness of a leg. The lady was as naked as I was.

The mattress was depressed . . . and suddenly an abstraction was transformed into reality as the whole nubile length of a female body assembled itself against my own. The soft weight of a belly was slung against my hip now; a breast teased my upper arm; an ankle hooked over my ankle and our two thighs were plastered together. The fingers slid higher up the inside of my leg.

I could feel myself hardening and lengthening. This was no time for conversation: the questions and answers could wait. I turned towards her, brought my hand up under the covers, and laid it on her body. Hot breath quickened suddenly against the skin of my shoulder.

I was touching the girl's waist – and clearly she *was* just a girl: the flesh was smoothly sculpted, the muscles taut; there was no sign of flabbiness or sag. I moved the hand further up, across a tightly-knit rib cage, and found a breast. This would be the moment of truth.

The breast was full, resilient, shifting only slightly under the pressure of my hand, the nipple hard and hot against my palm.

With a sudden small gasp she trailed her fingers across the upper reaches of my thigh and then wrapped them around my aching hardness. The fingers, tightening, caressing, sliding with dream-like ease up and down the shaft, were cool against the heat of my immediate desire for her. And that was something I remembered so clearly later: despite the heat emanating from her own body, the flesh itself remained cool, almost moist even, when she pulled me over and we lay pressed together from mouth to toe.

I felt the mounds of those breasts move beneath my chest as she wrapped her arms around my back and strained me closer still. Nails dug into me when I wedged a knee between her thighs. She was breathing now in short, hoarse gasps. I lowered my head, closing my lips on her half-open mouth.

The response was as immediate — and as electric — as the switching on of that bedside lamp I had been forbidden to use. The girl's tongue, scalding hot, wet and trembling, darted forward to meet my own. The two tongues wrestled together in the moist cavern of our sucking mouths, sending ripples of desire coursing through our two bodies. Her hips thrust up ferociously off the bed. The thigh clenched between my own legs ground hard against the rigidity of my stiffened cock.

My hands had delved beneath the supple body clamped to mine, clutching the twin globes of the girl's taut little bottom, drawing her closer, closer as our bellies slid lasciviously one over the other. Now, while the tension flaming within me threatened to become unbearable, I shifted one hand, jamming it between us so that the questing fingers could search for that female fortress my soldier was so anxious to storm. I had got as far as the springy thicket of hair shielding her loins when she suddenly released my back, reached up to her head and plucked with both hands. She shook her head forcefully.

For some reason I had assumed that my invisible

partner would have a helmet of the fashionably short hair that went with the tight cloche hat every woman seemed to be wearing. In fact, the hair had been pinned up, and now that it was unpinned it cascaded down as far as her shoulders, strengthening even more my desire to see this fascinating creature. But at that moment vision was the least important of the five senses: other desires, more urgent, clamoured for my attention.

With a small, almost animal cry, the girl raised her head from the pillows, searching for my mouth, demanding my lips and tongue once more.

The hard mound at the base of her belly ground hard against my own hardness. She parted her thighs, sliding one hand between our bodies to grasp for the second time the pulsating proof of my need. As those salacious fingers wrapped tightly around my shaft, I homed in finally on my target, fingertips smoothing through dry hair and then damp hair to the sweet wet folds of flesh flowering open to greet me. I prised apart the folds, caressing the satined skin inside. I heard a sharp hiss of indrawn breath. The girl opened her legs wider still, drawing up her knees. I eased myself across, lowering myself between them.

The grip constricting my shaft tightened, pulling, coaxing. I could feel knuckles, a wrist, a forearm moving against the heated skin of my belly. I flexed my hips. The girl arched up her loins. I held my breath, sensing the supersensitive head of my rigid wand slide through her wet hair, nudge heated flesh, stir aside the soft moist folds . . . and then abruptly plunge into the hot, hot clasp of her love canal, my whole stiff quivering length swallowed by the dark throat within those secret lips.

I released my breath with a groan of satisfaction, bunching the muscles of my behind, driving in deeper still, penetrating to the hilt. 'Oh, yes,' the girl whispered in my ear. 'Oh, yes; oh, *yes*! That's so good, so tight!'

I withdrew a little way and drove in again, the web of nerves sheathing my staff tingling with an almost unbearable satisfaction. And once more she arched up to meet me.

Slowly at first, and then with increasing rapidity, we established a reciprocating rhythm that was almost dream-like in its advance-and-retreat, insert-and-withdraw, in-and-out perfection. As the tempo accelerated and the wordless breathy cries from our two mouths coalesced in a single groaning ecstasy inevitable as the thudding of our hips, the girl began rolling from side to side under me. Her head thrashed wildly on the pillows. Her nails raked my back again. She scissored her legs over my hips and drummed imperative heels on the base of my spine to urge me even deeper within her heaving belly.

I lost all sense of time; we were an oiled machine, perfectly designed, working perfectly – the alchemists' concept of perpetual motion realised at last.

I had no idea how long it was before the exquisite tension within me began gathering to a point where the need was so agonizing that it imposed an involuntary hesitation in this perfect rhythm. Sweat was running in the hollow of my back and dribbling down my ribs to mingle with the moisture dewing the girl's skin where our bellies sucked and slapped. My thrusts, as strong as ever, nevertheless became sporadic. Throughout my body, it seemed, the nerves had disbanded to reassemble in the quivering depths of my loins. My cock felt ready to explode.

Happily, my companion found herself at the same time rising swiftly, inexorably, to her own release. A profound shuddering stirred her innermost depths. The movement intensified. While I continued to plunge, the ridged muscles clasping me contracted, the legs locked behind my back clamped fiercely over my waist, the whole pelvis beneath me convulsed and the girl mewed out her climax in a series of long keening cries.

That was enough to send me over the top. The tidal wave of heightened tension, of unbearable excitement on which for some time I had precariously been surfing, reared suddenly up, speeding me with it. The tip of the wave curled over . . .

And broke with the fury of all the world's thunderstorms about my ears as I spurted the proof of my delight deep into the unknown darkness below me.

My mind is again blank on the matter of how long it took me to come back to earth. All I know is that it was still dark, that the body beneath me, now totally relaxed with satiated desire, was nevertheless still pliant and trim, that the hot breath jetting into my ear had slowed to a deep and even pulse . . . and that I was possessed with an irresistable compulsion to see the mouth through which that breath was escaping, the owner of the body which had given me such joy.

Carefully, I eased myself away from her and rolled to the far side of the bed. This time she made no attempt to restrain me. I groped for the cord, found the switch, and flooded the room with light.

She was lying on her back, hands linked behind her head, gazing at me through slitted green eyes. She was beautiful.

The hair was red, a burnished red, halfway to chestnut. In that first bemused glance, I took in a wide mouth curved into a quizzical smile, a determined chin above superb breasts whose milk-white slopes still bore the rosy marks made by my exploring hands, a taut little belly sweeping down into slender legs. And the tawny bush, dark now with dampness, between those legs. I judged her age to be between twenty and twenty-two.

I had never seen this young woman before in my life.

I cleared my throat. 'Perhaps I should introduce myself?' I said inanely. 'My name is—'

'I know who you are, silly,' she interrupted, the voice still soft and mellifluous. 'Your name is Paul Mackenzie; your father makes motor cars in England; you lost your wife tragically in a Zeppelin raid during the Great War. You used to work as a designer in the old man's art department, but now you're a fashion artist illustrating the Paris collections for chic magazines. At the moment you are said to be working on the novelties to be revealed at Mado Laverne's show next month.'

I laughed. 'Well, I cannot fault you on that!' I said. 'But you have me at a disadvantage. I *don't* know who you are. Or why – I mean this was utterly, utterly delightful – but why should you secrete yourself in my apartment, smuggle your totally gorgeous body into my bed, and . . . and . . . well, why?'

'Maybe I like tall, lean men with dark hair, blue eyes and sharp, definite features,' she smiled.

'That's nice. I am flattered. But you haven't answered my question. Any of my questions.'

'I'll answer one,' she said. 'You can call me Rosette.'

'Is that your name?'

'It's what you can call me.'

I decided not to pursue that one. 'It will be a pleasure,' I said truthfully. 'A pleasure to be increased if you would give me just a *hint* . . .' I allowed the sentence to die a natural death.

Rosette sighed. She pushed herself upright against the pillows and folded her hands in her lap. 'Men are so *inquisitive*!' she complained. 'If you must know, there's a favour I might want to ask, something I could ask you to do for me. And I felt that you might be . . . well, more inclined to grant favours if you . . . knew me. I mean why should a perfect stranger—'

I laughed again, interrupting her. 'Perfect is right,' I said. 'Very well: let's have it. What can I do for you, Rosette?'

This time she ignored the question completely. 'I was so sorry to hear about your wife,' she said, unexpectedly. 'What a terrible thing.'

'It was seven years ago,' I said. 'I try not to think about it.'

'I know you never married again, but with what you have,' she slid a sudden roguish glance at my loins, 'I bet there have been plenty of girls happy to jump into your arms.'

I shrugged. She wasn't expecting a reply.

'How many lovers have you had?' she pursued, looking at me out of the corner of her eye. 'Do you *know* how many girls you've been to bed with?'

God knows why I should have answered her. Because I'd been counting them earlier that night, perhaps? Maybe in pique because she wouldn't give a direct answer to any of *my* questions? At any rate I looked her straight in the eye and said: 'Actually, yes. The number is forty. Forty-one if you count Laurence.'

Rosette leaned across to lay a finger against my lips. 'Forty-two,' she murmured.

Chapter Three

My studio was on the top floor of a tall seventeenth century building which leaned against a pre-war red brick apartment block off the Avenue de Versailles. Through its floor-to-ceiling windows you could look across an air-shaft and over a typically Parisian roofscape of mansards and chimney stacks to a curve of the river and the Eiffel Tower on the far side. Southwards, beyond the two-tier bridge carrying the blue and cream coaches of the Métro over the Seine, were the bleak workshops where André Citroën assembled his motor cars.

I loved the view. A hundred windows pierced dozens of crazy façades between me and the waterfront *quais*; beyond wrought-iron balconies and stone balustrades and geraniums in window-sill pots, the whole secret life of the city teemed on the other side of those grimy panes. On winter nights when the slates were shiny with rain, I could watch innumerable comedies and dramas played out in dumb-show between half-drawn curtains in the flaring gaslight. In summertime, with the shutters thrown back, the walls tiger-striped with sunlight and shadow and the windows flung wide, the sound of an accordion, a caged bird singing or the lilt of a woman's laugh rose sometimes above the rumble of riverside traffic. Of the forty ladies who had shared my bed (forty-one if you count Laurence), more than one had been netted after a casual exchange across the air-shaft or through sign language exchanged with the occupant of a distant balcony.

The room I slept in, along with a tiny morning-room, a kitchen alcove and the tub, was on the other side of the house, at the top of a rickety staircase spiralling up from the tiled lobby and a concierge's office. The windows here, starting modestly at chest height, looked out on the severe stone faces, blinkered with hooped blinds, of a row of town houses typifying the snob 16th *Arrondissement*.

By the time I had discovered the little Rosette was prepared to tell me, I could see through the half open door to the studio that the eastern sky was beginning to pale. Were we going back to bed? Was she the sort of girl who demanded coffee at six o'clock? Would she tell me now what 'favour' she wanted, or would she simply walk away and come back to me another day? The only way to find out was to ask.

I grinned. '*Chérie*,' I said, 'I'm not too sure of the next move, to be frank; I mean like there's no actual precedent for this situation. Would you—'

'No precedent?' she interrupted. 'What are you talking about? Wasn't I *preceded* by those forty girls you're so proud of?'

'Forty-one, if you—'

'I know, I know,' she cried angrily. 'Forty-one if I count this Laurence. Who *is* the wretched woman? Or was that the name of your wife?'

'Laurence is a was, rather than an is,' I said.

'Laurence was a very beautiful blonde — only it turned out that she was no lady.'

'You mean she was a prostitute, a whore?'

I shook my head. 'I mean she turned out to be a he.'

Rosette giggled. 'Oh, how gorgeous! How long did she — he — stay?'

'Long enough for me to open the door and indicate the stairway,' I said.

'And how was it that Laurence came to be here in the first place?'

'I asked her, of course.'

'You had no idea? It hadn't even crossed your mind that . . . that—'

'That I was inviting a transvestite home? No, none. Not until . . .'

'Not until the clothes came off? How gorgeous,' Rosette said, for the second time. 'What did you do: pick her straight off the street?'

'Certainly not. I'm not in the habit . . . well, actually, it's not a story that reflects too well on me,' I said uncomfortably.

'Good. Then you must tell it to me at once.' Rosette rearranged herself on the bed, punching the pillows into position. She sat cross-legged with her arms folded, the two breasts with their darkened nipples compressed between them. Seven floors below, the clip-clop of horses' hooves and the rattle of wheels on the *pavé* announced that the city's drays and delivery carts had started their early morning rounds.

I said: 'It was all pretty juvenile really. Laurence was sitting at a bar in a nightclub called the Black Cat, in the sleazier part of Montmartre. I was a little tipsy and I had this stupid row with a girlfriend of mine called Monika. She was a stunner but she had an appetite that was too big for any one chap to satisfy. I'd no right to tell her what to do with her life. Her latest lover was rich, though. I suppose it was that that made it worse. Anyway, they came into the Black Cat while I was there and we had this blazing row . . .'

'And you flung into a jealous all-right-I'll-show-you act,' Rosette supplied, 'and the most gorgeous person you could see was this blonde at the bar, so you picked her up and made it obvious that you were taking her home with you. Yah! Sucks to you, Monika! Is that the way it was?'

I nodded. 'Exactly. I wasn't really even *aware* of Laurence as a person at all, I was in such a rage. Otherwise, surely, I'd have noticed . . . well, something. But Laurence was just a stick to beat Monika with.' I laughed and shook my head. 'As if she cared!'

'Do you still see her? Monika, I mean?'

I shook my head again. 'It was two or three years ago, when I first came to Paris. Not long after the war.'

'You know,' Rosette said, 'the person I feel sorry for *is* Laurence. If she wasn't a professional . . . well, I mean it was probably just someone hoping to find somebody else who'd be loving and comfy for the night. And she gets chucked out before she even has her clothes off!'

'He'd taken off enough,' I said.

'Well, of course. Otherwise you wouldn't . . . But I still think the poor thing was badly treated.'

'Yes,' I said.

Rosette was staring at me, the half-smile animating

seized the two halves of her bottom, hauling her against me, fingers suddenly wet when I parted her legs with a knee.

There was traffic on the boulevard below: a grinding of gears and rasp of motor exhausts over the hoofbeats and the rumble of wheels. We didn't hear them. The hoarse panting of our quickened breaths was suddenly loud in the empty room.

When I dipped my fingers for the second time into the hot, sliding folds of moist flesh furrowed between her thighs, Rosette cried aloud. My own gasp of ecstasy followed as she drew up her knees, manoeuvred me between them, and engulfed my throbbing pride in the clasp of her body.

The rhythm we established, dream-like, inevitable, never-ending, seemed no more than a continuation, a prolongation − a projection, even − of that first timeless coupling. We schooled it, we nursed it, we husbanded it until at last we scaled together those peaks from whose summits the world takes on a newer, more marvellous meaning. And when it was over and the shaking of the blood had quietened a little, we lay for a long time wrapped together while the sounds of the city gathered and grew around us. Finally − a tug was hooting on the river − the smell of fresh baking drifting up from below reminded me that I was ravenously hungry. I got up, lit the gas, and put coffee on to percolate. When it was bubbling darkly below the glass dome, I dragged on a shirt and a pair of slacks and hurried barefoot to the corner shop to buy half a dozen croissants.

It was already quite hot. The Avenue de Versailles

her face once more, the green eyes glinting. I saw that the flesh above the slopes of her breasts was lightly freckled. 'Are you going to open the door, indicate the stairway, and chuck *me* out?' she asked.

'You have certain . . . attributes . . . that Laurence lacked,' I said. 'So not yet, anyway!'

The smile turned into a mischievous grin. She uncrossed her legs, slid down until she was lying at full length, and turned towards me. She placed one cool hand on the inside of my thigh. 'That scene that we rehearsed in the dark a little while ago,' she said slyly. 'Do you think we might play it for real, now that we can see?'

Through the half-open studio door, beyond my tilted draughtsman's table, the wide expanse of window revealed the Paris skyline etched black against the palest of blue skies. The bedroom was suffused with light. I switched off the lamp. 'I think that could be arranged,' I said.

And that is precisely what we did.

We repeated the performance virtually move for move, taking a perverse delight in recreating deliberately, almost immorally, what before had been an entirely spontaneous explosion of physical desire.

The delirious reminder of that sexual rapport had already been enough to stir me into an immediate, stiffened awareness. Now, rolling against me, she draped a leg over my shin, tracing arabesques across the tender skin of my inner leg with knowing fingers as I reached for her waist and then a breast.

She was massaging the rigid shaft of my cock. I felt the hairs on the nape of my neck prickle. We kissed. I was crowded with buses and motor cars and Unic taxis and two-horse delivery trucks. Errand boys on bicycles swooped in and out of the stalled traffic. A water cart was spraying the gutters, and storekeepers hosed down the sidewalk just as if it was an ordinary day.

Breakfast rendered my uninvited guest less inquisitive and a little more talkative. (I was going to say it loosened her tongue, but that could have been misinterpreted, and anyway the task had been carried out some time before.)

She had come in via the fire escape which snaked up the rear of the building between the forest of stackpipes, stuffing her clothes into a cupboard on the landing outside my door. Clandestine entry had not been difficult: I never used the antique lock.

She was, it seemed, the daughter of a wine merchant in Burgundy. She was in Paris for six months, supposedly at a snob 'finishing school', but her ambition — a passionate one — was to storm the fashion world. She wanted more than anything else to become a mannequin for one of the top houses; she was convinced, like thousands of other pretty girls, that given the chance she could master this difficult and haughty craft. 'All I need, Paul, is to bypass the queue,' she told me, licking flakes of croissant from her upper lip with the pink tip of her tongue. 'I *know* I can do it . . . but I have to sell myself to someone at the top; I won't be fobbed off by some don't-call-us-we'll-call-you cow with spectacles and grey hair in a bun.'

And that of course was the favour. Along with Paquin, Worth, Chanel and the others, Mado Laverne was one of the six top couturiers in Paris. Rosette wanted a personal introduction to my current boss; she wanted me to present her to Mado, with the warmest of recommendations, as an old family friend I'd known since she was in nursery school. 'It's the only way I can get someone who has the last word to look at *me*,' she said earnestly. 'Please, Paul.'

I allowed my eyes to roam over her still-naked body. It was an agreeable chore. She was slender enough and tall enough; her legs and hands and shoulders were good enough; with that tawny hair and slow, quizzical smile she was certainly attractive enough. Her breasts might be a shade too prominent for the ultra-boyish silhouette that was all the rage that year, but there was nothing I could do about that – and precious little that she could do. It was a chance she would have to take.

Pouring more coffee, I told her I would do it.

Her response was gratifying. It was not until after midday that we disentangled ourselves for the third time.

I scrambled some eggs and we drank a bottle of Bordeaux. 'This is not bad,' Rosette said, 'but you must let me send you a case of my father's wine.'

'That would be lovely. What part of Burgundy do you come from?'

'Oh,' she said vaguely, 'sort of in the middle.'

'I mean your father: what *Appellation* is he entitled to use? Nuits St Georges? Musigny? Chambertin?'

'He's . . . he's not a grower, he's a merchant; he gets his wine from all over.'

'Yes, but surely the labels on the stuff he markets must have—?'

'Oh, never mind Daddy,' she cut in. 'I'm dying to see

Reckless Liaisons

your work. Let's go into the studio.'

We went into the studio.

The collections that year were unbelievably rich – in every sense. The privations of the Great War had lingered on; as late as 1920 prices in Paris were rising alarmingly, sugar was scarce, butter only available on the black market and the use of milk in pastrymaking and confectionery forbidden. The continuing shortage of meat provoked fights outside butchers' shops. The Métro was still closed down at eleven o'clock each night because of the electricity shortage. In contrast to such penury, perhaps in defiant reaction against it, items that were not in short supply were used with an extravagance bordering on the extreme. And this was nowhere more evident than in the fashion world, where the current intoxication with the style known as Art-Déco already demanded a refined luxury based on the finest and most costly materials worked by the most highly skilled craftsmen, regardless of the final expense.

By 1922, scarcities were a thing of the past and we were back to normal. There was even an aeroplane passenger service between Le Bourget and Croydon in south London, with 'airliners' that could carry as many as eighteen people!

The lavishness of high-fashion creations was legendary. Whilst the jazz-age flappers with their bobbed and shingled hair kicked up daringly exposed legs in their short, short frocks when they danced the charleston and the tango in the afternoon, sumptuousness and magnificence were the bywords once night had fallen.

Our evening gowns – the Mado Laverne brochure I was illustrating announced – *are luxurious works of decorative art, each an exclusive and painstaking creation designed for a particular lady of society. Each is individually fashioned, piece by piece, with linings and interlinings and boning and thousands of hooks and eyes. Fabrics already rich in themselves are not permitted to rest on their laurels in our workshops but are trimmed by our expert seamstresses with fabulous gold lace and gorgeous, elaborate embroideries in beads and sequins and jewelled stones.*

Those of us employed to illustrate such exemplars of luxury and chic were expected to do so in a style – and with an imagination – as florid and lush as the designs we were promoting. It wasn't enough just to show in the tiniest detail the dress and the lady wearing it: she had to be *doing* something, or placed in a situation suitable to the design – by an expensive motor car, at a polo match, talking to friends at a ball. My own style was derived more from the Art-Déco exquisites of Iribe and Lepape and the incomparable George Barbier than the angular, Cubist-inspired drawings by the fashionably modern Thayaht and Charles Martin.

The design pinned to my drawing board featured two of Mado's most outrageous creations, which were destined together to form the highlight of her show when the collections were unveiled at the end of the month.

One of the models, a crop-haired brunette seated in silhouette, was playing a black grand piano; the other, singing, stood with out-thrust hip and one hand resting on the voluptuous curve of the instrument. In the background, a monocled man in evening dress leaned languidly against a Corinthian pillar.

The gowns were draped rather than tailored. The girl at the piano wore a heavy silk tube, cowled at the nape, in a bold butterfly-wing pattern of cinnamon and chocolate brown. The extra-low waist was emphasised by a loose sash in electric-blue, fastened by a huge bulbous rose made of green glass. The sleeveless garment was slashed from armpit to waist on each side to reveal a peach camisole, and the narrow skirt swirled out at the ankle to show off a hem trimmed in fox fur dyed the same blue as the sash.

The singer's orange *crêpe-de-chine* sheath wrapped her tightly, from the calves to just beneath her small breasts – which were covered, without a foundation, by two pleated panels of magenta satin rising from a peplum bunched around her hips, and hung from a rhinestone halter. A fringed overskirt covered in blue flowers fell to the floor from behind the model's knees. The backless dress was belted too, the buckle an enormous heart, spider-webbed with semi-precious stones.

'Marvellous!' Rosette enthused. 'I think it's absolutely ripping. I really do. What craftsmanship! What talent!'

'The rest of the stuff in the show is equally good,' I said.

'I didn't mean the dresses, silly – though they *are* lovely. I was talking about the picture. You're a real artist, I must say!'

'Thank you.'

'It's naughty when you really look,' Rosette said. 'You *know* that the moment that rhinestone collar is unclipped, the stuff will drop away and leaves her titties bare! And as for the bodice showing through the slit in the piano lady's dress — why it looks as if she's climbing half out of it already!' She studied my work with her head on one side — I'd worked in *gouache* on extra-heavy cartridge paper — and then added, 'I like the way you've handled the man: the figure is completely stylised, yet anatomically it's entirely solid; you can sense the bones beneath the cloth.'

I smiled. I thought it was a pretty good illustration too. 'I'm glad you like it,' I said. 'Although of course I shouldn't really be showing it to you at all: all the designs are supposed to be a dead secret until the collections are shown.'

Rosette was rummaging in a small sequin handbag she had recovered from the cupboard on the landing. She produced a long ebony cigarette holder with a gold tip, emptied the bag onto a chair and looked disapprovingly at the heap of small change, Métro tickets, lipstick, powder compact, mirror and keys. 'Blast,' she said. 'I must have left my fags at home. Do you smoke, darling?'

I shook my head. 'I'm afraid not.' She smiled winningly. 'Would you — could you possibly — would you be a *dear* and run down to the corner shop and get me a packet? I'm simply dying for the good old gasper!'

'For you, nothing is too much trouble,' I said. 'I may not smoke, but I may remind you that I have other vices equally bizarre!'

By the time I returned with the cigarettes, Rosette was fully dressed. The cupboard had yielded a square-necked blue dress with a low waist and a skirt that ended well above the knees. She wore stockings in thick white silk and black patent shoes with big silver buckles. The grey cloche hat, into which she had crammed her shoulder-length hair, was trimmed with moleskin. 'Very chic,' I said, handing her the packet. 'I see that I shall have to design a new brochure right away! I have to see Mado later this afternoon. Do you want to step into the shoes of my long-lost niece on a visit to Paris, and come with me?'

Rosette had torn open the blue Gauloise packet. She fitted a cigarette into her holder, and stuck the holder in the corner of her mouth. She took a box of Swan Vestas from a shelf in my kitchen, struck one, and lit the cigarette. The smoke swirled through a shaft of sunlight slanting through the window.

I waited patiently.

Finally she shook her head. 'Dear of you, sweetie, but I can't. Not today.'

'Why not? The quicker you get the introduction, the better chance you'll have of being taken on before the collections are shown. You know: strike while the iron's hot and all that.' I grinned. 'Besides, I might forget you . . . especially if Forty-three shows up!'

She tilted back her head and blew out a plume of blue smoke. 'That is one chance I *will* take. No, it'll have to be another time. Thanks just the same. I have to go now, anyway.'

Privately, I wondered why, if she was leaving in any case, it had been necessary to send me out for cigarettes when she could perfectly well have bought them on her way out. Then I remembered: 'one' did not smoke in the street, even in ultra-modern 1922! I said: 'Must you really? Couldn't I persuade you to have a drink?'

'No, really. I mean yes, really. That is, I have to meet someone.'

'Is it that important? Can't they wait?'

'No, baby, it's . . . it's a girlfriend. I'm meeting her at Passy, outside the Métro station, and I don't want to keep her hanging about.'

'As you like. What about this famous intro then? Leave me your address, and the next time an opportunity arises, I'll—'

'I can't do that,' she said quickly.

'Why ever not?'

'Well, it's . . . I'm staying with the friend, you see, and her lover is due back tomorrow and I'll have to move out and I . . . well, I don't know, frankly, where I shall be.'

'Is there nowhere I can telephone you? A place where I could send a message by *pneumatique*?'

Rosette shook her head again. 'Not at the moment.' She stubbed out the cigarette among the croissant crumbs on a plate. 'Look, sweetie — it's awfully kind of you. I do appreciate the offer, really. It *is* what I asked you for, after all. But we'll have to leave it that *I'll* get in touch with *you*. Then you can tell me when it's convenient. And I'll get in touch just as soon as I *possibly* can, I promise.'

'Well,' I said, 'it was a lovely night.'

'Lovely. We must do it again.' She picked up her sequin handbag. 'Now I really must be off.'

And that was all I could get out of her. Apart from the memory of three fairly hectic bouts of lovemaking — and the fact, as she had reminded me, that I could now say 'forty-*two* if you count Laurence' when I was trying to get to sleep — I knew no more about this extraordinary, oddly fascinating young woman than I had when the warmth of her body first interrupted my reveries on the subject of Monika.

It certainly seemed strange, on reflection, that a girl would go to that length to obtain a favour . . . and then turn down the offer of an introduction she had been so anxious, so desperately eager to arrange, at the first opportunity on the trivial excuse that she had a friend to meet.

Curious, too, that someone that determined to break into a highly competitive business should have found it impossible to leave even an address where she could be contacted with the person helping her to make the break.

The oddest thing of all, though, was that Rosette never did get in touch with me again.

Chapter Four

Mado Laverne was forty-one years old, although she could easily have passed for thirty. She was a tall, statuesque beauty with high, almost Slavic cheekbones, a finely chiselled mouth and brassy hair drawn tightly back into a chignon on the nape of her neck. Her father, Harry Levinski, who was killed in the first Battle of Mons in 1914, had married a Polish countess with money and set up a wholesale women's wear business in Lille, long before the Great War. At the turn of the century, the nineteen-year-old Magdalena Levinski had already been apprenticed to a lacemaker in Brussels and a *fabriquant* of rich silks in the town of Tulle, in central France. By the time war broke out she had worked as a seamstress for Paul Poiret, a cutter for Paquin and a designer – in association with the great Romain de Titiroff, known as 'Erté' – for the house of Worth. It seemed a good time, with property cheap and a deprived population hungry for luxury, to start out on her own. She bought a ninety-nine-year lease on a mansion in the Rue des Capucines, near the Place Vendôme. The discreet brass plate at the entrance announced simply:

Mado Laverne – Couture

The site was well chosen. Midway between the Opera

and the Louvre, conveniently close to Maxim's in the Rue Royale and the fashionable boutiques of the Faubourg St Honoré, Laverne's was equally accessible to the upper crust of the business community, the theatre world and the élite of Paris society. The business — with the help of a designer tempted away from Lanvin by the offer of a ridiculously high salary — was an immediate success. By 1922, Mado had not only eased herself into the top rank: she had quarried herself a specialised corner which singled her out even in that august company. The secret lay in the total contrast between her stunningly simple day dresses and the scarcely believable, breathtaking opulence of her evening wear. The socialites of *Le Tout Paris* — everybody who was anybody — were queueing up to pay absurd prices for her fabulous creations.

Two hours after the enigmatic Rosette had left my studio, I was walking down the Rue des Capucines on my way to the appointment with the famous *couturière*, an Imperial-size portfolio under my arm.

Apart from the brochure illustrations, there were designs to be approved for inclusion in the next issue of the expensive de luxe fashion magazine *La Gazette du Bon Ton* — the 'good taste gazette'.

There was a porter's lodge beneath the archway that led from the street to the courtyard around which the mansion was built. One of the porters — they wore a livery of tall hats and sleeved waistcoats in gold and black stripes — picked up an ivory-handled telephone to announce my arrival. I walked across the cobbled yard, past tubs of geraniums and a huge yellow Isotta-Fraschini limousine with a uniformed chauffeur drowsing at the wheel, to the broad flight of entrance steps. Mado was waiting for me in the vestibule, late afternoon sunlight sliding in through one of the tall windows burnishing her pale hair.

Personally, I had always thought that brassy hair was a mistake, the one slightly vulgar touch flawing the elegance of the composition. But in fact it was the result of neither peroxide nor henna: the colour was one hundred percent natural, as those privileged to see her pubic hair could confirm.

And, yes, I was one of that not-too-restricted clan. For Mado was a lady with an appetite. But her image as the unattainable, perfectionist goddess interested only in the aesthetics of beauty would be tainted if it were known that she had a regular lover − or, worse still, a husband − and so she was reduced to a series of affairs strictly in secret.

That's what Mado said. For my money, the explanation was simpler: I reckoned she was a girl who considered privately that variety was the spice of life.

At any rate it was made clear − subtly but quite decisively − at my first interview that any graphic work for the House of Laverne would be contingent upon certain extra-curricular activities being carried out in a satisfactory manner. No exclusive rights would be exercised, it was emphasised, but when the summons came to an interview concerned with work, it would be prudent to interpret the term in its broadest sense − and allow sufficient time for the vagaries of personal taste to be satisfied.

I accepted the conditions of course. She was a *very*

attractive woman, experienced sexually and unexpectedly adventurous. Besides, at the time I urgently needed work that would bring me before the eye of the public – especially the wealthy public.

So, a while back now, on her thirty-ninth birthday, unknown to herself my employer became Number Thirty-nine on my own private list.

'Paul,' she said throatily, as I bent to kiss her hand, 'how very nice! And you have brought the work? Splendid! We shall go up to my office at once.'

She led the way past the demure receptionist at her Louis-Philippe desk and up the gracefully curving staircase to the first floor. The house dated from the time when the *Préfet* Haussmann was restructuring the city, laying waste a tangle of mediaeval housing to drive the Grands Boulevards with their neo-classical façades and mansard roofs through the heart of Paris. The rooms were lofty and the stairways shallow. As I mounted, respectfully keeping a pace behind, I had time to admire, not for the first time, the sway of Mado's heavy hips, the straightness of her supple back and the slenderness of her ankles. She was wearing a severely cut, calf-length afternoon frock in black *moiré* taffeta, set off only by a large brooch and bracelets in Danish silver. Her bare arms and the creamy, parchment flesh of her shoulders were filmed by semi-transparent black organza.

We passed workrooms shrill with the whirr of machines and the chatter of girls, and traversed the great *salle* where the Laverne collections were shown – the mansion's one-time ballroom, now redesigned as a Greek temple, with Ionic columns and urns with tropical plants on either side of the central gangway.

Mado's office was a large room with French windows leading to two wrought-iron balconies overlooking a small garden. The huge desk, apart from two telephones, was bare. But an inclined drawing board and a work table between the French windows were littered with sketches, drawings and coloured patterns for model dresses already approved. 'Open your portfolio here, *chéri*,' Mado said, pushing the instruments to one side of the desk. 'Oh, my – yes! That model is really shown off with the girl at the piano. I like the way you've given importance to the fur hem by having her foot raised to the pedal.'

The illustrations destined for the *Gazette du Bon Ton* were quite different in style. The magazine – if you could call something that appeared only sporadically a magazine – was a limited edition luxury product, hand printed and individually coloured on handmade paper. The illustrations were produced by the *pochoir* (stencil) method – each one, in each copy of the publication, being laboriously built up by craftsmen using up to seventeen or eighteen different colour stencils to achieve the final result.

The final result was that the subtleties and nuances of tone and tint in an original watercolour could be captured in a way that was impossible with photographic or mechanical means of reproduction.

Three of Mado's models had been selected for me to illustrate: a girl in a huge wide hat leaning against an olive tree with a Mediterranean sea village in the background; a young woman and her cavalier walking two Russian wolfhounds beside the Grand Canal in

Reckless Liaisons

Venice; and a socialite in full evening dress mixing cocktails in a kitchen, the brightly lit interior viewed through a rose-covered trellis, as if the spectator was in a darkened garden.

As Mado studied the trio, I gazed out of the French windows at the real garden below. One of the seamstresses must have put out some crumbs left from her lunch basket, for there were pigeons clustered around a sundial in the middle of the lawn. Plumbago and oleanders and the flame-coloured trumpets of bignonia glimmered among the leaves of the border shrubbery, although the sun had now sunk below the rooftops. Behind Mado's desk was a doorway beyond which a recently installed spiral staircase led to her private apartments on the floor above. None of the couture house staff knew which of the office visitors climbed those stairs.

Speculation, however, was as they say rife. And I knew for a fact that the workroom girls ran a book on certain aspects of their employer's life.

Mado was holding the Venetian picture up to the light. 'Admirable, Paul,' she said. 'I love the way the reflections in the canal appear almost to mirror the motifs decorating that afternoon dress. And the concept of the trellis' – she picked up the kitchen scene – 'is quite brilliant.'

'Thank you,' I said. 'You think Lucien Vogel at the *Gazette* will accept them?'

'He'd better!' she said. 'Or he'll get no more exclusives from this house. They'll make perfect plates anyway.'

There was a knock on the door, and Patrice Delgado,

the ex-journalist who now worked as Mado's press and promotion officer, came in with a query. Was it all right to give Corinne Dubois of *Figaro* advance details of the gown the Comtesse van den Bergh would be wearing at the Viremont reception?

'Of course it is,' Mado told him. 'Dagmar van den Bergh loves to see her name in the papers. It will identify her anyway to likely conquests.'

Delgado, a short, dark, wiry man with a red-lipped mouth, nodded and withdrew. He smiled at me as he passed. I am not certain that he actually flashed a glance at the same time towards the door concealing the spiral stairs, but I would have laid money on the suspicion that he had passed through it more than once himself.

'Well . . .' Mado said, laying my designs down on the desk.

I cleared my throat. Mado didn't like to be thought of as a boss-woman, ordering men into her bed. Part of the charade was that *you* had to persuade *her* each time. 'My dear,' I said, in my best Sasha Guitry manner, 'do you not find the atmosphere a trifle heavy down here?'

'Heavy?'

'Why, yes.' I looked out of the window and up at the cloudless sky. 'A matter of atmospheric pressure, no doubt. I was wondering perhaps whether a change in altitude would render the evening less oppressive.'

'Oppressive?'

'There is of course the Eiffel Tower, but taxicabs are difficult to come by at this hour.' I switched my gaze to the door. It was flanked by a Matisse still life and a framed Bakst costume design for Diaghilev's Russian Ballet. 'A height difference of even one storey,' I said, 'might make *all* the difference between an evening of solitary reflection and one full of infinite promise.'

Maco decided to come into the game. 'Monsieur Mackenzie! Are you venturing to make me an improper suggestion? Let me not think you have designs on my virtue!'

I let pass the opportunity provoked by the word virtue. '*You* are the designer,' I couldn't resist saying, nevertheless; 'I am no more than a craftsman only too happy to translate the designs into action!'

She reddened. 'To the devil with you, Paul. You know very well I want to go to bed with you. Now. This minute.'

I strode to the door and jerked it open. Careful — don't crow because you made her admit it; don't spoil the game forever by putting every card on the table. I remained silent, head lowered, until she had passed me.

After that, once the opening move had been played, it was routine. But the routine was a delight: we had worked on it for several years.

I don't mean that the ritual was — forgive the term — hard and fast; it was no I-do-this-then-you-do-that sequence, like a chess match systematised with diagrams at the wrong end of a newspaper. Rather it was a loose framework, a base on which details could be improvised in the manner of a game of tennis, or the wire armature of a sculptor, capable of being 'fleshed out' with clay in a number of different ways.

As with tennis, the rules were unvarying: service, cross over, serve again; receive service; change ends at the end of the set, and so on. In our case this translated into a standing encounter, fully clothed, which was restricted to kissing and the caress; a transfer to the sofa, where the caressing became more intimate; a break for champagne; the mutual undressing scene with revelation of treasures to be enjoyed; and the final move to the bed, or end-game, which could be prolonged indefinitely.

It made an agreeable enough contrast to the tempestuous, more explosive action of a fresh conquest or the spontaneous combustions of unbridled passion. The excitement lay in the knowledge of what was coming – but not knowing precisely how and when. Anticipation was the name of the game.

The black taffeta skirt of Mado's dress was fairly tight; she was obliged to hoist it halfway up her thighs to negotiate the spiral stairway. Climbing behind her with my head at the level of her heels, I was afforded an enticing view of cool flesh above black knee-length stockings – with an occasional glimpse of lace frothing higher up – as her legs scissored around the circular path above me. The sibilant hiss of those criss-crossing black silk stockings was louder in my ears than the distant rumble of rush-hour traffic in the Rue des Capucines. By the time I reached the top of the stairs there was already a certain tightness about my loins.

The stairway emerged behind a curtained arch at one end of a small vestibule. On the far side of this, a wider arch led to the 'official' stairs, which swept down to the professional floor below. Somewhere above, lit by dormers in the mansard roof, were servants' quarters, but I had never penetrated that far.

Mado was smoothing down her skirt. She smiled at me: small, very even white teeth between the thin but voluptuously curved lips. 'You know where everything is, Paul,' she said. 'Perhaps you would be kind enough to prepare us some refreshment?'

The ice, delivered in fifteen-pound blocks every morning, was kept in an insulated chest in the kitchen. I took the pick from its hook above the scrubbed table, chipped off enough to half fill a silver bucket, and withdrew a bottle of Veuve Clicquot *demi-sec* from the wine rack. I lowered the bottle into the bucket and gave it a preliminary twirl before I carried the bucket into the sitting room to rejoin Mado. She was standing beside an Empire occasional table inlaid with ivory and gingerwood on which, I noted, two champagne *flutes* on a silver tray had already been placed. I moved them to one side and put the bucket on the tray.

Now was the time to commence. I could almost hear an invisible umpire call: 'Play!'

I moved towards her and stood very close. I shook my head. 'My God, Mado,' I said – and meant it – 'you look more seductive, more desirable, every time I see you!' It was true: success suited her; she *was* a most desirable, beautiful woman, quietly confident in her mature sexuality.

The smile widened. She said nothing, holding my gaze with large, curiously pale blue eyes. Slowly, gently, but very deliberately, she swung one heavy hip against me.

I put my hands on the black organza veiling the flesh of her upper arms, drawing her still closer. There was no need to say any more.

I was aware of weight, a soft pressure against the hardness now constricting that part of me anxious to make contact. The upper half of her body sagged slightly against me, so that I could feel the thrust of her breasts against my chest. I lowered my hands to the padded cushions of her hips, bent my head and kissed her.

She responded instantly, almost greedily, raising herself on her toes to fasten her mouth, limpet-like, on mine; her lips clasped, clung; her hot tongue darted between my teeth, across my gums, up into my cheeks. Our tongues met in a twining, muscular joust.

Mado's hands were laced behind my head, holding me down on her as we kissed with increasing abandon. A knee jammed itself between my thighs; her belly swung even harder against my hardness.

My own hands, rising to cup the rounded swell of her breasts, now dropped again and snaked behind her to grasp, through the layers of material, the curved spheres of her bottom. I eased them slowly apart, pressing her against my loins. Her breath, quickening with every heartbeat, jetted through flared nostrils against the skin of my face. The backs of her legs were trembling.

That was one of the entrancing things about Mado: she could hold herself, and hold herself, and hold herself in . . . but all the time, beneath this restraint, you were excitedly aware of the smouldering fires stoked up within, just awaiting the opportunity to erupt. She was like a firework waiting to explode. Light the blue touch paper and retire.

I reckoned it was time to terminate Phase One — but on this occasion she was there before me. Suddenly she freed her mouth, leaning back against my embrace. Lips glistening with moisture pouted and then parted in a smile. 'Oh, Paul, Paul!' she murmured breathlessly.

Reckless Liaisons

I bent my head to kiss her again, but she pulled away, leading me across the room to draw me down beside her on an upholstered *chaise-longue*.

She lay back against the sloping end of the sofa, stretching both legs along the padded seat. The pale blue eyes were glittering.

Phase Two. Let battle commence.

Perched on the edge, I leaned over her recumbent body and stared down into the fathomless expression now masking her face. Beneath the organza, the shadowed contours of her breasts rose and fell rapidly. I placed a hand, still holding her gaze, deliberately on one of them, kneading the soft flesh, rotating the palm until I felt the nipple harden through the diaphanous cloth.

A small sound escaped through her half-open mouth.

The organza swathing her bare arms and shoulders fastened in front with small studs concealed beneath a trimming of black braid. I hooked the fingers of both hands through the gap between two studs and wrenched the covering apart to expose the creamy flesh. I seized the top of the taffeta corsage, ripped that open and tore away the camisole under it to reveal her naked breasts. They were small, with extra-large nipples. I squeezed up one breast, lowered my head and took a nipple in my mouth.

Mado gasped aloud. While my tongue traced arabesques around that stiffened bud of flesh, she rolled her hips from side to side on the *chaise longue*. Her head turned this way and that on the cushioned back. A low groaning noise gurgled deep in her throat.

I held the nipple between my teeth, teasing it, applying pressure to the puckered skin of the areola with my lips. Supporting myself on one hand, I stretched the other to feel the heat of her pubic mound through the stuff of the skirt hitched up almost to her waist. Very gently, palm flat against the base of her belly, I massaged the mound through her dress, tightening, stretching and then loosening the flesh so that it tensed and then relaxed the skin sweeping down to the hairy furrow of her secret parts.

'Oh, *yes*!' she cried hoarsely. 'Oh, Paul! My dearest, give it to me; let me have it now!'

I continued my ministrations. Whatever she said, whatever I said, leap-frogging several phases to reach the end-game ahead of time was definitely against the rules.

My hand flipped quickly beneath the hem of the skirt to meet a complex of lace and silk and elastic that was already damp. At the same time I felt fingers graze the rigid bulge at my crotch that was beginning to feel uncomfortably tight. The fingers scrabbled, turned between our two bodies and trailed pointed nails up the throbbing outline of my stem.

I lay across her, plunging my hand in among the lacy frills, drawing aside elastic to permit my fingers, probing, smoothing, exploring, to home in at last on springy hair and the sliding folds of hot wet flesh. I transferred my sucking mouth to her other breast.

Mado uttered a small yelp of delight at the touch of my hand on her hidden treasure. The groan in her throat turned into something that was very nearly a purr when I parted her secret lips and felt for the rubbery, now suddenly erect, button of nerves and tissue and skin that was the source of all her innermost joy. Seizing my wrist, she held it there in place while she pulled down her skirt to cover both our hands. Visible sex was for later.

I raised my head to kiss her mouth once more. Our clinging lips devoured one another. And then abruptly her caressing hand dived between buttons and forcibly yanked open my fly. As I caught my breath, she hauled aside shirt-tails and underwear, grabbing my heated shaft to pull it out into the open air. Normally this would signal the end of Act Two.

Nothing untoward scarred the existing blueprint.

She pushed aside my groping hand and sat up straight, staring with wide eyes at my loins, where the stiffened, quivering proof of my desire, with its engorged and bulbous head, speared obscenely naked from the gaping fly of my slacks. 'I think we'll save that for another time,' she said in a calm, quite normal voice. 'Meanwhile, darling, perhaps you would like to pour us a drink?'

I levered myself off the *chaise-longue*. I knew that it pleased her to eye this rude, nude testimony to carnal lust spiking out of my clothes while we shared a decorous apéritif. I sprang the champagne cork, poured, and brought the two glasses over to her.

She was sitting with her ankles demurely crossed and her skirt pulled right down again, a picture of sobriety in the curtained luxury of her room . . . if it wasn't for the sight of one naked breast exposed between the savaged edges of the ripped dress.

It was dusk outside now. A faint illumination from the street lamps below filtered into the room between heavy, half-drawn drapes. Costly oriental rugs glowed in rich colours beneath a crystal chandelier whose electric candles had been dimmed to an amber flush that blurred hard lines and suffused with warmth the elegant outlines of Louis Quinze *fauteuils*, an imported Sheraton escritoire, and a huge Ming vase on a marble-topped Directoire commode.

The champagne was still a little warm too, but it gave us time to catch our breath and allow the thudding of the heart to slow down to a normal rhythm.

'You won't forget the programme cover, darling, will you?' Mado cooed, as she sipped her second glass. 'Hurok has to have the maximum of time if he's to organise the right number of *pochoirs* for the fan.'

That, I thought, is my girl! Nothing like a spot of romantic dialogue to heighten the excitement in the privacy of the love-nest!

Hurok was her fine-art printer. The programme, a work of graphic art in itself, would list, with illustrations and brief descriptions, the models to be shown in the forthcoming Laverne collection. My cover, a wrap-around, front-and-back design on laminated board, was to feature, against a solid black background, a spread-open Japanese fan, on each thin leaf of which a detail of one or another of the gowns to be exhibited would be depicted.

'Hurok,' I said, draining my glass, 'like everyone else in this business, wants everything the day before yesterday. The people working for him are perfectly competent. They'll be happy if they get my artwork next week. You'll get your cover in plenty of time.'

'Well, that's all right then,' she said. 'I think there's a taste still in the bottle. If you wouldn't mind, *chéri* . . .'

Reckless Liaisons

In stark contrast with the opulence of the sitting room, the bedroom – where we found ourselves ten minutes later – was a bare and modernistic shrine. Framed originals by Chagall and Brunelleschi hung on the walls, which were a darker violet than the curtains. The carpet was white. Printed designs by Raoul Dufy curtained off a walk-in clothes closet, and there was a Bauhaus chair by Mies van de Rohe in front of a tubular dressing-table with a black glass top.

As a showcase for the pale beauty of its owner, the ten-foot wide divan was fitted with black silk sheets and a black velvet bedcover.

The revelation of that beauty was slow to manifest itself that day. Mado was in a teasing mood, prolonging everything to the last possible second. Having unbuttoned my shirt and lifted up the vest beneath it, she slid her cool hands around my back, kneading the muscles of my waist and then caressing my nipples for what seemed an age before she would even remove my jacket. And as for the eager staff lewdly projecting through my fly, it might as well have been on display behind glass panels of her Lalique china cabinet for all the attention she paid to it.

My own hands, meanwhile, had achieved no more than a repeat performance of the *décolletage* obtained on the *chaise-longue* in the other room. Three times, as my fingers snaked down towards the loose waist of the taffeta dress, the hand was grasped gently but firmly and guided back to the snowy slopes of her breasts. After the third, she rose on tiptoe – we were standing beside the divan – and bit the lobe of my left ear. 'It is better to voyage hopefully than never arrive at all,' she misquoted, in her most mischievous voice.

But while she was thus slightly off balance, I seized the opportunity and speeded up the script a little. I dropped my hands to her hips, spun her body around, and faced her away from me, at the same time wrapping both arms around her from behind and crushing her back against me so that my hard, pulsating length bored into the taffeta-covered crevice between her buttocks.

Mado uttered a small gasp of surprise. She writhed her hips, rotating her pelvis, rolling my shaft from side to side as my hands now grabbed the skirt, hiked it up above her waist, and then dove under the elasticated waistband of whatever she wore beneath. I pushed the garment halfway down her thighs and then dragged the torn dress up and over her head in a single swift movement.

She turned to face me again. She was wearing no suspender belt: the stockings were held up in the French manner with a coin rolled into the top just above the knee. Wide-legged black lace knickers bunched around the pale flesh between those stockings and the tight white slip that still hid the triangle of hair furring her loins. In a moment, smiling wickedly, she had stripped off my shirt and vest, baring me to the waist. It was the beginning of the symphony's slow movement!

We stood eye to eye, like opponents squaring up in the ring. I reached forward and very deliberately tore open the remains of her camisole, exposing again both of her naked breasts. She unbuckled my belt, pulled open the waistband of my slacks and unfastened the rest of my fly.

I dragged down the white slacks and underpants,

freeing my stiff cock to shaft towards her. Very slowly then, each of us with hands on the other, we bent our knees and crouched down in unison, sliding of the remaining clothes until they pooled around our ankles and we were nude from there upwards. The end-game was ready for play.

We kicked off the remnants and moved on to the divan.

Mado's luscious body was milk-white against the sombre sheets. Coco Chanel's revolutionary precept — after too much sun on a Mediterranean holiday — that brown was beautiful had yet to influence the arbiters of taste in the world of *La Mode*, and the paler, the creamier the skin, the more we enthused.

Certainly, against that black silk, the female amplitude of my companion's hips, the smooth sweep of belly curving down to the straw-coloured thatch between her fleshy thighs, the small high-set breasts with their rosy tips, were set off to perfection, like jewels in a velvet lined case.

I stretched myself out beside her prone body. At once — and at last! — the hand nearest me reached for my throbbing staff, wrapping expert fingers around its heated length, gently teasing the distended skin up and down the ridged muscle within.

I didn't immediately return the compliment. In our game, what Dr Freud of Vienna had termed the foreplay could be drawn out indefinitely. I cradled her head in one palm, turning it towards me so that I could brush her lips with my own. My free hand roamed the contours of her body, trailing fingernails up the inside of one thigh, rounding a hip bone, caressing a breast. I was a sculptor fashioning her out of the darkness of the bed; I scooped out the hollows, built up the fleshy mounds. I plunged the hand beneath her to perfect the heated crevice between her buttocks.

Mado slid out the tip of her tongue, flickering it snake-like between my lips. She caught the lower lip between her small white teeth. The hand wrapped around me started a slow, a dream-like milking movement.

My palm was now hard against her pubic mound, the blonde hair crisp and springy under my touch. Her teeth nipped my lower lip, and I moved the hand beneath her head away, past the neck, below the shoulders and down along her spine until it was wedged under her bottom.

I thrust her hips and pelvis upwards, against the pressure of the palm cradling her mons. I sank the middle finger of that hand into the cleft between her thighs, brushing it through wet hair, until I felt the hot, sliding clasp of her secret lips. I rotated the hand, drawing the finger up again to part the lips.

Mado was breathing fast once more; the rhythmic pumping at my loins quickened too. A second hand reached over to clutch the wrinkled and fleshy sac pouched beneath my hardness, kneading the sensitive glands within.

As she shifted her position to turn towards me, my fingers worked wildly at her genitals, spreading the outer lips, stroking the inner, searching for and finding that bud of flesh between them, whose manipulation could induce in her such shudderings of ecstasy. The fingers of my hand trapped under her hips parted the cheeks of her buttocks, probing upwards into the scalding depths of that hairy furrow.

The lighting in the bedroom was discreet and indirect, glowing from behind ground-glass screens placed low down on either side of the divan. Reflecting from the violet walls, it cast a mysterious, purplish illumination over the distended, darkened flesh of Mado's nipples. I sucked one breast and then the other, drawing the resilient mounds up into my mouth, tonguing the erectile tips.

We were both groaning softly now, nerve ends quivering with desire as the practised quartet of our respective hands coaxed sensuous music of infinite joy from the instruments of our pleasure.

I raised my head and we kissed again, languorously, lasciviously, the hands still working their magic . . . and each of us knowing, with a particular and salacious anticipation, that at any moment now we would switch positions and allow our mouths the satisfaction of taking over the tasks those hands were so busily perfecting now.

By the time Mado rolled over onto her back, flung her arms wide and spread her legs, crying 'Come to me now, *chéri*; oh, come to me now!' the evening was well advanced.

I lowered myself between her thighs, my cock bursting with tension, and slid into her, shivering with delight as the head, and then the whole rigid length, was engulfed in the dark velvet depths of her belly. She thrust up her hips, hooked her heels behind my knees, and wrapped loving arms around my back.

I smiled down into her eyes. 'Happy?' I murmured.

'What do you think?' said Mado Laverne.

We started it then; we became what a Welsh poet was to describe as the two-backed beast.

Our two bodies fused into a single entity, we moved, slowly, deliberately, into that easy, sensual, reciprocating rhythm that goes on forever yet threatens to stop at any minute.

I thrust down; she arched up her hips. I withdrew a little; the ridged muscles of her innermost throat tightened as if to retain me. I plunged once more; she rose to meet me. We rolled this way, we rocked that. Her breasts moved under my chest. Our tongues interlaced. We could prolong it all night, this timeless and tremulous delight. And yet — here once more was the breathless anticipation! — at any moment, quite independent of our conscious wills, some indefinable line would be crossed, some mysterious reaction triggered, and the wave would rear up.

The wave was irresistible; we were powerless before its force. Once it had lifted us, there was nothing we could do but let it surge on and then crash down to send us spinning among the stars, gasping out our shared release.

At the moment, though, no wave was in sight; only the ripples of exquisite delight stirred the dark surface of the night. I was suddenly aware of the fact that this was the fourth time I had made love in the past twenty-four hours.

I hoped, when we came back to earth, that Maxim's would still be open and prepared to find us a table.

Chapter Five

The profession in which I found myself – fashion illustration inventive enough to be considered an art form in its own right – owed much to such 'modern' painters as Matisse, Braque, Dérain and Modigliani. Adjusting the onlooker's apparent point of view in relation to the picture, the tilting up of the foreground to make any middle-ground disappear, the use of curvilinear figures against a grid-like rectilinear background, the adoption of flat colour without shading on garments – these were all tricks learned from them. Bakst's fabulous costume designs for the Russian Ballet in 1909 also played their part.

The public and the critics too had been conditioned by Art-Nouveau to accept that 'art' need not be confined to pompous galleries and museums but could equally well relate to furniture, tableware, glass, fabrics . . . and clothes.

The dress designer Paul Poiret provided the original impetus for our new profession before the war, when he commissioned two luxury albums cataloguing his creations. Executed by Iribe and Lepape, the illustrations, hand printed on Imperial Japan paper by Jean Saudé, went through thirty different hand-colouring stencil processes with gouache paints matching the artist's original. These albums were the forerunners of such publications as the *Gazette*, the *Journal des Dames et des Modes*, and *Art, Goût, Beauté* – art, taste and beauty, which could have been the motto of our movement.

By 1922 Vogel's *Gazette*, which was published by the Central Library of Fine Arts, had established its own team of fashion artists, seven of them, all graduates of the famous Paris School of Fine Arts. The group, which included Iribe, Lepape, George Barbier and Charles Martin, became known collectively as the 'Knights of the Bracelet' – because the wearing of bracelets formed part of their exquisite, fastidiously stylish and immaculate image.

Although my work was occasionally accepted by the *Gazette*, I was not, of course – as a foreigner from 'Perfidious Albion' – accepted as a full member of this august club. With my friend the sculptor Tom Crawford, who designed solid silver mascots for the radiators of coach-built luxury motor cars, I formed a rival group which christened itself the 'Knights of the Bottle'. The five other members included Bertrand Laforge, who produced outrageous hand-crafted sporting bodywork for his father's touring cars, an architect named Hans Bohl, and a randy young Parisienne woking as a social columnist on *Figaro*.

The columnist's name was Corinne Dubois. It was she who had introduced me to my late wife, Camille, while I was on a visit to Paris in 1912. Corinne was what was known as 'a sport' – which, being interpreted, meant: if you wear trousers, watch out, or they'll end up around your ankles!

Two or three days after my tryst with Mado Laverne, I was sitting with Tom and Corinne outside the Café Haarg on the Place St Michel, dribbling water through a sugar lump into a small glass of absinthe. A striped awning shaded the crowded tables from the August sun; across the road, the Danton fountain splashed busily into a stone basin.

'I hear this new designer is aiming to upstage the Top Ten,' Corinne said, 'putting on a show a week before the Collections start.'

'Really?' I said. 'Who is this, then?'

'His name is Ahmed Simbel. He's a Lebanese — or so he says. Bit of a mystery, if you ask me.'

The green absinthe was turning milky. I raised my eyes and looked at Corinne — a dark girl in her early thirties, a little on the plump side, with a bee-stung lower lip and bright eyes behind spectacles. 'What do you mean — a mystery?'

'A touch of the swarthy Levantine there!' said Crawford, who restricted his conversation whenever possible to clichés, puns and catch-phrases.

'Surely you must have heard?' Corinne said. 'He appeared out of nowhere. A month or so ago. Started hiring seamstresses, tailors, cutters, beaders, milliners, furriers and embroidery queens all over the shop.'

I shook my head. 'If I did hear, I've forgotten.'

'Took a whole floor of that empty mansion in the Rue St Roch. The one with the big courtyard. And they've been working like stink ever since, the whole lot of them. But in total secrecy, that's the thing. Most of the staff are non-French — and they talk about their work on pain of *death*, I promise you!' Corinne grinned.

'They actually have, would you believe it, some sort of *guards* to check that nobody smuggles out details of any of Simbel's designs!'

'What's he worried about?' I said. 'Dash it all, don't tell me the man thinks people like Mado or Jean Worth or Paquin need to *steal* ideas from other designers!'

Tom Crawford laughed. He struck an heroic attitude and declaimed: 'The time has come, designers say, to talk of many things: of shoes and furs and lingerie, and if one flares or clings; and where the waistline ought to be, and whether hats have wings.'

Corinne chuckled. 'Can I use that, Tom?'

'It's not original,' I said.

'Of course it's not: it's a paraphrase of *The Walrus and the*—'

'No, I mean the paraphrase as quoted has been used before. It was used during the war. In *Harper's* or *Vogue*, I think.'

'I never claimed it as my own,' Crawford said. 'Now come on, you Knights of the Bottle: who's game for another round?'

A steamboat on the river hooted at Notre-Dame. I raised my hand. 'On me,' I said.

What with the absinthe and the sun and the good company, I forgot all about Corinne's revelations concerning Monsieur Ahmed Simbel. My mind was too occupied anyway with thoughts of a meeting later that day that could conceivably jack up my score to forty-three.

That particular lapse of memory was to cost me, as Tom would say, dear.

* * *

Françoise Dupuis was twenty-two years old. She had actually been born while the bells of Paris were ringing in the new century. She was a tall, willowy brunette with the slender, fashionably boyish figure the dressmakers loved, and a bust that was scarcely noticeable. Her features were quite large: a big mouth, a strong chin and a nose that was fairly prominent. She was in fact handsome rather than pretty. But there was a magic in her touch, an electric thrill provoked by her fingers that would send a shiver coursing down your spine, even if the fingers had only been laid momentarily on the sleeve of a jacket or shirt.

Françoise, in short, was what the Americans call a sexpot.

She was also rather shy, a little timid and on the defensive, not at all out of the same box as Corinne.

I had met her at a party thrown by her brother Denis, who was one of the Knights — ours, not theirs — and fallen at once. The mixture of extreme sexuality and a reluctance to acknowledge it added up to a paradox (yes, another — it seemed that I collected them!) that no serious insomniac could afford to ignore.

We met in Toni's Bar, a fumed-oak sink of iniquity not two hundred yards from the Opera and the Chaussée d'Antin. She was wearing a lime-green, loose waisted tube of a dress with an oversize dupion bow of the same colour low down on the left hip.

I toyed with a whisky-sour while she sipped that most innocuous of all cocktails, a White Lady. She answered my questions readily enough as I tried to draw her out a little. She lived at home, near the Luxemburg Gardens. She had spent one year at the Sorbonne. She was mad about the cakewalk and the charleston. She preferred the bus to the Métro — you met a better class of person — but Papa was teaching her to drive. That was really wild.

Her first contribution to the conversation — the first that wasn't a comment on something I'd said or an answer to a question — floored me. 'Paul,' she said, 'you're in the fashion business, on the inside. I wonder would you do me a great favour? I'm dying, simply dying to be a mannequin. Do you think you could possibly introduce me to Mado Laverne?'

I was staggered. 'Oh, *no*!' I exclaimed. 'Not you too!' I'd spoken loudly enough to startle the barman. Two businessmen nursing dry martinis turned around on their stools to stare at our table. Françoise looked abashed. 'Oh, my!' she faltered. 'Did I say the wrong thing? I'm awfully sorry; perhaps I shouldn't presume—'

'No, no. It's not that,' I cut in hastily. 'Forgive me. I didn't mean to bite your head off. It's just that . . . well, I guess it's no more than a coincidence, but you took me by surprise.'

'I don't understand.' She was almost tearful. 'I didn't mean—'

'You didn't do anything wrong, Françoise. My fault entirely. It happens that you're the second person in a week to ask me that, and the first, who . . . who took a lot of trouble . . . never followed it through, that's all.' I glanced across the table, not for the first time. Ye-es. Frankly, being tall and relatively flat-chested, this girl stood a much better chance than the busty Rosette of being taken on by Mado. 'Of course I'd be delighted to introduce you,' I said. 'I can't promise anything, but I'll do my best.'

'Paul, that's really dear of you. That's *wild*!' Suddenly she was animated again. I signalled the barman for another round.

We had dinner at Drouand's, two hundred yards away in the Rue des Augustins. I liked eating there because if the fish wasn't as good as it should be or the chef had made a mistake with the *cassoulet*, the waiter would tip you off. We shared a half bottle of champagne while we consulted the menu. As the level of Gewurtztraminer sank in the tall green bottle of Alsatian wine that followed it, Françoise became confidential.

Yes, it was nice living at home, but it did cramp your style a little. She loved the theatre, she really loved it, but going to the opera was more of an *occasion*, wasn't it? Deauville in the summer was still quite chic, but winter sports at Gstaad were much more fun. The *aprésski* parties there were just wild. Yes, she had had a couple of boyfriends; once she had even been engaged to be married, but the young man had been a provincial and he was mean with money. Apart from which, if one was used to Paris, one simply could not consider the *idea* of living in Clermont-Ferrand, could one?

'Absolutely not,' I said. 'Waiter! We'll have two Armagnacs with the coffee – the Bézaudun '08 if you still have it.'

'Oh, do you think I really should?' Françoise said. 'I feel a little tipsy, you know. Do you think I really should?'

'I'm convinced of it,' I said.

Waiting for the doorman to call up the cab was the critical moment. Living with her parents, she would have no apartment of her own available. Very few young girls in Paris did. On the other hand, a bold invitation to 'come back to my place' might be considered a little forward and frighten her off. A third choice – simply to give the cabbie my address and say nothing – would almost certainly be construed as 'taking her for granted'.

I solved the problem with a few hasty but well-thought-out phrases. I keyed the situation in with her wish to be a mannequin. Maybe, I said craftily, she would be interested to have a look at the clothes she would be modelling if Mado did take her on? She would? Well, it just so happened that some of the designs were on the drawing board in my studio this very night . . .

I told the cabbie to go to the Avenue de Versailles.

I showed Françoise the designs. She thought they were wild.

I made a pot of coffee. I thought it could be considered a mite too obvious if I proffered another drink. In any case, the groundwork had been done at Toni's and chez-Drouand.

Françoise swallowed coffee and returned to the sketch on my drawing board – a tiered evening gown featuring forty yards of heavily pleated lavender chiffon topped by a silver lamé bolero. 'Paul, do you really think I could do it?' she asked. 'Model for M-Mado, I m-m-mean?'

'No doubt about it,' I said.

'Let me show you how I'd do this one.' She

pirouetted away from the board and minced back and forth in front of me, one hand flouncing an imaginary skirt of lavender chiffon. She spun around several times – the legs below the short afternoon frock she was wearing were slender and splendid – paraded once more, and stopped in front of me with one hand on an out-thrust hip. 'Will I do?'

'You're smiling,' I said. 'Look haughty and disdainful; look down that admirable nose at the fools stupid enough to buy it. Stick out your hip a little more.'

She contrived a repeat performance. I sank into an overstuffed armchair beside the studio couch. Françoise turned and swayed back towards me, veered off course, and stumbled against the chair, collapsing across my knees with her legs draped over one arm and her back against the other. She smiled up at me, giggling. 'Silly me! Oh, Paul, you are sweet. Why are you so nice to me?' An arm rose, a hand stretched out, and cool fingers brushed a strand of hair off my forehead ('Fell into your bloody lap, you lucky beggar!' Tom Crawford said later).

The touch of her hand sent this galvanic thrill flaming through me. Involuntarily, I felt myself harden. I don't know if she was aware of it or not, but she wriggled her hips slightly, stiffening me more than ever. The hand smoothed over the top of my head and dropped to cradle the nape of my neck. The whole length of my spine tingled.

Françoise was still smiling. 'Oh, my!' she said, sleepily. 'Alone in a gentleman's apartment at this hour of night! I shouldn't be doing this, should I?'

'Definitely not,' I said.

'But I will, won't I?'

'I hope so,' I said.

The touch on my neck became a grip . . . and the grip, subtly but unmistakably, transformed itself into a gentle tug. I bent forward swiftly and kissed her on the lips.

It was a chaste enough kiss to start with. No tongues were involved. But her lips, clinging, clasping, held promise. I slid one arm around her shoulders, laying the other hand on her hip. I moved the hand into and then out of the hollow of her waist, gliding it up onto a breast. The breast, flattened even further by a tight bust bodice, scarcely swelled the stuff of her dress, but I could feel the nipple, unexpectedly large, hard already against my palm through the two layers of material.

I wasn't sure — yet — what the 'this' that she shouldn't be doing implied. Did it refer to what the young people of Paris were beginning to call 'going the whole way'? Was it restricted to kissing and a cuddle? Or did it merely mean her presence in this place at this time? There was only one way to find out.

I drew back my head to look at her face. Her chest was rising and falling rapidly; the brown eyes staring at me were expressionless.

There was no clue there. Her winey breath played warmly on my face. I rotated my palm against the stiffness of that nipple and then raised my hand to caress her cheek. 'You're beautiful,' I said huskily. 'You . . . really . . . are . . . the most fascinating—'

My words were choked off. With a sudden savage grasp, Françoise jerked my head down and crushed my lips to her open mouth. This time the tongues had their say. And this time there could be no doubt about it: the taut curves of her buttocks were definitely and deliberately screwing against the aching hardness at my loins, shifting from side to side rolling the rigid shaft between those fleshy mounds.

This, too, was about the time that I realized I had had quite a lot to drink. There was a period about which my memory remains oddly vague. Confused even. The exact order of things even today is unclear. I do recall though that — prompted perhaps by some vestige of gentlemanly concern — I asked at some point whether it was all right for her to stay out so late. Would her parents be angry? Worried? I had no wish to get her into trouble at home.

I remember that she laughed. She was over twenty-one, she said. She had her own latchkey. In any case she was out late quite often with friends, paying a visit to the Folies or dancing at one of the nightclubs in Montmartre.

It was here that the big blank intervened.

My next clear recollection — and sadly a whole exciting chapter must have been lost for ever — my next clear recollection is of Françoise kneeling on the floor, with the top half of her body leaning forward over the couch. And the lower half, from the waist downwards, being lewdly, salaciously, delightfully, completely naked . . .

Her dress, shoes, stockings, and a pair of white little-girl knickers with elasticated legs were strewn about the floor. Whether I had torn them off or she had, I had no idea. I was still fully dressed myself, except for my jacket and necktie.

The bust bodice, camisole top and short, lime-green lace underskirt that was rucked up around her waist served only to emphasise the obscene nudity of that slender, tight little bottom offered so shamelessly to my gaze, and the darkly furred crevice between its taut pink cheeks with the hint of moist flesh so enticingly exposed at its centre.

The sexual areas of women vary enormously. I can find no correspondence between physical types and genitalia. There are however, I would say, three broad headings under which the innumerable variants can be classified — at least from the external point of view. They seem to have a direct link with the pattern of the pubic hair, or so my own forty-one experiences confirm. This, the forty-second — and, no, this time we do *not* count Laurence! — was no exception.

In one type there is simply a slit in the smooth flesh at the base of the belly, the lips virtually invisible, a thin scythe of hairs forming a crescent between the vulva and an area just below the navel. Quite different are the organs, usually below a thick triangle of hair spreading as far as the crease of each thigh, which show two definite pads, or cushions of flesh, with a sliver, a wafer of creased pink skin caught between them. A third example, associated with a tangle of more straggly hair, turns the flesh outward in what can only be termed a pout. With arousal, of course, all this changes and both inner and outer labia flower open like a summer rose.

Françoise was in the second category — and it was definitely summertime.

She was murmuring something that sounded like a

request, a plea, her voice muffled by the rug into which her face was pressed.

I decided at any rate to interpret it as such. And given her stance and position, added to the fact that the legs suddenly parted slightly, dilating the half moon of pink flesh, it seemed to me that there could be no doubt whatever about the subject of that request. I mean, she wasn't going to be asking could I bring her another cup of coffee.

I whipped off my shirt, unbuckled my belt and shoved slacks and pants down to my thighs. I dropped on my knees immediately behind her, placing my hands on her buttocks.

Françoise shivered slightly in expectation. A faint flutter of muscles trembled the skin at the base of that narrow-hipped, boyish bottom. Amongst the dark hairs the crescent of flesh, dewed now with a single pearl of moisture, opened wider.

I was breathing hard myself. The stiffened lance of my cock speared out from my loins only inches away from her. Gently, I eased apart the quivering cheeks. Below the small, tightly wrinkled ring of her anus, distended labia gaped like a cut melon. Wine-dark beyond palely glistening outer and inner lips, the mysterious centre of her sexuality called me. I lunged forward and went into her.

Like the bright blade of a sword slamming into its scabbard, my throbbing staff forced its way up into the hot clasp of Françoise's belly. A throaty cry — of surprise? of pain? of delight? — escaped from her mouth. Her body jerked convulsively; her clenched fists pummelled the rug spread over the studio couch.

I leaned back, pulling her close against me, to savour that first delirious sensation of completeness, of being swallowed, ungulfed within the warm grasp of alien flesh.

But my tingling nerves refused to allow me to remain still. I backed off slightly, hands on her hips, pushing her away a fraction, then plunged forward, dragging her hard back against my pelvis so that my shaft once more penetrated the darkest hot depths of her body, the sword buried again up to the hilt.

I repeated the process, withdrawing, thrusting, retiring, advancing, establishing an accelerating rhythm that alternately rocked me back on my heels and then jammed me forward to meet the hips that were now bucking frantically to meet each stroke.

What bliss it was to feel the super-sensitive, inflated skin of my maleness massaged by the hot, wet, clinging clasp of those innermost lips!

I leaned forward over Françoise's back — still sliding easily in and out of that lubricated passage — and unbuttoned the camisole top, wedging my hands beneath her to push up the bust bodice and fondle her small breasts, fingering the thickened nipples while she moaned her pleasure into the rug.

Soon afterwards, heaving beneath my weight, she raised her head and uttered the first of a series of sobbing cries, shuddering out her release as interior muscles contracted around my hardness and I was clamped wetly between her jerking thighs.

Later, when the remaining garments had been discarded and we were both entirely naked, she lay spread-eagled on the day bed, crucified with her arms and legs flung wide, beseeching me to take her again — now, roughly, any way I liked. I was kneeling between her parted thighs. I looked down at her willowy, almost angular body, at the spread legs and the mat of dark, damp hair between them, the still dilated sexual lips and the big brown areolas with their oversize nipples . . . and I thought, well, just now, the way I liked was the way she was.

I inserted my hands beneath her buttocks, pulled her hips a little way up off the bed, and lowered myself to penetrate savagely the fleshy oval glistening among her pubic hair.

Françoise expelled her breath with a sound that was half sob and half sigh. As I pumped in and out of her, her hands raked down the length of my spine, between my buttocks and up each side to circle my armpits. The fingers still disseminated that extraordinary electric effect that spurred me to ever more violent exertions in the pelvic region and sent the blood thundering through my veins. But this was purely a matter of touch, and I recalled that in fact she rarely used the hands in an *adventurous* way or permitted them to be directed by her imagination. When, quite soon, I became seized with the intensity of my own excitement, convulsed, and squirted my tribute to her appeal high up into Françoise's belly, she had drawn up her knees and grasped an ankle in each of those hands.

It didn't matter that this time it had been for my pleasure and not hers. Despite the fact that there had been no lead-up to a second release for her, she climaxed at once when she felt me spurting within.

Some time afterwards — she was lying in the chair

with her legs lewdly spread and hooked over the arms — I raised myself from her loins and for some reason slapped her once, hard, across the face. She came instantly.

By then of course I had realised: the paradox was easily explained.

The Mackenzie Chart for the Classification of Female Genitalia is paralleled by a sister document, Female Approach to Sex, the result of my own unaided research. Following the experiences with which you are familiar, I had reckoned that a number of separate headings — five, in this case — could broadly cover the types of women a libidinous male might normally be expected to meet.

There were those who considered sex a chore, often a distasteful one; those who would have liked to play — often did play — but were naturally frigid; the enthusiasts in favour in principal, but who could never unwind sufficiently to enjoy it; those who regarded it as a pleasure to be indulged in *with* someone; and those for whom it was something, however enjoyable, that was done *to* you.

Françoise was in the last category. Like many women, she found her excitement in situations where she was *forced* into intimacy, where she was obliged to submit. Her natural diffidence, her prudishness even, was a stockade, a barrier which had to be scaled before that electric sensuality which had so impressed me could be *taken advantage of*. She was a spectator of her own defilement in what Dr Freud would have described as 'the rape fantasy'.

Once I had come to terms with this, I played the game her way.

I took her in every possible manner. I ordered her to perform every whorish task I could think of. I told her what to do with those inactive hands and instructed her in the use of the mouth, slapping her occasionally if she proved a backward pupil.

It was three o'clock in the morning before I stole down the stairs and out into the Avenue de Versailles to find a cab, so that I could take her home to Maman and Papa.

Chapter Six

Before I married Camille, she shared an apartment with the *Figaro* gossip columnist, Corinne Dubois, in the Rue St André-des-Arts, on the Left Bank. Tom Crawford's studio, converted from an abandoned bakery, was on the ground floor of the same old building. The sculptor was still there, but Corinne had moved to a smarter quarter: she lived now in a modern riverside block in Passy. The three of us had remained good friends, however, and we still, ten years later, met fairly frequently — were we not, after all, fellows and founder members of the Knights of the Bottle?

There was a closer link that bound me to Corinne. She had been on my private and personal bedtime list before it ran into double figures. Once, at a masked society ball given by the couturier Paul Poiret, I had spent a whole lustful night with her under the mistaken impression that she was the room-mate I was subsequently to marry. On another occasion, Crawford joined us for a minor orgy at one of Paris's most famous brothels. And although her roving eye normally searched out new conquests, it occasionally still settled on me if there was nothing more fruitful in sight. If I couldn't get away in time, that is.

It was natural enough therefore, when a prospective

escort chickened out, that she would ask me if I'd care to use the spare invitation she had to the pre-collection show given by the mysterious Monsieur Simbel.

'Love to,' I said. 'I'd be fascinated to see what all the fuss is about. What time and when?'

'Seven o'clock on Thursday.'

'Jolly good. Why not pick me up at the studio? Mado's whip keeps the old nose to the grindstone, you know, and I'm having a job finishing her stuff on time. Come around about six, and we'll have a snifter before we go.'

'I'll do that,' Corinne said.

Only she didn't, of course. Come around about six, I mean. She came at five fifteen, while I was still in the tub. And since — I think I mentioned it — I never use the antique lock, she just opened the landing door and walked straight in.

'Who is it?' I called.

'Me, darling.'

'Oh, Corinne!' I protested. 'Come on, now. I'm still in the bath, and I won't be ready for—'

I broke off. She was standing in the bathroom doorway, her generous figure swathed in blue *voile*. Behind the spectacles, her hunter's eyes gleamed.

I'd tried to make a quick exit from the hot water and dash for the towelling bathrobe behind the door. I was too late: she caught me standing up, with one foot on the edge of the tub and nothing but a small hand towel to cover . . . well, whatever I thought needed covering. With Corinne that would have to be a bath sheet!

'Paul! How nice. What a pleasant surprise.' The eyes rested on the equipment between my legs. She snatched away the hand towel. 'How *very* nice!'

'Look, sweetie,' I said hastily. 'I don't really think—'

'I've never done it in a bath, hot water and all that,' Corinne said. 'At any rate not with a man.' She stood very close to the tub, reaching out a hand towards my damp genitals. 'I think it's a wonderful idea.'

'It isn't *my* idea. I really don't want . . . I think—'

'Don't think,' she said, the hoarse, sexy note already in her voice. 'Just relax.' She was stroking my cock, fingertips idly promenading the shaft.

'Corinne . . .'

'I can't think of a nicer way to begin an evening.'

'I'm all wet.'

'I just *love* wet men!' Corinne enthused. She let go of me and crossed her arms. Corinne could undress more rapidly than anyone I ever met. She whisked the blue dress over her head, unbuttoned some kind of bodice and shoved a pair of lacy French knickers down to her ankles before I'd stepped out of the bath and onto the mat.

'Sweetheart,' I said. 'I love you very much, but I don't want—'

'Of course you want to. I know you do; I can see you do; I can *feel* you do!' She felt me. It was true: despite my resolutions, I was stiffening, lengthening. There was nothing I could do to stop it. Blast!

Corinne bent down. Shoes, knickers, stripped-off stockings skittered across the floor. She stood naked beside me: the breasts were large and loose but they hadn't dropped; the stomach was rounded and the hips fleshy, but she had managed to keep a small, trim waist.

Quite suddenly, she leaned against me and shoved.

Reckless Liaisons

Caught off balance, I stumbled against the edge of the tub and fell back into the hot water with a huge splash.

Corinne leaped in after me, sending a soapy wave slopping out over the rim and onto the linoleum covering the floor. She lowered herself, while I was still spluttering, and sat facing me with her back to the brass taps. Her two feet shot forward between by thighs and homed on my crotch. Her toes curled; she was rolling my shaft between the soles of her feet beneath the surface. She grinned at me impishly.

'Look, this is all very well . . .' I began weakly.

'Isn't it?' said Corinne. 'We should have tried it ages ago!' She took a cake of Roger-Gallet from the soap-dish and lathered the swelling slopes of her breasts. One of her heels jammed my genitals hard against my pubic bone . . . and I was forced to accept it: it was no longer any use denying the fact — proximity and touch and the sight of that lush nude body had rendered my cock as stiff as a plank.

I jammed my hands on the curved edges, levered myself upright, and stood up in the bath. Like it or not, the girl was going to have to realise that *I* called the tune in my own place; I wasn't going to be seduced into a sex scene I didn't want by this indecent display; I would step out of the bath, dry myself, and start to dress. Now!

She had hitched herself forward on her haunches. Water swirled. She wrapped both arms around my upper thighs. The slippery breasts grazed my knees. She tilted back her head, smiling up at me, and I saw with surprise that she was still wearing her spectacles, the thick lenses dewed with drops of water.

I saw too that the spearing proof of my unwanted

virility throbbed a fraction of an inch from her mouth. The tip of a pink tongue moistened her upper lip and the lower one. Before I could make a decisive move, the lips opened, her head bobbed forward, the mouth closed . . . and I shivered with involuntary delight as the familiar hot clasp closed tightly around me. Teeth grated gently against the sensitive skin of my staff; a tongue licked busily at the underside of the throbbing head. I groaned aloud.

There was nothing for it. My legs were shaking. I looked down at her hollowed cheeks and sucking mouth. 'Oh, God,' I said, 'Corinne, you are a dreadful woman!'

She freed her head and grinned up at me. 'Aren't I?' she agreed cheerfully.

She stood up to face me, the soft belly slung against my hardness, soaped breasts squashed to my chest. Slowly, lasciviously, she lathered me too, practised hands sliding the slithery foam over my shoulders, down my back, around hips and haunches, between my buttocks and then around to the front to milk my shaft. I took the soap and massaged the rest of her. We were clamped together, belly to slippery belly, the oiled flesh moving easily as we squirmed and writhed. Both of us were breathing hard now.

And suddenly she broke free and turned her back on me. Supporting herself with her two hands on the taps, she leaned right forward and looked over her shoulder to gasp: 'Give it to me, Paul. Put it in. I want to feel you inside me *now*!'

A froth of soapsuds surrounded the drops of water spiking the hairs clustered thickly in the furrow between the wet globes of her buttocks. Her secret lips gaped open. I stretched forward over her back. The heavy breasts hanging from her chest dropped like shelled eggs into my hands, I took the weight of them on my palms as I flexed my hips and drove into her, straight as a die. She expelled her breath in a shuddering sigh.

For what seemed an age we held that pose — the bathwater, rapidly cooling now, swashing around our ankles, our two bodies scarcely moving as I thrust fractionally in and out of her, Corinne heaving back minimally to meet each thrust, my hands fondling those ripe breasts with their hardened nipples.

And then all at once she pushed me away and straightened up, pressing her hands to the base of her spine. 'Oh, Paul darling,' she gasped, 'my *back*! I'm so sorry . . . it's *awful*, isn't it? So damned unromantic! . . . but one isn't as young as one was.'

Privately, I was as grateful for the respite as she was: hinged into the shape of an L, one is not in the most relaxed of positions for lovemaking. But by now she had got me going, and I wasn't just ready to call it a day and give up. I sat down in the water again, pulling Corinne, still with her back to me, into my lap. Another soapy tidal wave swamped the floor.

I slid straight up into her as her fleshy haunches settled on my thighs. 'My God,' she breathed, 'it's never been in so deep!'

It was her turn to grip the edges of the bath. She pushed herself up a few inches and then sank down again, impaled on the quivering spike that was jammed up into the hot depths of her belly. I caught my breath each time she lowered herself, the aching focus of my desire tunnelling into her flesh as easily as an index into the finger of a velvet glove. Water sloshed up the enamelled sides of the bath each time she lunged down on me. 'Dreadful,' I moaned. 'You *are* indeed a dreadful girl . . . but, my goodness, it's so good!'

After a while, she tired again and lay back, still with the cock trapped inside her, against my chest. Her damp head was on my shoulder. I plucked away the misted spectacles, twisted around slightly, and kissed her. Our lips clamped and clung and sucked and gobbled greedily. It wouldn't be long now. I sensed the exquisite pressure in my loins starting to spread . . . upwards and outwards, into the belly and the tightening chest, the blood thundering in the ears and behind the eyes.

I wrapped my arms around the wet body plastered against me, my left forearm supporting the weight of those heavy breasts, the right hand searching, finding, spreading underwater lips. I caressed the tiny shaft of flesh within them, manipulating it against the hard column of my own engulfed stem until a growl deep in my companion's throat signalled the mounting approach of her jerking orgasm.

At the same time – Corinne could do this – she made me come, ecstatically, wildly, simply by contracting and relaxing alternately the ridged muscles of her vagina.

We made the show with minutes to spare, but we never did have time for the promised drink. We were both (as Crawford would have said) as *clean* as a whistle – but it was too late for the whistle to be wetted!

Monsieur Ahmed Simbel was indeed (Crawford again) a

swarthy Levantine. He was a short, spare man, about forty years old, with a dark, lined face and patent leather hair that looked as though it had been glued to his round, Semitic skull. He was wearing a beautiful, pearl-grey Savile Row suit, white *glacé* kid shoes, and a Paisley silk scarf knotted into a large bow instead of a necktie. His cuffed trousers were very wide.

The show was on the first floor of the Rue St Roch mansion. The huge room had been decorated in oriental style, with rich hangings and Ispahan rugs on the wall. A Turkish carpet covered the turnaround at the end of the narrow gangway and there were occasional items of *chinoiserie* among the gilded chairs on either side of it. At the far end of the room from the archway through which the mannequins would enter, a small Negro band played ragtime on a dais banked with hibiscus and lotus blossoms.

Turning convention on its head for the second time, Simbel had organised the reception and cocktail party *before*, rather than after, the showing of his collection. The drinks were served in an anteroom already packed with people, and the high-pitched waves of conversation beneath the crystal chandeliers were deafening.

Corinne had a column to fill and work to do, interviewing anyone she thought worth a mention. I relinquished her, took a glass of pink champagne from a tray carried by a waiter in a white jacket, and looked around the crowded room.

A few of Paris's minor − or younger − designers (Doeuillet, the Callot Sisters, Patou) had accepted invitations, but Mado and the rest of the Top Ten had pointedly stayed away to mark their disdain for the interloper who was daring to upstage them and preempt the Collections. Paris society as a whole, though, was well represented. Curiosity is inevitably a draw; snobbery even more so. If the Duchesse of X was going to be there, the Marquise of Y could not possibly afford to miss the occasion . . . and Madam Z would pull every string she could lay hands on to ensure that she too received an invitation. In fashionable Paris of 1922, 'one' could not conceivably afford to be left out.

There were quite a number of people at the reception whom I knew myself. Friends such as Crawford and fellow Knights Hans Bohl and Bertrand Laforge; rival illustrators like Barbier and Lepape; technical workers and craftsmen from the industry on the lookout for anything new; newspaper folk in search of a story.

I saw a couple of bankers and their overdressed wives. I saw Françoise with a good-looking older woman I took to be her mother. I exchanged greetings with Dagmar van den Bergh, a red-haired divorcée *Comtesse* who had been, a dozen years ago, one of the leaders of the fashionable lesbian cult known as the *Amazones*. I had a drink with a woman known simply as Milady, who was the owner of a high-class brothel next door to Tom Crawford's studio in the Rue St André-des-Arts.

Milady – who had been given that name when she was young by fellow street-walkers, because of her airs and graces – was now a well-preserved fifty, a Junoesque figure with upswept pale hair, still tightly corseted in this revolutionary period of loose clothes and no foundations.

'Paul, *chéri*,' she chided. 'How long is it since you have been to see me? A year? Eighteen months? The girls are pining away for the lack of their *beau anglais*!'

'Darling, I've been busy,' I said. 'And, let us be frank, a lot of people — a lot more people — are giving it away free now!'

She swept the room with her scornful glance. 'This kind of *canaille*? The world is not what it used to be. You remember, Paul; you were here before this dreadful war, when folks could mingle with their own class. Don't tell me you find this preferable . . . In any case, Nellie desolates herself that you come to visit her no more.

Nellie Lebérigot, the daughter of a Breton fisherman, was the voluptuous senior girl at Milady's — and her oldest friend. 'Is Nellie here?' I asked, glancing around at the throng of drinkers.

Milady shook her head. 'Impossible. The Arch-Duke is in town. The ex-Arch-Duke, I should say.'

'Can one be both "ex" and "Arch"?' I queried.

'Dear boy,' said Milady, 'you can be anything you want if you have the money.'

The Comtesse van den Bergh was with a tall, dark, beetle-browed German Baroness — a species of which she appeared to have an inexhaustible supply. 'Paul, darling,' she cooed. 'An eternity. Why is my *salon* no longer blessed with your presence?'

(All right, she was Number Thirteen if you must know — in a moment of heterosexual aberration on her part. I don't count the professionals; they are, as the French say, *hors-festival* — in a separate category.)

'My apologies, *chère Comtesse*,' I said. 'I abase myself.'

'Quite right, too,' Dagmar said. 'For a male. There

Reckless Liaisons

are people coming on Friday. There is a young woman who might interest you. I shall expect you at any time after four.'

'Your wish, Madame,' I said, 'is my command. You sexy trollop!'

Dagmar grinned and towed her glowering Baroness away.

I circulated. A word here, a light-hearted quip there. Tom Crawford was with a peroxide blonde, bowed in a gold lamé dress beneath a vast feathered and flowered hat. 'When is a lampshade not a lampshade?' Tom demanded, eyeing this confection and that of an elderly socialite standing nearby. 'When it is a hat . . . with blue flowers growing on it in woolly cloth, and worsted tassels hanging down.'

I smiled dutifully and passed on. He had misquoted that one too. At one time I thought I saw the enigmatic Rosette. But the crowd closed in and it was announced that the show was about to begin before I could get to her.

Despite all the ballyhoo, and a certain amount of speculation in the press – after all, the man was completely unknown in Paris, London and New York – Ahmed Simbel's Collection was nothing out of the ordinary. At least not until the final models. When the lid was at last lifted on the past few weeks' carefully orchestrated secrecy, the pot was shown to be fairly empty.

'It looks,' whispered Corinne, who was sitting next to me, 'as if all this stuff was copied from a 1913 edition of *Harper's Bazaar*, with eighteen inches chopped off the hem of each dress!'

The designer himself gave the commentary, in a passionless, reedy voice. I hadn't talked to him during the reception, but I had received the impression of a smug, self-important and over-assertive person – a little man, in every sense of the word, trying to be big. Several of the top fashion journalists left before the show was halfway through.

The jazz band played suitable tunes as each model was announced and the mannequin catwalked along the raised gangway – *Valencia* for a flounced Spanish number; *On The Alamo* for three linked frocks, morning, afternoon and evening, featuring star and stripe motifs; *Ostrich Walk* when the model was swathed in a pagan, African-style shift fashioned from gaudy fabrics in harsh colours. Perhaps the most daring was a pure white, skirted bathing suit with long legs and an excessively low-cut back worn by a dusky girl from the French colony of Martinique. The band welcomed this with *The Black Bottom*.

This produced a ripple of amusement, but the applause on the whole was polite rather than enthusiastic. Until the end, that is.

'And now, ladies and gentlemen,' Simbel intoned, 'for the high point of this modest incursion into the territory of the famous. The clothes you have seen so far have been designed for the everyday, the ordinary occasion. We are not, here, pandering to the exclusive or the avant-garde, but simply to the lady of taste who wishes to complement her natural beauty with something that is wearable but at the same time original. For my last two presentations, however, I allow myself a bow – a deep bow – in the direction of the unusual

Reckless Liaisons

and the opulent. Ladies and gentlemen . . . *Estrellita* . . . and *Foxy*!'

The lights dimmed; a single spot lanced through the gloom to illuminate the space immediately behind the archway. The band pianist launched into a slow-drag version of the *Elite Syncopations* rag.

Framed by the arch was a black Bosendorfer grand piano. A mannequin was posed in the sweeping curve of the instrument; another sat at the keyboard. Behind them, a monocled man leaned negligently against a Corinthian pillar.

The standing model wore an outrageous orange *crêpe-de-chine* sheath, with her small breasts barely covered by two pleated panels of magenta satin which rose from a peplum bunched around her hips. The panels were attached to a rhinestone halter, and a fringed overskirt fell to the floor from behind the girl's knees.

The piano player's gown was a cowled, heavy silk tube in a bold butterfly-wing pattern of cinnamon and chocolate brown. Above an extra-low waist, emphasised by a loose electric blue sash, the dress was slit up to the armpits each side to reveal a peach-coloured camisole. The narrow skirt flared out at ankle height into a wide hem that was trimmed with blue fox fur.

The man glided forward, took each girl by the hand, and led her down the gangway to the turnaround, where they pirouetted and then bowed to the audience. This time the burst of applause was genuine. From somewhere at the back, a man's voice called in English: '*Very* smart!' Corinne was clapping enthusiastically.

I didn't join in.

These designs were no copies filched from a pre-war fashion magazine.

They were copied, panel for panel, stitch for stitch, colour for daring colour, from the designs on the drawing board in my studio a couple of weeks ago — designs that nobody but Mado Laverne and myself was so far supposed to have seen . . .

Chapter Seven

Mado Laverne found out about the pirated designs from the next morning's newspapers. I had intended to be waiting when the day staff opened up the workrooms at eight o'clock, but a flustered messenger was knocking at the door of my studio at seven fifteen, with a peremptory demand for me to go to the Rue des Capucines 'at once'.

I went. Mado was in a towering rage. The pale hair was drawn back more tightly than ever; the chiselled lips were set in a hard line. It was difficult to remember that only a few days ago my hands had been on the breasts quivering with anger beneath her severe black silk suit.

'What have you got to say?' she grated. No Paul, no dear or darling, not even a good morning.

The papers — three of them — were spread out on her desk.

'Simbel's' sensational evening gowns had been given a lot of space. They were only photographs of course, black and white, but I knew the fashion editors must have had the prints long before the show if they were to have blocks made and get the pictures into the early editions.

I swallowed. 'Mado, I don't know what to say.'

I knew that her entire collection was built around

those two models. Now that they had been stolen — and shown, with plenty of publicity — there was no way she could use them, or any variation of the designs. Not only that: apart from the loss of income involved, she would have to rethink the whole show, including the creation, design and making of two replacement models, with little more than a week to go before the Collections.

'How *could* you?' Mado said. 'You knew perfectly well . . . how could you do such a thing?'

'I didn't *do* anything,' I said wretchedly. 'I don't know how on earth that beastly little Lebanese got hold of your designs. I can't think how—'

'He got them from you. Or through you. He must have. *You* had the original sketches, the samples of material, the only copies of the patterns; you are the only person it could have been.'

'Mado, it's not true.' I cried. 'Couldn't one of the girls, a seamstress perhaps, or a *vendeuse*, have talked out of turn? Or told him—'

'You can't copy something in *this* detail' — she tapped one of the photographs viciously with the back of her hand — 'just by being told about it. He must have had sight of the material confided to you.'

'I brought you my gouache a while ago, and returned all the stuff at the same time,' I said reasonably. 'Maybe someone at the printer's . . . ?'

'Your design hasn't *gone* to Vogel yet.' She was still pale with fury. 'I put it straight in my safe with the rest of the originals. It's still there. I checked.'

'And there's nobody else with access to the safe?'
'Nobody.'

I bit my lip. 'And the actual models, the gowns themselves?'

'They are not made up yet.'

'Mado,' I said, 'I swear to you—'

'Madame Laverne, if you please.' The voice was icy.

'Madame Laverne, I give you my word of honour...'

'That is not a word I am inclined to take. In the circumstances. Oh, I am not suggesting that you were actually bribed, that you *sold* the designs; but you were indiscreet, you talked too much, you allowed someone to see them while they were in your possession. And that kind of betrayal is unforgivable.'

'Have you spoken to Ahmed Simbel?'

'Naturally. I had him woken before seven. I accused him of theft. He had the effrontery to feign indignation!' Mado gave a sharp bark of laughter. 'He was impudent. Arrogant too. He even admitted that the designs were not his own. They had been sold to him, he said, by a young Chilean designer who was passing through Paris and needed money to get home to South America. A likely story,' she sneered. 'Especially as this convenient Chilean is said to have left already — and to be on his way back to Valparaiso or Concepçion aboard the *Rex*!'

'There is nothing you can do legally?'

'Nothing. Since the pirated version has been shown first I am helpless. And if I used my own, *I* could be accused of plagiarism.'

I sighed. 'What *are* you going to?'

'Hire a new illustrator,' Mado said. 'One that I can trust. Good day to you, Monsieur Mackenzie.'

*   *   *

I was shattered by Simbel's duplicity. And astonished beyond reason. But the surprise derived less from the jolt of seeing my own pictorial design reproduced in three dimensions in the Lebanese's showroom than from a realisation of my own naîveté. Because of course Mado was right. The fact that Simbel had repeated *my* invented décor as well as her dresses proved that it was from my studio that the designs had been stolen. Because nobody but Mado had seen the gouache since it left there.

And while I was doing it I *had* been indiscreet; I had talked too much and I had allowed someone to see what was on my drawing board.

Rosette.

Someone had talked all right, but only in general terms, in the sense that two brilliant designs existed . . . and that they could be found in my studio.

Simbel must have heard about this and hired the little bitch to get them.

Given that proposition, a lot of pieces of the puzzle slotted into place.

No wonder Rosette had never contacted me again!

No wonder she shied away, with such a limp excuse, when I offered to introduce her at once to Mado; no wonder she never gave me a surname and persisted in her refusal — on the shakiest grounds — to provide me with her address.

It was no surprise, either, given the circumstances, that she couldn't answer my innocent questions about the wine supposedly marketed by her invented father. Or that she was caught off balance and unable on the spur of the moment to think of a town in Burgundy where she might have been born.

As for that odd request for me to run out and buy her cigarettes when she was hurrying away herself a few minutes later, that was the easiest one of all to answer . . . when you knew the real aim of the operation.

While I was away she would have produced a camera – probably hidden in the cupboard on the landing – and taken as many photographs of the design as she thought necessary. And that could have been plenty because, using her body as bait, she had been careful to make sure that she remained in my place until the summer sun, pouring through the floor-to-ceiling windows, filled the studio with brilliant light.

The pictures would have been black and white, of course, but she could have taken notes – or even snipped off the tiniest strips from the material samples. Simbel would then have had the models made up, and photographs taken of the actual garments to circulate to the press before his show.

For me the unkindest cut of all was a note from Corinne pushed under my door. *Figaro* had not received copies of the publicity photos. *Paul* – she wrote reproachfully – *you might have told me! After all, you did come as my guest: you could easily have tipped me off and slipped me one of those pictures well before. Next time you want to sell out a copyright, try and remember who are your friends*.

The bitch had taken it for granted right away that I was the guilty one!

So I was out of a job, and my name would be mud in

the fashion business – because I dare not admit what had really happened. Especially since I had seen a small full-face portrait photo at the head of a column in one of the papers running the pictures. The column was headed simply *La Mode – the Latest from our Fashion Expert Desirée Schneider*. The photograph, complete with know-all expression and slight smile, was of the columnist.

It was slightly smudged but there was no possibility of a mistake. The face of Desirée Schneider was the face of the girl I knew as Rosette.

Not only had I been indiscreet; I had been indiscreet with a newspaper gossip columnist!

In the circumstances there was only one thing to do. I went to the nearest post office, climbed the stairs to the public telephone room, and gave the woman behind the counter two numbers. I called two fellow Knights of the Bottle, Bertrand Laforge and Hans Bohl. 'Gird up your randy loins,' I told each of them. 'Tonight a great deal of champagne must be drunk, and we're going to the One-Two-Five to chase up the sexiest girls in town . . .'

Chapter Eight

The One-Two-Five was the brothel owned by the woman known as Milady, so called because it was at No. 125 Rue St André-des-Arts, next door to the seventeenth century house where Tom Crawford had his studio.

Milady's was a newer building, dating from the early 19th century – a one time *hotel particulier* or town mansion, built around a cobbled courtyard which was entered through an archway closed by tall wooden doors. The establishment was not equipped with such extravagant, almost surrealist, opulence as houses like the famous No.6 Rue des Moulins, once the home of the painter Toulouse Lautrec, or Mme Kelly's Chabanais. But it was comfortable, Milady was a splendid hostess, and the carefully chosen girls were intelligent and companionable as well as beautiful. As was the case in many of Paris's hundred-odd licensed brothels, it was not obligatory to avail yourself of the talent; you could meet friends there for a drink, flirt with the beauties at the bar, or discuss the declining standards of behaviour with Milady over a bottle of champagne. But if you didn't take one of the girls upstairs, the drinks of course were liable to be dearer.

Hans Bohl and Bertrand were already there when I

arrived. They were sitting over a bottle of Pol Roger at one of the low tables scattered around the lofty first-floor reception hall. Two or three girls in glittering evening gowns cut low to show off their breasts were joking with a group of blue-uniformed Spahi officers in an alcove beneath the stairs. An elderly, distinguished-looking man in evening dress leaned over the brass and mahogany bar conversing with Jules, who had been dispensing Milady's drinks for years.

It was early in the evening, the slack time: business would be much brisker later on; for the moment, below the chandeliers in the big, panelled room, there was only the discreet hum of conversation punctuated by an occasional laugh from one of the girls.

Hans Bohl, tall, blond and muscular, looked up and grinned as I joined the table. 'Greetings, Sir Paul,' he drawled, the German accent barely noticeable. 'Now what brings three Knights together in solemn conclave in this gaudy bawdy house? What triumphs do we celebrate? Enlighten us.'

I enlightened them. 'I'm out of a job,' I said. 'The name of Mackenzie stinks in the nostrils of the world of fashion. I have no prospects. I suppose you could say that we're celebrating my freedom!' I signalled Jules to bring us another bottle.

'But, Paul, what on earth happened?' Bertrand, small, dark, wiry, and the perfect complement to Hans, looked concerned. I told them what had happened. All of it. Including the duplicity of Desirée/Rosette.

When I had finished, Hans laughed. 'Oho! "Somebody's been sleeping in *my* bed!" squealed the baby bear. "And they fucked up my whole career." I tell you, Sir Paul: they are not like horses — you should *always* look a gift girl in the—'

'But, Hans, we must help him,' Bertrand interrupted. 'There's always work in Papa's design department. Of a kind. Or maybe Corinne could suggest something in the newspaper line?'

'There is only one thing Corinne would ever suggest!' Hans observed.

'True, O King. Spoken like a true prophet,' I said. I recounted the saga of the bathroom assault, embroidering the story a little. In this revised version, Corinne had arrived at *four* fifteen. Perhaps fortunately, the climax of the account — if the term can be excused — was cut short by the arrival of Milady, bursting out of a coffee-coloured lace sheath and gleaming with gold bracelets.

'Paul, *chéri*!' she cried, throwing her arms so wide that the bracelets clattered. 'And your dear friends! At *last* my salon is favoured with your company. What a joy to see you again . . . a joy, just for once, to be able to mingle with folk of one's own class. What are you all drinking?' She peered at a bottle. 'Ah, the Pol Roger. A good choice. Now tell me: are you going to be gallant enough to bring pleasure to my girls as well as to me? Nellie will be free later, and I am sure that Candice or Suzette would wish to—'

'It depends on the effect of your champagne,' I said.

'Then you had better have another bottle, dear boy,' said Milady. 'On the house.' She raised a beringed finger to summon Jules.

The place was filling up. The noise level had risen. There was a lot more laughter now. And a lot more girls. A pianola was playing in one of the back rooms.

The distinguished-looking man had moved to a settee, where he was fondling a fresh-faced child who looked no more than sixteen. 'That's the ex-King of Montenegro,' Hans told us.

'It never reigns but what it paws!' a sepulchral voice intoned behind us. Tom Crawford had joined the Knights at the round table.

'Tom,' I protested, 'you've been using that line since before the war, when they weren't even ex!'

He was unrepentant. 'A good pun,' he said, 'is hard to come by. We owe it to the dear things, once they do arrive, to get as much mileage out of them as possible.'

'Well, that one must be nearing the end of the road,' Bertrand said, 'because any day now you're going to run out of kings.'

'Then I'll have to conthentrate on the queenth,' Crawford lisped, in a mincing, limp-wristed voice.

Nellie Lebérigot — to my relief — was standing by the table. She was a well-built woman, dark and busty, about the same age as Milady. The gossips said that, twenty years ago, they had both been streetwalkers; Nellie was rumoured to have been one of the several hundred young girls who paid twenty francs a month, at that time, for the privilege of parading their charms every night in the huge *promenoir* at the back of the stalls in the Folies Bergère. Tonight, statuesque and yet still nubile, she was swathed in a velvet dress of midnight blue. The black hair, unfashionably long, was pinned up with a Spanish tortoiseshell comb.

I invited her to sit down and have a drink. Nellie and I were old mates — in more than one sense. She squeezed my hand, glancing appreciatively at Bertrand and Hans. 'Perhaps your friends would care to meet my friends?' she murmured, nodding her head at two young women hovering nearby. I raised my eyebrows. Yes, please, they would.

Candice was a tall and willowy blonde with shingled hair. She wore a fringed knee-length dress that seemed to be made mostly of pale blue sequins. Quite naturally she gravitated to Hans's side of the table. Suzette's plump little body was encased in skin-tight crimson taffeta with a scooped-out neck. She had chestnut hair and smiling eyes. It was clear that Bertrand found her entrancing.

Crawford had drifted away. He was deep in conversation, on the far side of the room, with a thin, wiry brunette named Lily Leblanc — the White Lily — who was rumoured to have acquired a number of extremely recondite techniques during a visit to the Far East.

There were differences in the way the girls at the One-Two-Five — and anywhere else, I suppose — related to their clothes. For some, clearly, they were no more than what happened to be covering the important element: their body. Others appeared to be cosseted by their clothes. Still others preened, flaunted themselves or manipulated garments to show off their better features. There were different words for these different attitudes. Milady, for instance, could only be said to be *caparisoned*. Candice was decorated by; Nellie and Suzette were dressed in; Lily simply wore. What she was wearing tonight was a short, tight black skirt, a black leather corset, and high-heeled black boots which reached halfway up her thighs. Crawford, who was drinking beer from a silver tankard, held one of her black-gloved hands.

At our table, Milady's bottle of champagne was finished. Hans and Candice exchanged glances. She placed a hand on his arm. My German friend smiled, nodded to me, and rose a little unsteadily to his feet. Candice steered him towards the curving, shallow stairway that swept up to the two floors above.

The four of us exchanged idiotic pleasantries for a while; we discussed the latest news with becoming gravity — Roald Amundsen's ship, the *Maud*, would carry a crated seaplane to help reconnaissance on his current exploration of the polar regions; a meteorological report, forecasting the coming weather, was to be read out each day and broadcast by radio-telegraphy from the transmitter on the Eiffel Tower.

Finally there was a silence. Tom Crawford passed us on the way upstairs. He had taken Lily's arm and seemed to be scrutinising with great attention the wrinkled leather at the wrist of her elbow-length glove. 'Well . . .' Bertrand said, with a sideways look at his companion.

I rather fancied the roly-poly, laughing Suzette myself — but he was obviously so taken with her that I hadn't the heart to break up the party the way it had arranged itself. What the hell . . . I could see Suzette another time; Nellie and I were old bedmates. Nice, comfortable, warm and loving Nellie was probably just what I needed. After the shock of Rosette's betrayal and the interview with Mado, I needed the warmth, I needed reassurance and sympathy and a touch of the old there-there with a cooling hand on the brow. I did not, for once, want to play the all-conquering male, the scalp-hunter, the seducing Casanova; I wanted security and an understanding ear. A tiny shred of admiration wouldn't come amiss either.

Maybe I felt I had some expiation to do. A psychologist, I guess, would say that I was looking for a surrogate mother. The point, anyway, was that Nellie could – and would – give me all of those things.

I took her hand and stood up. Bertrand and Suzette chose the same moment for an identical manoeuvre. We grinned goodnight and went our separate ways.

Nellie made sure that we were given the Blue Room. This was on the top floor, at the back of the house, where the tinkling of the pianola was less intrusive and boisterous laughter from the bar muffled.

The moment old Marthe, the maid who had been with Milady since she opened the place in 1910, had deposited the hot water and left the room, I knew I'd made the right decision.

Nellie's welcome-back smile was a life-saver, full of tenderness and complicity. 'My poor Paul,' she murmured, 'you're not yourself. You're all tense; your smile is forced. There's something the matter isn't there?'

I nodded wordlessly. For some reason – probably too much to drink and not enough to eat – there was a tightness constricting my throat. My eyes pricked almost as if tears were gathering.

'Tell me about it,' Nellie said.

I swallowed. 'Later,' I said. 'After we have . . . later on perhaps.'

'Just as you like, darling. You know you can confide

in Nellie. Nothing you say here goes beyond this room, you know that.'

'I know I can trust you,' I said.

'Good.' She sat on the wide, brass-railed bed. 'Now help me out of this dress and we can relax.'

I got on the bed and knelt up behind her. From the neck to the base of her spine, the blue velvet was fastened with innumerable hooks and eyes. One by one, the fingers a little clumsy, I slid them apart. As the edges of the dress gaped, a widening triangle of creamy skin, crossed by the lacy band of a bust bodice, appeared.

The nape of her neck looked, as they so often do, curiously defenceless. One tendril had escaped from the Spanish comb holding up her hair. I bent my head and kissed the nape, running my lips a little way down her spine. She gave a slight shiver, uttering a small sound of pleasure — and I felt at once the unmistakable tightening of the loins signalling that shortness of breath and adrenaline flow and thumping of the heart summed up in the three letters S-E-X.

It's amazing, astonishing how quickly the cares and worries, the hates and jealousies, the hurts and slights and disappointments of life fly out of the window once that finger of flesh and muscle at the bottom of our bellies stirs . . . and stiffens . . . and points unerringly at the object of our desire!

I eased the velvet dress off Nellie's plump shoulders, sliding the sleeves down her arms. When the clinging, cat-like material was around her waist, I wrapped my arms in front of her and cupped her breasts, the rough indentations of lace cradled in my palms contrasting with the smooth, soft weight of flesh within. She leaned back against my hardness as her nipples erected under my thumbs. 'Oh, my!' she breathed. 'There's a soldier eager for standby duty in there! Undress, relax, and bring him out into the open air while I nip into the douche a mo.'

She freed herself from my embrace, pushed down her dress, stepped out of it, and walked into the *lavabo* cubicle wearing nothing but the bust bodice, stockings and wide-legged, white lace French knickers. I tore off my own clothes hastily and lay on my back on the bed, the proof of my desire, engorged with anticipation, spearing up from the black thicket of pubic hair between my thighs.

There was a knock on the door and Marthe came in with warm towels, a silver bucket on a three-legged stand, and a bottle of champagne 'courtesy of the house' — which I knew would be on my bill anyway, but what the hell! The old woman took a couple of glasses from her pocket, polished them on her apron, and put them on the night table. '*Soyez bénis* — bless you, Monsieur Paul,' she said. She went out and closed the door.

When Nellie came back she was naked except for the black silk stockings rolled down to just above her knees. I looked at her with approval.

I said that she was well-built, statuesque but still nubile. That didn't do her justice. She was a big lady, certainly, but her proportions were, well . . . magnificent. The shoulders and hips were well padded, but the skin was unblemished and smooth as parchment. The waist, sculpted still into a corset silhouette, flowed into a belly that was soft and rounded and almost

Reckless Liaisons

pneumatic. The big breasts with their rosy tips, sagging only very slightly with the advancing years, were taut and resilient.

The thatch of dark hair covering Nellie's loins was springy and crisp; below it, noble thighs tapered to shapely calves and slender ankles.

What you are looking at here, I told myself, is eternal *woman*.

'Stay just where you are, *mon amour*,' she said throatily. 'Such a splendid soldier, surely, is wasted on sentry-go. The cavalry . . . riding . . . would be better suited to his special talents!'

This was a game we had played often before. Nellie climbed on to the bed. She swung one silk-stockinged leg across me and settled herself down to straddle my hips. Then, grasping my cock firmly in one hand, she lowered herself still further and manhandled the pulsating tip to part her pubic hair and nudge the moist secret lips it concealed. The tip, extra-sensitive now, eased itself between the warm wet folds and I arched my pelvis so that gradually the entire throbbing length of my stem was engulfed in the close hot clasp of her inner flesh.

The sensation was exquisite.

Sitting now on my hips, with the two tight globes of her buttocks pressing me down again, Nellie smiled wickedly. 'A little ride, Paul darling, will do you good!' she confided. 'Make you frisky and bring the colour to your cheeks!' And she began that favourite movement of hers, alternately raising and lowering herself to massage my staff with her whole body – rising and falling in invisible stirrups, as I liked to think of it.

I caught my breath; it was almost too much. Every

nerve end in my own body seemed to concentrate its sensory receptors within the length of that eagerly quivering shaft. I reached up my hands to take the weight of her breasts, groaning aloud each time that fleshy belly thudded down onto me. I thrust up savagely, following every upstroke and ready for the following slide down that swallowed me to the hilt. She was rising higher now, quickening the pace, withdrawing further, retreating until only the very tip of my cock was caught between those sucking lips . . . and then careening down to take the whole length again.

Fascinated to watch the rigid emblem of my lust tunnel into her, reappear, and then vanish once more, I was reminded not for the first time of that image: the index finger and the oiled glove.

Nellie was exciting herself too. She was breathing very fast; a thin rivulet of sweat trickled down the valley between her breasts. 'That will do for the walk and the trot,' she panted. 'And now, my steed, we shall see how your cavalier fares . . . in the canter . . . and the *gallop*!'

I cried aloud. The suddenly quickening rhythm, accelerating, pumping, sucking up and slamming down, was inducing an exquisite agony in my loins. Nellie's hands, flat on my chest, mashed the nipples as she frenziedly levered herself ever more swiftly from the base to the tip of my heaving cock and then back again. Her head threshed wildly from side to side; the Spanish comb flew away and her hair tumbled down. The large breasts jerking against my palms were slippery with moisture. Faster, faster! cried the Red Queen.

And then all at once I could go no faster, not even, as

Reckless Liaisons

the Queen would have said, to stay in the same place. My hips were unable to rise and fall rapidly enough to meet Nellie's thrusts. I stayed rigidly arched while all the forces of my desire gathered themselves within me, concentrated on that throbbing point on which she was impaling herself, blossomed with breathtaking speed, and . . .

. . . and Nellie abruptly withdrew, rose half upright and then rolled across to lie beside me on her back. 'This way now, my *beau*,' she panted. 'I want you here, between my thighs.'

She had left me just in time. I allowed the hammering of my pulse to quieten a little, my lungs to fill with air. I rolled over in my turn and gazed down at her. Her legs, gleaming in their black silk, were drawn up. The thighs, obscenely spread, showed milk white between the dark stockings and the tufted black bush in the centre of which wine-coloured lips gaped hungrily open. Her arms were flung wide; her hair spread fan-like on the pillows; her breasts rose and fell with the heaving of her chest.

I jacked myself up and then turned over to subside between those thighs as instructed. A hand inserted itself between our two bodies and grasped the wet, quivering length of my stem, guiding it to the hot throat in which it had so recently been swallowed. I flexed my hips gently . . . and thrust. The lips clasping my eager flesh slid slowly, languorously down. Nellie's sigh of fulfilment and my own could have been a single breath.

Bliss.

Now all was easy and relaxed and gentle. The mountain torrent had flowed into the deep, wide stream of the river. The muscles of Nellie's stomach fluttered as I laid my body along hers. Her resilient belly moved with the pressure of mine. I felt her warm arms wrap around me.

In a lazy, dream-like motion, I started to rock in and out of her, feeling the columned thighs clamp over my hips each time her pelvis rose to meet my measured strokes. 'Oh, Nellie . . . !' I whispered.

This was what I wanted, what I needed. Here was peace and security and reassurance and delight. Here — as we moved easily and rapturously together — was joy.

Nellie laid her cheek against mine. 'Come to Mama,' she crooned.

Chapter Nine

It was on the Friday of the following week, when I was on my way to the Comtesse van den Bergh's house in the Avenue Kléber, that I saw what the Yankees call 'the can'.

The term, although slangy, is specific. It embodies the rear aspect of the female anatomy from the top of the thighs to the lower lumbar region, including the gluteus maximus and medius, the buttocks and the cleft separating them, the posterior elevation of the hips, and the *stance* and working of these fleshy components as a whole, in relation to the rest of the body. The ensemble is not covered by the word 'bottom'; a can is more than just a bottom. Nor is the English Anglo-Saxon term 'arse' sufficiently precise. A man does not have a can (unless you count Laurence and his ilk).

It may seem odd to single out this double feature of the structure of the fair sex, but so much – or, as the case maybe, so little – can be deduced from its observation that it seems to me worth the digression . . . if only to explain my reaction on that particular Friday.

The can – I suppose behind or *derriére* would suffice if you dislike Americanisms – the can moves in a mysterious way. Its wonders to perform, do I hear someone say? Well, yes. Because its varieties are legion, and the classification subdivides again once the item's operation and movements are taken into account. It would be rash to postulate a separate characteristic for each posterior in every walk of life — both literally and metaphorically. But there are enough variations to fill a sizeable reference book.

Can cans and can't cans, will cans and won't cans, cans that wriggle and those that writhe, tight little cans that grind, like the mills of God, exceeding small . . . they are all part of that beguiling parade: the only procession that is best seen from behind!

I was early for my rendezvous with the Comtesse, you see, and I had stopped at Fouquet's, in the Champs Elysées, to fill in time with a *bock* — and a glance, admittedly, at the talent passing my sidewalk table.

I saw pert cans and saucy cans, rude cans and sad cans, huge cans meatily swaying that threatened to overbalance their owners at every stride, and jaunty cans — watch it! — that rolled with the hips. I saw cans that dimpled the thighs with a deep crease each time the silk-clad legs scissored, and cans the two hemispheres of which alternated in a yo-yo rhythm like the pistons of an engine.

And then finally I saw *the* can.

A girl of medium height with raven-black hair parted in the middle, plaited into pigtails and coiled over each ear. She was wearing a cream silk shirt and one of the new, rather daring, 'divided' skirts: a brown knee-length sheath whose pleats concealed the fact that it was cut like *culottes* with a central gusset. And moving easily within the material was this entrancing behind.

Reckless Liaisons

She was walking quickly uphill towards the Arc de Triomphe. I threw coins on the table and started off in pursuit.

The avenue was crowded. Late sunshine gilded the plane trees as the fringed and flowered and deeply smocked frocks of flappers and tourists and homeward-bound shopgirls eddied and swirled in the sombre groundswell of men in business suits and slouch hats. Now here, now there, the brown skirt appeared discreetly, vanished, and then reappeared each time the girl with hair coiled over her ears zigzagged swiftly between knots of strollers on her way uphill.

The roadway too was thronged with traffic. Green single-deck motor buses, their open rear platforms jammed with office workers, snarled and panted among the suicidal taxicabs. Expensive landaulettes and *sédan-cas-de-ville* honked imperiously at impertinent Renaults and Citroëns. Horse-drawn delivery vans hugged the kerb.

Twice, I almost lost my can. The first time was when I stumbled over one of the darting street urchins employed by the posh boutiques to shovel up the horse droppings; the second delayed me as I was about to dash across a side street, the Rue Bassano. A pastry-cook's cart with a hooped canvas top was just pulling in to the sidewalk when something frightened the horse, and it reared up, neighing, between the shafts. The carter cursed, cracking his whip, blaming me for the incident. I shouted back, stepping hastily up on to the kerb again. By the time I had dodged around the rear of the vehicle, swerved past a cab, and gained the opposite pavement, the can was seventy yards away.

I started to run. What elegance! What effortless mastery of mechanics, I mused as I reduced the distance between us. In the case of your average *derriére*, the movements and countermovements of each separate and fleshy half appear to be no more than the *result* of the action of walking. With this girl it was different: so subtle and well-drilled was her action, so smooth the muscular coordination, that one could almost believe the can itself was the power unit, the engine *driving* limbs and torso and head and hands in their complex progression. I put on a spurt to close the gap between us.

We were a few hundred yards from the Arc de Triomphe when a chattering crowd of Italian tourists spilled down the steps in front of a bank and piled into a parked charabanc, separating me from my quarry. I extricated myself as rapidly as I could . . . to find, by one of those freaks that control the random movements of crowds, that I was faced with a stretch of empty sidewalk all the way up to the arch. Of the girl in the brown divided skirt there was no sign.

Was she in a shop? Had she gone into one of the buildings? Did she accelerate and whip around the corner at the Étoile? Or had she plunged down the narrow, curving length of the Rue Presbourg?

There was no way of telling. I ran past the shopfronts, peering into each plateglass window. No luck. I hurried to the Étoile. Whirling traffic and anonymous crowds. It was too late now to try the side street: the girl had vanished as quickly as she materialised. What a pity; what a shame!

In any case I was late now for my appointment. I took

the Rue Presbourg myself, and cut through it into the Avenue Kléber, where it ran down from the Étoile to the river.

Dagmar van den Bergh had been married to a Belgian Count at the turn of the century. But the gentleman, who had extensive banking interests in Liège, had learned early in the relationship of his wife's Sapphic preferences and returned hurriedly to his native heath, leaving the Comtesse — so the gossips said — the mansion in the Avenue Kléber and a very considerable income on the strict condition that she stayed out of his life.

The house was certainly splendid. Its classical façades looked over a courtyard separated from the avenue by an archway closed off by gold-tipped, black wrought-iron gates. An elderly man in the porter's lodge picked up a gilt and ivory telephone to announce my arrival. Once through the gates, I crossed the cobblestones and climbed marble steps leading to the glassed-in portico. An enormous Delaunay-Belleville limousine and a rust-red Benz racer with no windscreen stood among the magnolias in tubs surrounding the yard.

The liveried footman who flung open the double doors and took my card led me across a black-and-white squared marble hallway and up a curving staircase with glass banisters and a brass rail. The décor had been changed since I last paid Dagmar a visit: the classical busts flanking the first floor landing had been replaced by curvilinear art-nouveau furniture in exotic tropical woods and a cubist Virgin in pink granite supported by an onyx stool. The tall white double doors leading to the salon were sheathed in beaten copper. The servant knocked, opened them gracefully, and announced: 'Monsieur Paul Mackenzie!'

At first the room seemed crowded. Dagmar separated herself from a group in front of the French windows and advanced with outstretched hands and a beaming smile. 'Paul, *cher ami*! How kind of you to come!'

I took a hand glittering with diamonds and kissed it. Magnolia perfume scented the creamy flesh. The burnished auburn of Dagmar's hair was darker now, and streaked with grey. But considering that it must have been some years since her fortieth birthday, she was still pretty stunning. Her figure was partly hidden by a high-necked, sleeveless cocktail dress of multicoloured beads which fell sheer from the points of her breasts to her knees. The silk-stockinged legs, though, were as slender and graceful as ever, and the skin of her arms was smooth and firm. 'You're a little late,' she said reprovingly, 'so you must drink up at once to catch up with the rest of us. What shall it be — a Manhattan? A White Lady? Whisky-sour? Gin-fizz? Come to the bar and choose.'

The bar? I noticed then that it wasn't just on the landing that the décor had been changed. Dagmar's gracious, panelled salon had been transformed. Garish African rugs strewed the parquet floor; the furniture was white leather and tubular steel; instead of gold-framed family portraits, the walls were hung with Futurist landscapes, a Chagall still life, lithographs by De Chirico and Klee.

The horseshoe-shaped bar had been installed at one side of the French windows. It was fashioned from chrome and black glass, backed by a jazzy mural repeating the stylised figure of a Negro with a saxophone. 'With so charming a hostess,' I said, in answer to Dagmar's question, 'what could I choose but a White Lady?'

She signalled to the barman, a mulatto in a white linen jacket who picked up a silver cocktail shaker and began to prepare the drink. 'You must meet my friends,' she said, gesturing towards the group by the French windows. 'Guy is a painter; Mimine has written a scandalous . . .'

I wasn't listening. My attention was riveted by a couple sitting on high stools at the bar. The man, who was facing me, could have been a diplomat from the Quai d'Orsay — smooth grey hair, silver tie, double-breasted blue pinstripe suit, gold watch-chain looped across the waistcoat. But it was his companion on whom my eye was fixed.

I couldn't believe it. She had her back to me, but there could be no mistake: cream silk shirt, brown skirt with pleats, black hair in plaits coiled over each ear . . .

It was the girl I had seen — and lost — outside Fouquet's in the Champs Elysées!

She must have ducked into the Rue Presbourg while I was blocked by the Italians, and cut through into the Avenue Kléber only a couple of minutes before I arrived myself.

But, now that she was visible in close-up as it were, my God, I could see how right I had been about that superb rear elevation!

She sat squarely on the stool, elbows on the bar counter, sucking something from a frosted cocktail glass through a straw as she listened to whatever idiocy the diplomat was pushing her way. The ensemble of hips and buttocks, spread slightly now on the flat seat of the stool, was entrancingly broad, solid, entirely without flabbiness or fat; leaning forward, she filled the whole space between her thighs and the top of the bar with *her* — no bulge, no belly, no paunch, just a firm citadel of flesh that was taut and tight and, yes, *pliant*!

And somehow that very width, that depth, underlined the fact that between those heavy, separated halves there would be a tender furrow hazed with dark hairs that concealed lips eager for a hungry mouth. My goodness, I thought in the second it took for Dagmar to steer me to the bar, kneeling in front of that earth mother with arms locked around that and the face buried, a man could feel, would feel *safe* . . .

'Janine,' Dagmar said, 'Victor — I'd like you to meet Paul Mackenzie, whose pictures decorate the *Gazette* and *Modes*. Paul, this is Janine d'Arcy and Victor Houbigant.'

We shook hands. The Chinese are said to recognise no more than two types of female face: the horse and the button. Janine was a button, with large dark eyes, a snub nose, and the hair that wasn't plaited arranged in a bang across her forehead. Her hand was cool.

Houbigant was no diplomat: it turned out that he managed a wholesale dress business. I was happy to see that he appeared to have no special interest in the girl. After a few minutes of banal conversation, he excused himself and joined the group by the windows, where the women were more expensively clothed. Among them I recognised the beetle-browed German Baroness, the

Reckless Liaisons

actress Gabrielle Dorziat, a couple of men I knew by sight, and Bertrand Laforge's mother, who had been seduced into the *Amazone* camp by Dagmar as a way of getting even with her husband, whose infidelities were the talk of Paris.

I switched my attention back to Janine d'Arcy. She had a pleasant, rather high voice. Her small mouth was painted a vivid, very dark red that was almost crimson. The silk shirt was cut loosely, but so far as I could see, her breasts were unremarkable, small too, and a little pointed.

Never mind. It was that wide and solid centre-section that held my interest so fast: each time she moved, it settled on the stool more enticingly. Mentally stripping away the clothes, I was aware already of a tightening sensation at my loins. I don't know what we talked about: my imagination was too busy. But by the time Dagmar returned and obliged us to circulate, I was on my third White Lady and I had extracted a promise from the girl that she would allow me to escort her home — or maybe take her to dinner, it depended.

'It depends on what?' I asked her.

'On how I feel when the party's over,' she told me.

'The way *I* feel, the party would only just be beginning!' I said.

The flesh around Janine's eyes crinkled as she smiled up at me. She slid off the stool (I held my breath as that heavy flesh moved) and went to join Gabrielle Dorziat without saying any more.

I stood by the window with Agathe Laforge. Below the narrow wrought-iron balcony, the chestnut trees shading Dagmar's town garden were gilded by the setting sun. Classical figures on plinths, I was glad to see, still flanked the paved walk crossing the lawns, and there was a blaze of geraniums, begonia and blue lobelia above the stone urns which stood in front of the brickwork walling in the garden. An indoor figure on a plinth stood behind my companion. It was a tall assemblage of cubes and discs and spheres by Brancusi which represented — according to a small brass plate on the plinth — a *Seated Woman*.

The sculptor, I reflected, could never have seen Janine d'Arcy at a bar.

Agathe was a well-preserved — very well-preserved and richly pampered — sixty. She wore a severely styled, long-sleeved tea gown in midnight blue organdie that swathed her soft body in elegant folds. Her grey hair was expensively cropped.

The body, I knew, was surprisingly adaptable and she used it expertly. I 'knew' her, you see, in the biblical sense: ten years ago, during a weekend house party at her manor near Evreux in Normandy, she had slotted into my list somewhere between the numbers seven and eleven. As a reward, she had confided in me a secret formula of her husband's that permitted my father to rustproof the bodywork of the lightweight sports-racing cars he manufactured. We had remained friends ever since.

I was telling her of my fall from Mado's grace, when Dagmar joined us with refills. 'We were talking about the Ahmed Simbel farce,' I said. 'You told me then, when you invited me, that there would be a young woman here who — and I quote — might interest me. Would that by any chance be Janine d'Arcy? Or has the subject of your recommendation yet to arrive?'

'By no means,' Dagmar said, smiling. Her green eyes glittered with mischief. 'Janine is the girl, all right. I think you should find her very interesting indeed.' She turned to Agathe. 'Wouldn't you agree, *chère amie*, that Mademoiselle d'Arcy was . . . interesting?'

The two women exchanged glances. Agathe's lips twitched. 'Very,' she said drily.

I couldn't get any more out of the Comtesse. She hurried away to greet some new arrivals. Mme Laforge turned to exchange pleasantries with Victor Houbigant. The big room was filling up. The manservant entered to switch on the electric chandeliers. Light flashed from the chrome cocktail mixer as the barman shook and shook. The noise level of brittle party conversation swelled to a subdued roar.

At a quarter past seven Janine d'Arcy caught my eye and indicated by a nod of the head that she was ready to leave. My pulses quickened.

Dagmar left a man in a white sharkskin suit and two girls who seemed to be wearing nothing but sequins and came to the door to bid us goodbye. In front of the marble chimney piece a woman wearing a wide-brimmed black hat, a gold frock with an exceedingly short skirt and even less top, and high-heeled gold slippers was screeching with laughter. She was apparently on her own.

'Darlings, I *know* you are going to enjoy one another,' Dagmar enthused when we had made the usual polite noises of thanks. 'It's so very nice,' she added, with a look that I was unable to interpret, 'when one can bring people . . . together.'

Reckless Liaisons

I shepherded Janine out of the house and offered my arm once we were in the street. We were both a little tipsy. Because it was so near, we went back to Fouquet's for an absurdly expensive dinner.

Nothing of special interest emerged during the meal: the conversation in fact reminded me of the evening I had spent with Françoise, chez-Drouand a few days before. There were to be other similarities . . . and one big difference.

There was no chance of an exploratory footsie-footsie or an opening move in the knee-trembler game at Fouquet's: the table was too exposed. But I had thought that maybe I could make at least a tentative approach towards those hips in the dark intimacy of a taxicab — although here again the question of which address to give the Jehu arose.

In the event the problem was a non-starter. She lived just around the corner in the Rue de la Boétie. And she felt that a short walk would clear her head. So my studio and the Avenue de Versailles were out, at least for tonight.

Crossing the busy Champs Elysées, I took her arm, allowing my hand to fall as it were accidentally to her hip as we approached the far side of the avenue. The padded flesh moved easily beneath the loose material of her skirt. I was not sure whether the nimble leap with which she gained the kerb was an evasive action to distance me or a subconscious escape from a bus, seen from the corner of the eye, roaring towards us from the Rond Point.

The house was one of a row, five storeys high, with tall wooden double doors opened after dark by a buzzer

Reckless Liaisons

set in the surrounding stonework. Inside was a tiled hallway, a bank of wooden letterboxes, and a staircase curving around the latticed shaft of an old-fashioned, hand-operated lift. The outer doors banged shut behind us. I was holding Janine's hand. 'Are you going to ask me in for a coffee?' I said.

Well, no she wasn't, actually. That would be quite impossible.

O, God! I thought. Not another one living at home with Mum and Dad?

No, not that. But her apartment — it was on the top floor, under the mansard roof — was shared with two friends. And one, she knew, was in that evening and would be 'doing' her hair. 'Never mind,' I said. 'It's still early. Come to my place and *I'll* make *you* a coffee. It's in the Avenue de Versailles. We'll get a taxi, and I'll bring you back later.'

The head with its two spiral buns of hair shook again. She had an interview tomorrow morning. Early. She couldn't afford to be up late; there was a lot to do.

I resigned myself to the fact that whatever happened would have to be confined to the stairways, public corridors, dark corners or even the lift of this apartment building. Oh, well: half a loaf . . .

'I'll see you to your door,' I said.

The lift was operated by pulling on a counterweighted hawser which passed vertically through the mahogany and brass car. Beside the hawser was an enamel plate bearing the words: *Please pull rope to return lift to ground floor after use.*

I ushered the girl in and closed the doors. The car was small and we stood necessarily close together. Between the second and third floors, I reached behind me with one hand, grabbed the rope, and dragged the lift to a halt. 'It stopped!' Janine said. 'Paul, did you do that?'

'Guilty,' I said.

'But . . . but why?'

'Because you are a very desirable young woman, and I want to kiss you.'

'Oh, Paul! . . . No, but I mean *really* . . . !'

'Yes, but *I* mean really,' I said. I moved towards her.

The lift rocked slightly on its shock-absorbers. The building was very quiet: I could hear the rumble of traffic from the street. On an upper floor, someone was endlessly playing scales on a piano, and there was tinny music from a wireless set in the distance. I put my hands on those hips and drew the girl against me.

'Paul! Please. You mustn't. I really don't want . . .' The high voice died away. The last few words, I noted with mounting anticipation, had become rather breathless. I reckoned I was dealing with another Françoise – the other side of Mado's coin – someone who wanted the man practically to force himself on her. I bent my head and kissed her forcefully on the lips.

For a moment there was no response. My mouth was clamped over hers. I speared my tongue between her teeth. Hot breath jetted from her nostrils against my face. I feasted my hands on the swell of flesh below her waist, crushing her body even closer.

I was wearing those wide-legged flannel trousers known as Oxford Bags. There was thus no constriction around my loins, but I was aware, had been aware for some minutes, of the gradual lengthening and stiffening of that part of me most eager to get to close quarters with Janine. I knew too that it was thrusting out the flannel in a definite and unmistakable fashion. I wanted her to know this as well, so I rammed my own hips hard against her pelvis.

This time there was a response all right. A soft little tongue darted forward to meet my own. The breath against my cheek quickened. As I moved my hands around to grasp — and press harder still towards me — those splendid muscular buttocks, I felt a tentative palm against the small of my back. Slender fingers stole up to cup the nape of my neck.

Now our two pairs of lips clasped, clung, sucked and nibbled. Our tongues writhed and twisted, jousting in the hot wet cavern of what seemed a single shared mouth. My loins ached. The girl's belly was slung against me. Two pairs of hands began to explore.

Three floors below a door banged. 'Where the devil's that dam' lift?' a man's voice shouted angrily.

I separated myself from Janine, cursing under my breath. 'We can't stay here!' she whispered, eyes wide in the dim light. I nodded. I hauled on the rope, stopping the car at the third floor level. I opened the doors and pushed her out onto the landing.

'Coming!' I called down the shaft. I jerked the rope the other way and sent the lift creaking down to the ground floor.

'I should think so!' the angry voice complained. 'I don't know what the hell this place is coming to, what with the dustbins and the electricity and this bloody lift . . .' The words died away in a furious mumble.

We were at the far end of a corridor. I heard the lift doors close. In the shaft, the rope quivered, the counterweight came into view and sank from sight. I shoved Janine past double doors that led to the emergency stairs. We climbed to the next half-landing.

I backed her against the wall. 'Paul,' she panted, 'I think—'

'Don't,' I said. The stairway was poorly lit. The expression in the large eyes staring at me was unfathomable. I put my hands on her upper arms and kissed her again. This time there was a small wordless exclamation deep in her throat, and the tongue came out at once.

Our mouths were fixed together for ever; we were eating each other up. My fingers unbuttoned the silk blouse, plunged inside the constriction of a bust bodice, touched smooth skin. The breasts were small, fitting neatly into the palm, the nipples large and very hard.

I rolled the nipples between forefinger and thumb, the tips of my fingers passing from the wrinkled circles of the areolas to the stiffer buds at their centre. A slight tremor passed through Janine's body. And now, suddenly, there were hands at my waist . . . inserting themselves between us, fumbling at my belt. My cock, jammed through two layers of clothing against a thigh which had advanced cautiously towards me, positively quivered in response.

The hands at my waist were burrowing like little animals. The end of the belt pulled through the buckle; buttons slid through buttonholes. The waistband was loose. Scrabbling busily, the animals seized shirt-tails, underclothes, and jerked them free. I felt cool air play on the heated skin of my belly. I freed one of my own hands.

In turn, I pulled the silk blouse out of the waistband

of Janine's divided skirt. The flesh of her waist was cool and slightly moist, smooth, pliant and yielding to the touch.

The skirt fastened at the side. I found the catch, but I couldn't open it: it was some kind of patent clip that my fingers were unable to find their way around. I stretched down to locate the hem of the divided skirt and yanked one leg up to the top of the girl's thigh.

We were still kissing and I still had one hand between her breasts. She was breathing very heavily now, the chest heaving as I fondled the two small mounds of flesh.

There was a knee between my thighs. The fresh night air of the stairwell was abruptly chillier still against me; the animals had homed in on their target; fingers wrapped around my throbbing shaft, dragging it out from a tangle of underpants to spike out obscenely from my gaping flannel bags!

I drew back my head with a gasp. 'Oh, God,' I groaned, 'Janine . . . you're so . . . I have to; I must . . . Oh, *darling*!'

The hand grasping my cock began lasciviously milking the rigid stem, sliding from the engorged head to the base and back again as fluid eased out of the tip into her palm to lubricate the movement. Her other hand caressed the sac below, rolling the glands gently within the fleshy envelope.

I had both hands under her skirt now, one up each leg, crawling up the backs of her thighs to the taut half moons of those luscious buttocks, pulling them gently apart so that my heated imagination could dwell on the hairy cleft between them.

The raping fingers of my right hand tore aside the lace edging the leg of her French knickers. They plunged in further, to the base of the belly, the crease at the top of the thigh. I caught my breath.

Damp hairs grazed my fingertips; I felt the sliding clasp of wet flesh. I plunged my hand deeper still, separating the creased lips, probing for the rubbery bud between them. Janine's pelvis jerked and she uttered a small cry as I found it. She was still staring at me with those wide eyes, still expressionless in the dim illumination.

For a timeless moment we remained frozen in that position, clamped together, a little contorted, hearts beating wildly as we pumped each other's secret parts. There was no sound in the stairwell but the labouring of our breath and the slight, sly, suck and squelch of stealthily manipulated genitals.

I moved my left hand around a curve of buttock and reached the fingers into the warm wet furrow so that I could enter her from behind. The big hips shuddered and the milking hand increased its rhythm to a point where I felt my cock was about to explode.

I tilted back my head, groaning with ecstasy . . . and suddenly, brutally, the animals ran away.

The air played cold on my tortured staff. Janine's hands were against my chest, struggling, pushing me away. Her head thrashed from side to side. One of the coils over her ears shook loose, and hair cascaded down over her shoulder. Violently she twisted her hips to escape my hands. 'No!' she panted. 'No . . . we mustn't. Not here. Not now. No more . . . *please*.'

'What the devil . . . ?' I said angrily. 'Janine . . . ?'

I tried to retain my grip in the crevices of that fleshy body, but those hips, that torso, those thighs were muscular and strong. She leaned forward, twisted away and ducked out of my encircling arms. '*No!*' she cried again in a hoarse whisper that was almost a scream.

She broke free, tearing the waistband of her skirt, and raced away up the stairs, holding the damaged garment up with one hand.

I let her go, watching the flash of white thighs and the smudge of dark between them where the black knickers bunched over her flesh. She disappeared around a curve in the staircase and the clatter of her high-heeled shoes receded. What the *hell*!

I walked slowly down to the ground floor, stowing myself away, stuffing in shirt-tails, refastening belt and bags. The wet patches on my underclothes were cold against my skin.

I was thinking, not too kindly, of Dagmar. What in heaven's name was so 'interesting' about a girl who looked — and at first acted — as sexy as all get-out, but turned out to be nothing but a PT, a tease?

I was to find out later, but I didn't know then.

The emergency doors at the bottom of the stairs led to a yard at the back of the building. The angry man had been right: the overflowing dustbins hadn't been cleared for days. The night air was rank with the smell of refuse and rotting fruit.

I came out into a narrow lane. Back in the Rue de la Boétie, I hailed a cruising taxi.

'Where to, M'sieu?' the cabbie asked, reaching behind him to open the door.

I settled against the worn cushions with a hand on my

disappointed crotch. 'Take me to number one-two-five in the Rue St André-des-Arts,' I said firmly.

Chapter Ten

It was a busy night in the Rue St André-des-Arts. Nellie was at Maxim's with the ex-Arch-Duke and wouldn't be back until late. Lily was practising her oriental wiles on an Admiral of the French fleet. The other girls were all occupied one way or another. Finally it was Milady herself who graciously offered to accompany me upstairs. This was a rare privilege. The *patronne* was accommodating, extremely expert, and at times hilariously bawdy. She it must have been of whom the London poet wrote at about that time: 'Uncorseted her friendly bust/Gives promise of pneumatic bliss'.

Unfortunately that wasn't what I really wanted.

Certainly my immediate need was satisfied, the bleeding from my wounded heart temporarily staunched. But I had seen myself as the dashing Lothario that evening, the Casanova of the *quartier* — and the affront to that desire for conquest never far from the male psyche was not to be eradicated by hired help, however charming. Buckling in fact was what my swash still craved.

I trolled the Latin Quarter, crossed the river and walked as far as the Opera, dropped in and then out of several cafés and bars. No luck; nothing but business girls again, and cheap ones at that. By three o'clock I was back at the studio, alone and ready for bed.

By then of course I was no longer tired: fatigued but not sleepy. There was nothing for it but to count the ladies with whom I *had* been successful.

This didn't work either. By the time I got to Françoise I was wider awake than ever. I fixed myself a stiff brandy and selzer, climbed back into bed, and went back to the beginning. Only this time, instead of just counting, I recalled in as much detail as I could manage the actual details of each encounter.

Evelyn was the first. I was sixteen and still at boarding school. It was in the summer term: a junior master had taken a dozen of us for a ramble on the heath. We were picking blackberries to take back for high-tea and I had got separated from the rest.

The girl suddenly appeared on a pathway between two tall clumps of gorse. I knew her by sight: she was the daughter of the school porter, an ex-sergeant-major by the name of Shoebridge, known to one and all as Shoebugger. Evie Shoebugger was one of two sisters who used to stare boldly at us with prominent eyes when we went for walks. We called the sisters Lusty and Busty. This one was Lusty — although, as I soon found out, the other nickname would have suited her just as well. She was a big, strapping country girl with loose breasts — she called them titties — wild hair and very strong arms. I guessed she must have been at least eighteen.

'Hallo, boy,' she said. 'What are you doing all alone?'

I told her what I was doing. 'I tell you what,' she said. 'Show me your thing, and I'll show you mine.'

Naturally I was shy. I positively bridled. Like all of us I was dying to get to close quarters with a girl, but when it came to it . . .

When it came to it, Lusty was equal to the occasion. She reached out with one of those big hands and yanked open my fly. 'Take it out and show me,' she commanded. She hitched up her flowered cotton skirt, pushed close-fitting, peach-coloured elasticated knickers down to her ankles, and stepped out of them. I stared with fascination and a rapid tightening of the loins at her smooth belly and the furry slit between her thighs. Hastily, I pulled out what I had. It was bigger than I'd ever seen it.

Evelyn pulled the skirt up around her waist, lay down on the grass, and spread her legs. 'Do you know what to do?' she demanded.

'Of course I do,' I said hotly. I'd been told how babies came by Peter Goddard when I was eleven. 'The man rubs his tool up and down the girl's slit until—'

'Well, get down here and do it,' she said. And then, a few moments later: 'No, silly! Not up and down the *outside*! When it's stiff enough you put it in. Here — let me show you . . .'

I realised later of course that she'd been 'doing it', as we said, for ages, probably with lots of chaps. She was already wet and ready. And of course I spent after the first few strokes. But I shall never, ever forget the ultimate thrill of that very first scalding clasp of flesh closing over my shaft as I shoved it into her body.

My first taste of commercial sex was vicarious. A crowd of cricket enthusiasts had been taken up to Lords by the Sports Master to watch the Varsity Match.

Reckless Liaisons

Oxford won by three wickets. Two days later my chum Rhodes cornered me behind the Fives Courts and asked, 'I say, Mac – did you hear what Davies did while we were at Lords?'

Davies was something of a hero: Head Boy, Captain of the Sixth, and the 1st XI fast bowler. You weren't allowed to speak to him unless you'd been there at least six terms and had earned the right to wear your blazer unbuttoned. 'What did he do?' I asked.

'Why, he cut out during the lunch interval,' Rhodes told me, 'and took a bus down to Piccadilly and picked up a tart!'

'He *didn't*!' I exclaimed.

'He did too. Davies told me so himself. The tart took him back to her place and they undressed *completely*. Then the tart told Davies to get down on all fours and put it in from behind like a dog, so Davies lifted his leg and pee'd against the leg of the bed. And when they were doing it the usual way, the tart said she'd give him an experience he'd never had before. And she rolled up a few feet of string into a ball and stuffed it up his hole, and when Davies came she jerked the whole lot out . . . and Davies said he never *had* had an experience like that before!'

'My God!' I said admiringly. 'But at least I didn't have to pay for my first experience.'

'No,' said Rhodes, 'but you forgot you'd crammed Lusty's knickers into the pocket of your blazer, and Matron found them and you got twelve black marks and a beating.'

'That was another six black marks!' I said. 'How much did Davies pay the tart?'

'I think it cost him over a pound,' Rhodes said.

I shook my head. Six strokes of the cane against all that money? But which of us came off best?

That was a digression, though. I drained the brandy glass and moved on to Margot. Margot was Number Two, but she was the first I really talked into it myself, my first conquest. It was during a New Year's Eve dance at the Hog's Back Hotel, near Guildford. Rhodes's people had lent him their Sunbeam saloon and we drove out there, three of us wearing hired dinner-jackets with black patent dancing shoes in paper bags, and three girls. Margot was mine.

I got her out there while supper was being served, and I can still feel today the cold shine of the leather seat against my bare skin as I tried to undress her in the back of that car. Pushing my hands down the front of her dress was no problem; she even seemed to become enthusiastic when I got one leg of the knickers entirely off her and felt the springy hair and the soft lips between her legs. But when I draped her legs over my shoulders and pushed down my trousers to lean over her doubled up body she began to complain.

'Please, Margot,' I groaned. 'Please let me. I want to so much. I love you, Margot . . . please. It won't take long, I promise.'

'It's cold,' she complained. 'The seat's not comfy. The others'll miss us.'

'No they won't,' I urged. 'Please, Margot. You're so lovely.'

'Oh, all right,' she grumbled at last. 'But hurry, do.'

I hurried. I plunged. I was right: it didn't take long.

Not only that: two days later, when the parents had

Reckless Liaisons

gone to a wedding and I had the house to myself all afternoon, Margot wouldn't let me at all. 'Tim Oates knows how to do it *properly*,' she said scornfully. It was my first intimation that the fair sex were not content to play cylinder to the male piston.

Claude, a French girl on holiday with an English family, explained. 'You are quite — how do you say? — quite pretty, my Paul,' she told me. 'And your . . . your *appareil* is formidable. Also you do use it quite well. But for us, you must understand, it is not sufficient just to be pump up like the tyre of the bicycle. We can be really interested like you, but it take maybe longer; it is not enough just to be, to see; it take a little stroking, a little caress, a little *love* to prepare us, no?'

I talked this over with Rhodes and he had been told much the same thing, but it was Duggie Thomson, an American friend of his whose guv'nor was some kind of diplomat, who finally put us right. 'You wanna pay attention,' Duggie said, 'to the boy in the boat.'

'The . . . boy in the boat?'

'Yeah. You know. Slang for the clit. That's what it looks like, a kid sitting at one end of a canoe — the gal's whatsit, between the lips in front of her cunt. Works like a little prick too. I mean like, it erects, gets a hard on, and that. What you wanna do,' Duggie said, 'is like when you jack yourself off in the john, well you wanna jack her off with that pint-size prick. After that, she'll do anything you say.'

Of course we had all left school by then and were working at one job or another, so there were no long holidays and it wasn't always easy to find the time, but when finally I put the advice into practice with Claude in the back seat of a Packard, I couldn't seem to find the right spot. And although she agreed in principle and even took my finger to guide it, the finger still kept slipping off. Rhodes tried it out with Duggie's sister, though, and he said it worked a treat.

Part of the trouble was that I never actually got naked and into a bed with anyone until fat Frieda came into my life and filled the Number Five slot. Frieda was a nurse. She was a German refugee; it was a couple of years before the Great War, not long before I came to Paris for the first time. Because she was a foreigner, the sister in charge always put her on night duty – but it was a small cottage hospital, and this meant that when she slept during the day, three or four times a week there was nobody with her during the afternoon in her room in the nurses' home. Nobody, that is, but me when she could smuggle me in.

Frieda was all bust and bottom and big legs, with fair hair that unpinned and fell over her top half like a tent. Inside the tent were thick lips and big rubbery nipples and one of the most lewd tongues I ever met; outside it was the great hot cavern of her sex, eager to slide in and suck dry anything I had to offer.

Frieda loved the heat; she liked to lie with her legs locked over my back, heaving and squirming under me as our two bodies became slippery with sweat and I rolled and slid among the swells of her flesh. She was bossy too, telling me exactly what to do and where to do it, instead of allowing me to play the game my way. But in fact she was doing me a favour, giving me a first-hand lesson in female anatomy . . . and detailed instructions on How To Please which I was to find invaluable later on when I came across ladies who were, well, hard to please.

How different, my God, were Frieda and Tamara, the sixth victim on the bedtime list! Tamara was dark and sinewy, with a lean acrobat's body and a wide, wide mouth. She said she was born in Hungary and I believe she once worked in a circus. Personally, I think she had gypsy blood. She was certainly an adept contortionist, and she could induce an orgasm in me simply by contracting and relaxing her inner muscles in a marvellous accelerating rhythm. But in the end, whatever extravagant positions she had coaxed our limbs into, there was basically only one thing she really wanted: to suck and be sucked. I don't know that I ever actually saw her face.

Irene was the first girl with whom I had an affair that lasted any length of time. She was a peaches-and-cream English rose — excuse the mixed metaphor — who liked nothing better than to lie spread-eagled all afternoon (or all morning, or all night), cupping her generous breasts and holding them up for me to kiss while she moaned: 'Oh Paul, Paul — why are you so good to me?'

Nellie was the first genuinely experienced woman I knew. I count her because the first time we made love I didn't know she was a whore and no money changed hands. (In fact she *had* been paid — by my fellow Knight Bertrand Laforge, who wanted to worm a manufacturing secret out of me and thought it might help if I was seduced. But that is another story, and anyway I was unaware of it at the time.)

I forgot Heather with the limp, a snub-nosed, wide-eyed and nubile friend of my sister's who narrowly avoided a family scandal. I was in my last year at school, staying at home in the summer hols, when apparently she took a wild fancy to me. Heather had a club foot. She clumped down the passage to my room in the middle of the night, climbed into bed with me, and untied the tape of my pyjama bottoms before I was fully awake.

I know: shades of Rosette. But this time I was petrified. My parents were sleeping in the next room and the door wasn't completely closed. My old man was strict as hell — and a churchwarden too! My hysterical whispers had no effect and the girl refused to go back to her own room. She already had my cock out. I did the only thing possible: I flung aside the covers, got out of bed, took her hand and crept downstairs with her to the scullery — the part of the house furthest from my people's room.

Heather liked it shoved into her from behind while she was kneeling. I only ever shafted her that one time, but I shall never forget the sight of her secret place — two cushions of flesh darkened with hair between the white columns of her thighs as she knelt on a kitchen stool in the light from a street lamp, with her elbows on the wooden draining board.

She was the first female I actually heard shout when she was seized by her release. I say shout: she roared, she bellowed, she practically screamed through the hand I clapped over her mouth while I was still embedded in her from behind.

'Those dam' cats next door woke me up again,' my father growled irritably at breakfast. 'I'll really have to speak to Ransome about it; this will not do.'

Reckless Liaisons

Heather, dark circles beneath her eyes, exchanged glances with my sister and then stared steadily at Sunny Jim on the packet of Post Toasties.

Thinking of Bertrand, the two occasions on which I went to bed with his mother were absolutely stunning. It was during this house party. Her husband had insulted her by bringing down Milady at her brassiest — as a retaliation to the fact that Agathe Laforge had been having an affair with Dagmar van den Bergh. Among others. And I knew perfectly well that her sudden passion for me was no more than another riposte aimed at him. But, goodness, that first night was an experience! It had everything: a ripe and seductive woman of forty in a diaphanous negligée, soft lights, a four-poster bed covered by a white bearskin rug, champagne in an ice bucket and a coal fire burning in the grate; the whole romantic formula, perfectly staged!

The woman was marvellous too. Everything about her was soft — the breasts, the belly, her waist, the flesh of her thighs, the generous cushions of her lips; yet all of it at the same time was resilient and firm. And did she know what to do with it! She was quite extraordinarily expert: lewd and obscene and lascivious and coquettish and shy all at the same alluring time. Everything about *me*, I tell you, was hard! It was really wild.

Wild?

Oh, my God! Françoise! I'd promised to introduce her to Mado. What was I going to do about that now?

Through the open door to the studio, I could see that the eastern sky was lightening. At some time during the night I had poured — and drunk — a second brandy. It must now be almost six o'clock and I was no further in my licentious litany than the early teens. And still very wide awake.

'Mackenzie,' I told myself severely, 'this . . . really . . . will not . . . do! You must take yourself in hand at once.'

Chapter Eleven

It wasn't as difficult as I had expected — arranging a meeting between Françoise and Mado Laverne, I mean. Once the contact was made, of course, there would be nothing more for me to do: either the girl would strike Mado as suitable or she wouldn't. It would be up to her.

I reckoned there was only one way to do it. Françoise had asked *me* to use *my* influence, and I had promised to do just that. Going through a third party — in any case, who? — would be as much of a betrayal as if I had forgotten all about it, whatever my personal relations with the *couturière* had become. I summoned up what courage I had, went to a post office and telephoned the Rue des Capucines.

My heart was thumping as I asked the operator for the number. To my astonishment, once the connection was made, I was put through to Mado at once.

'Paul!' she exclaimed. 'What a surprise! It's good to hear from you. How are things?'

'Madame Laverne,' I began nervously, 'you must forgive me for intruding like this, but it is not on my own account that I—'

'Madame *Laverne*?' she cut in. 'What is this, Paul? Are we not the oldest of friends? Why so formal all at once?'

My God! I thought. Women! Admittedly, her astrological sign was Scorpio – quick to take offence and as speedily forgetting all about it – but even so . . .

I made a fresh start.

'Mado . . . I'm sorry to disturb you, but there's this young woman, very much your type, I think, who is dying to meet you. She's tall and slender, with strong features. She's convinced she could make a career as a mannequin, and I fancy she may be right. The thing is, I promised her—'

'She's a conquest of yours, and you promised you'd put in a word? But you must bring her to see me, Paul. Of course.'

'That would be most kind.'

'Bring her tomorrow. After . . . well, about three. I am having lunch with a Welsh mill owner who produces the most fabulous lightweight worsteds, divine for the winter collection.'

'I'd appreciate that. It's awfully good of you.'

'I shall look forward to seeing you,' Mado said.

I left a note with the maidservant at the house where Françoise lived with her parents, asking her to meet me at the Opera Métro station the following day. She arrived on time – always a good sign when one is a little concerned, recommending one friend to another – and we walked round to the fashion house.

Mado was wearing pale mauve, the hair piled on top of her head this time, the boat-necked *crêpe-de-chine* afternoon dress looped around shoulders and waist. Her lip make-up was bright orange.

I guessed the Welshman had lunched her – and wined her – well, because her eyes were very bright. A swatch of thin, vividly coloured woollen patterns lay on her desk.

'Yes,' she said when the introductions had been made, 'you might do, at that. You have the height, the carriage, the narrow hips; you have strong features, as Paul points out . . . Just turn around, my dear, would you? . . . H'mn. Yes. Splendid. The only thing, Mademoiselle . . . ?'

'Dupuis,' Françoise supplied. She was looking her best, in a very simple white frock and white court shoes.

Mado nodded. 'The only thing is, I always leave the final decision to my head *vendeuse*. It is she, after all, who has to use our girls to sell the product!'

She banged an ivory button on top of the brass bell on her desk. 'Please ask Madame Solange to come in, Cecile,' she instructed the white-overalled seamstress who answered the call.

I knew the *vendeuse* slightly. She was young for so responsible a position, perhaps thirty-two or thirty-three — a gaunt woman, ramrod straight, with dark, cropped hair and horn-rimmed spectacles. She was wearing, as usual, a plain black dress with wide sleeves caught at the wrist. 'Oh, Madame Solange,' Mado said when she came in, 'Mademoiselle is a candidate for the gangway team! Perhaps you would care to take her away and see what she has to offer?'

The woman inclined her head. 'If you would come this way,' she said to Françoise, holding open the door.

'Remember, when you show a gown,' Mado called after Françoise, 'to look at the fools idiot enough to pay my prices as if they were pieces of shit!'

Françoise grinned, flashing me a grateful look as

she left. I wondered if she would pass the test. Watching her leggy stride and the imperious tilt of her head, I thought she might. I remembered too, very vividly, the way those legs had been hooked over the arms of my easy chair – and subsequently over my back – only a few days ago. If I was right and she was accepted, I hoped I might look forward to a repeat performance before too long!

Now, however, I was alone with Mado . . . and I didn't quite know which way the interview would go. For once I was at a loss for words.

Happily, Mado wasn't. 'I'm grateful to you, Paul, for bringing the girl along,' she said. 'I think Solange will approve. In any case we are always on the lookout for new talent: the mannequin wastage, through marriages to millionaires and maharajahs, is something cruel!'

She pushed back her chair and rose to her feet, stumbling slightly when she caught her hip, rounding the corner of the desk. It must have been a *very* good lunch. 'I'm happy that you c-c-came,' she said. 'I had been m-meaning to get in touch. My spies tell me that all kinds of strange things go on *chez* that dreadful man Simbel . . . and maybe I was a little hasty: it seems that you might not have been as much to blame for the stolen designs as I thought.'

'It *was* partly my fault,' I burst out. 'But only partly. I'd welcome an opportunity to explain exactly what I think did happen. I think it must have been while the drawings were—'

'Another time, Paul,' Mado interrupted.

'But I think you have the right . . . I really want you to know . . .'

'Yes, yes, dear boy. All in good time. But this is more important. What are you w-w-w-working on n-now? Are you very busy?'

I shrugged. 'A couple of coachwork designs for Bertrand Laforge's father. Fashion drawings for *Figaro* that Corinne kindly put my way. Why do you ask?'

'My winter coats,' she said. '*Modes and Manners of Today* want to run a colour feature. The garments are made, but I'm not too happy about the materials. What I need is a series of *gouaches* illustrating *them* . . . but imagining they're made in some of *these*.' She gestured towards the patterns on her desk. 'You're the only person who can d-do it, Paul. Will you find the time and help me out?'

My heart had leaped as she made, rather diffidently, the offer. 'Why, Mado, I'd be delighted,' I said. 'Of course I will.'

'That's good then.' She was standing by the door that led to the spiral staircase rising to her private apartment. She unlocked the door and opened it. 'Perhaps you'd like to come upstairs, and we can discuss the details over a bottle of champagne . . .'

You know who went upstairs.

It happened the following day. Late the following afternoon, to be precise. I was sitting at a sidewalk table outside the Café de la Paix. There were a lot of people about. Beyond the Métro station, on the far side of the big square, the gilded dome of Garnier's Opera House was resplendent in the light of the setting sun.

Reckless Liaisons

I didn't notice her at first: there were flappers all over the shop — homeward-bound shopgirls, pretty young students, suburban housewives up to see what the big stores had to offer. She was older than a flapper anyway, a tall, mature brunette with close-cropped hair and a lean figure two tables away. I wouldn't have noticed if she hadn't been looking my way with more than casual interest. Then I realised: it was somebody I knew. I smiled and she smiled back.

I picked up my glass of beer and went over to her table. She was sitting alone. 'I'm so sorry,' I said, 'I didn't recognize you at first.'

She smiled again. 'You have only seen me before in a completely different setting,' she said.

Yes, I thought, and in a completely different mood! I was used to seeing her in self-effacing black, with a rigidly expressionless face, and here she was animated, wearing a bright flower-print dress with a white turnover collar, white patent belt and white silk stockings. It was in fact Madame Solange, the head *vendeuse* from Mado's show-room in the Rue des Capucines.

'Won't you sit down?' she invited, pulling a chair back from the table.

'It would be a pleasure,' I said and sat down. 'Perhaps you would allow me to refresh your drink?'

'That would be very kind, Monsieur Mackenzie.'

She was drinking a three-tiered concoction of crème-de-menthe, pastis and blackcurrant syrup — green, grey and red stripes in a tall glass. I raised a finger to summon a waiter. 'A *perroquet* and a beer,' I told him. I turned to Solange. 'My friends call me Paul,' I said. 'It would be nice if I could count you among them.'

For the third time she smiled. 'It would be a pleasure for me too . . . Paul.' The mouth was wide, with well-shaped lips; the voice warm, a little husky. I realised suddenly that this was a very attractive young woman.

'You don't need to use them when you're, so to speak, off duty?' I blurted out. 'The spectacles, I mean; the horn-rims.'

Solange shook her head. 'Just part of the job. The lenses are plain glass,' she confessed. 'When you are trying to sell expensive items, it is essential not to distract the clients' attention away from the mannequins; it is they, after all, who are showing Madame Laverne's creations. The less emphatic and the more businesslike the rest of us look, the better.'

'You don't look in the least unemphatic or businesslike now!' I exclaimed.

I got the smile once more — with a slight wrinkling of the nose and a creasing of the flesh at the corners of the eyes. The eyes were violet, very wide, with long dark lashes.

We talked of this and that. We were on our third drink when she said: 'The girl you brought in yesterday — she has a good walk and a sufficiently haughty stare. I think she will do. At any rate, Madame has decided to give her a try-out. She will start next month.'

'I am pleased to hear it,' I said.

'She is your *petite amie*?' — A sudden glance from under arched and pencilled brows — 'Your, how do you say, girlfriend? Your fiancée?'

'No, not at all. Just a friend. I know her parents,' I lied. 'I promised them I'd help her if I could.'

'Just so. I was so happy to hear,' she said, with an abrupt change of subject, 'that you will be working for us again. Your work, you know, is quite exceptional.'

'You are very kind; I am flattered.'

'I know what I am talking about,' Solange said. 'I took an art-school course, I wanted to be a designer myself, before I got this job. I still amuse myself at weekends: street scenes and an occasional watercolour landscape. You know.'

I nodded. 'I used to do that, when my job was making the designs for motor car bodies look pretty on paper. I never seem to be able to find the time now.'

'Oh, but what you do professionally must be so *interesting*! The techniques you use are so personal. You use watercolour mainly yourself, don't you?'

'*Gouache* actually.'

'Even more astonishing. The subtlety, the nuances of your representation of different materials amazes me. There's a certain way you handle gauze and organza – oh, and any semi-transparent medium with *appliqué* brightwork . . . well, I'd just love to know exactly how you do it. Really, you must show me one day. If it isn't a dark secret, that is.'

'No secret.' I grinned. 'The only secrets are Mado's designs – and I don't seem too bright keeping those, do I? I tell you what, though: I'd be happy to show you how it's done. And since there's no time like the present, why don't you have dinner with me tonight, and we can pop into the studio afterwards, where I will Reveal All!'

'I think that would be lovely, Paul,' said Solange.

* * *

I took her to a small restaurant in the Rue Fantin-Latour, only a few hundred yards from the Mackenzie residence. By the time we'd gone through fluffy quenelles of pike in a lobster sauce, roast quails, a splendid white Graves and a Château Léoville-Barton to wash down the cheese, I was finding this young woman very desirable indeed. 'We'll have coffee and brandy in the studio,' I said, 'before my hidden talents are exposed.'

We did have coffee. I poured brandy, but we hadn't drunk it yet. Solange was leaning against the tilted drawing board on its stand. The board was covered with scraps of paper, sketches, half-finished colour trials. I had laid various colour washes over rejected figure drawings in Indian ink; I had demonstrated some of the tricks used to represent different types of material on different gauges of cartridge paper. A dozen camel-hair brushes stood in a beaker filled with water which had turned deep violet. Unscrewed tubes of *gouache* littered the table next to the stand.

Solange was fascinated. She scrutinised the samples, asked questions, exclaimed in admiration, picked up the pieces of paper after I had daubed colour on them. I was fascinated too, but not by what I was doing or what I produced.

Her lean, spare body was almost boyish in its elegance as she bent over my board. Beneath the flowered linen dress, a trim waist and tight haunches led the eye gracefully to the slender tapered legs exposed from knee to ankle. The slightest curve below the white neckline of the dress hinted at delicate breasts.

I had only realised as we rose from the table outside

the Café de la Paix that she was as tall as I was. Looking at her now, I reflected that despite the ten years difference in age, she could easily have held her own with the pampered beauties whose sartorial assets she paraded before Mado Laverne's rich clients.

I went into the other room to fetch the brandy balloons. I gave her one and stood beside her at the drawing board. She turned to face me, raised the glass, and touched it to mine. 'Here's to a real professional,' she smiled. 'Paul, I'm most grateful for the lesson!'

'It's nothing,' I said, feeling rather foolish. 'Here's to a lady — a most delightful lady! — intelligent enough to know what I'm talking about.' I drank.

She carried her glass back into the other room. I followed with mine. I was just through the doorway when she turned back towards me, swinging around unexpectedly, about to say something.

The movement took me by surprise. I was too near her, maybe following too fast: we had, after all, been drinking quite a lot. I was unable to stop in time, and walked straight into her, knocking the brandy balloon out of her hand.

The glass smashed on the tiled floor, soaking my trouser leg with spirit. Solange stumbled under the impact, almost falling backwards. I shot out my free arm, grabbing her around that slim waist, pulling her upright.

I don't remember sliding my own balloon onto the table. I only know that I kept that arm around her waist and that it was joined virtually at once by the other. I drew her gently against me, my arms circling her waist. 'Oh, Solange . . .' I murmured.

Her face was level with mine. Warm, winey breath played on my mouth and chin. Her wide violet eyes were inscrutable – but she made no movement to draw away, there was no reflex of rejection. I bent my head a little sideways and kissed her on the mouth.

The response was not instantaneous, the way it had been with Françoise and even Janine; rather it was slow and considered, as if the action had been contemplated, weighed, and then judged permissible. In any case I wasn't aiming to force things. This young woman was no eager-beaver flapper out for a quick thrill; this was a personality labelled *Fragile: Handle with Care*. An adult, in fact.

On the other hand, I sensed no *Danger: Keep Off*! notices.

I had kissed her very gently at first, the lips clinging with butterfly-wing softness as I concentrated all my awareness of her allure, her desirability, in the muscles of my mouth. It was not until I felt her own lips relax and open that I allowed my tongue to venture between them.

It was met, not immediately but tentatively, with a hesitation that was overcome the moment I explored the inner surfaces of her lips, her teeth, the hollows of her cheeks. Then she thrust hard against me, tongue to wrestling tongue, as our mouths clamped more forcefully together. Eventually it was she who invaded my mouth. By this time the blood was pumping fiercely through my veins; I could feel the wild beating of her heart against my chest. My arms tightened around her pliant waist as the long, lean body was draped against me.

When at last we drew apart, she leaned back in my embrace and whispered breathlessly: 'I'm *so* sorry!'

'Sorry?'

'Your beautiful glass. I smashed it. That was unforgivable.'

'My dearest, darling lady,' I said, 'don't even think about it. It was sheer clumsiness on my part. Anyway — look where it got me!'

I tightened my grip. The violet eyes were fixed on my face. And this time the flesh at the corners crinkled and she flashed me a marvellous smile. 'Kiss me again, Paul,' she said.

The kiss was longer this time, the tongues more venturesome. Since she was pressed firmly against me now, I withdrew my hands from the small of her back and passed them up her sides, sensing with a particular thrill the soft swell of breasts caress the tips of my thumbs.

The breasts, as I had imagined, were small and tender, but well shaped. I felt the nipples harden against my palms as I cupped them.

There was hardness too at my loins, becoming more rigid every moment. The kiss was developing into a marathon, the breathing heavy and the wet lips clasping, sliding, opening ever wider each time the two tongues thrust and probed. I judged that this was probably the moment of truth — the time to find out was this no more than a thank-you-for-dinner-and-what-a-nice-evening cuddle, or was she serious, would she go the whole way? After all, I knew nothing, really, about her: the whole evening had been opportunist, a spur of the moment affair.

My cock, stiff as a plank now, was shafted up against my belly. I moved my hands to Solange's buttocks, pressing her even closer towards me. At the same time I rammed my hips against her pelvis, thrusting into her softness with the unyielding outline of my staff.

The reaction was unmistakable. She squirmed her own hips slowly, lasciviously from side to side, rolling the length of my desire this way and that between our two bodies, savouring the hardness clamped to her belly. A deep 'Mmmmm!' of pleasure purred in her throat.

Very good. So far, in fact, so good — but only so-so! We couldn't stand up all night kissing. It was time to make the next move.

I didn't want to risk the possibility of bathos — 'an unintentional lapse in mood from the sublime to the absurd', my school dictionary had told me years before. And this could happen, I felt, if the two of us, still locked together, were to teeter all the way across to the bed. The backs of my knees were against the seat of the armchair which had been so successful with Françoise. I dropped into the chair and pulled Solange down onto my lap.

The manoeuvre passed very neatly, with no clumsy positioning to overcome. She was leaning against me, with my left arm around her shoulders and my right hand free to roam. We were sitting cheek to cheek, and the first thing I did was turn my head and resume the passionate kiss.

Long fingers clasped the back of my head and combed through my hair, pressing my mouth even harder against hers. I realised that this was in fact the first time she had touched me with her hands, and a chill of anticipation prickled the nerves at the nape of my neck. I began unfastening the buttons between the collar and the waist of her flowered dress.

As soon as there was enough space, I slid my hand inside to attack her bust bodice. Surprise, surprise — women are both adept and adroit at these things! — it was already loose. I eased up the strip of cloth and felt cool, scented flesh, a satined swell of skin, the puckered circle of an areola and a stiffened nipple. I abandoned the kiss, squeezed the delicate, pointed breast up into the gap in front of her dress, and lowered my head. I fondled the breast, feeding the nipple into my mouth, rolling it around with my tongue. I held the sensitive bud gently between my teeth, licking it with a quick, fluttering movement.

Solange uttered a deep sigh. She licked the lobe of my ear, nipped it between her teeth, thrust her tongue into the interior. I shuddered with delight.

My mouth was still busy with her breast, but I had freed the hand to pull her short skirt up around her hips. She made no move to stop me. She was wearing skin-tight knickers with no lace trimmings, elasticated at the waist and legs. I passed my hand over the soft curve of her belly, trailing fingertips down the crease above each thigh, lowering the palm between them. Her mons was hot against my hand, the padded swell already moist where I stroked the well-defined cleft at its centre.

Solange's hips jerked under my caress. She was breathing very fast. She spread her thighs a little and reached her free hand down between them to touch the hard throbbing bulge at my loins which had been crushed beneath her buttocks. 'My!' she murmured lazily. 'We're well stacked in there, are we not?'

I sat up straight and smiled at her. 'Solange,' I said, 'you are gorgeous!'

There was a wealth of complicity in her returning smile 'And what, my Paul, are you?'

'I'm Alice,' I said crazily. 'I'm in Wonderland!'

She continued staring at me, the violet eyes wide, but said nothing. Her hips writhed slightly against the proof of my desire, my lust for her, as my finger continued its caress.

'The thing,' I said, deciding to keep in the Alice vein, 'the thing is: will you, won't you, will you, won't you, won't you join the dance?'

Solange chuckled. The pink tip of her tongue appeared, brushing the width of her top lip so that it glistened with moisture in the artificial light. 'I am rather fond of dancing,' she observed.

'Then let's have a ball!' I said recklessly. Adding, a moment later: '*Madame* Solange? You don't have a suspicious husband waiting at home?'

'I am not married.'

'Bravo!' I decided to get all the cards out on the table. 'And no *beau*? No extra special boyfriend?'

'I treasure my independence,' Solange said. 'My job is well paid. I like to do what I believe is called playing the field.'

'A girl after my own heart,' I enthused. 'Let me replace your brandy at once.' I stirred in the chair, but she placed a finger on my lips. 'Later perhaps. It's . . . comfortable here.'

'How much later? Do you think I might be able to twist your elegant arm and persuade you to remain with me all night?'

'I think you might.'

'Then I know a place that's far more comfortable,' I said huskily. 'I propose that we leave this chair and go to bed . . . now.'

'Do let's,' said Solange.

'Is this your bathroom?' Solange asked, with fingers on the handle of the door.

'Among other things,' I replied, remembering Corinne Dubois's incursion in the middle of my ablutions on the dread night of the Ahmed Simbel show.

'I'll be with you in a moment,' my current object of desire said. She opened the door and went in, holding the gaping edges of her dress together with one hand. Female modesty is a curious thing. I heard water running.

When she returned, Solange was wearing nothing but the white stockings. Her body was surprisingly dark — a warm, dusky tint shown off to perfection by the pale, bright shine of the sheer material sheathing her slender legs, and emphasized by the thick black bush triangled between her thighs.

I had undressed down to my white underpants — maybe there is some strange modesty, the first time at least, in men too! — and was lying on the bed. 'How lovely you look!' I exclaimed. 'Did you spend the whole summer on the Riviera?'

She glanced down at herself and smiled. 'You mean the tan? No — very late winter sports at Zermatt. The ski slopes were open until Easter, and I stay brown once I've been exposed.'

I raised my eyebrows. 'The whole body exposed?' There were no paler patches delineating pelvis and bust.

'I said I liked to play the field. That includes snowfields,' Solange said. She sat on the edge of the bed. The proximity of that slender naked body had already re-induced a massive erection that was thrusting out the front of my underpants like an army tent.

Lips curved into an enticing smile, she stared me straight in the eye, reaching out a hand to hook her fingers into my waistband. Quite slowly, she dragged my underpants down so that my cock sprang free. Quivering slightly, with the veins bluish-red under the distended skin, it rose from my loins like a flagstaff.

'*Well*!' Solange said. 'That's something I'm sure you should be proud of, Paul . . .'

She yanked the underpants down to my ankles, dragged them off me, and threw them onto the armchair. Then she climbed on the bed and stretched out the lithe length of her body beside me. I reached out my arms and drew her close.

There is nothing like that first ecstatic moment when you hold a nude and nubile female body against you – belly to belly, soft breasts crushed to the chest, the hands closed over the taut swell of buttocks, cool skin against the heat of a throbbing cock. In an instant, like the pieces of a puzzle locking into place, knees wedge between thighs, mouth seeks mouth and the hands fill with flesh as the mind becomes dizzy with delight.

The moment of course is just that: it is short-lived.

It has to be savoured perhaps within seconds, because

almost at once the lustful impulses, the sex drives of the individuals involved, spurred on by the lewd urge of nakedness, compels them into movement.

To touch, to feel, to stroke, to stimulate reaction becomes all-important.

Certainly for Solange and me on that first night the joys of the kiss and the caress seemed never-ending.

Chapter Twelve

My hands traced the outline of Solange's body, moulding the narrow hips, sculpting the hollows between ribs and waist, smoothing the muscled planes of belly and thighs.

I fondled the small, pointed mounds of her breasts, sucking on the rosy tips while my exploring fingers dabbled in the moist delights half hidden amongst the dark thatch between her legs.

She lay on her back as I knelt beside her on the bed, uttering small mewls of pleasure each time the marauding hands touched a sensitive spot or startled a shiver, a jerk from her super-responsive nerves. Her skin was smooth as velvet.

One of her hands was wrapped around the thickness of my pulsating staff, pumping it slowly and seductively up and down in a dreamy rhythm; with the other fingers spread across the base of her belly, she had parted the fleshy lips of her cunt, offering up to me the dark, wet secrets of the interior.

My breath quickened as I feasted my eyes on the slim frame so enticingly stretched out before me, on the glistening lips, angled forward beneath that prominent mons in subjection to my hand and . . . yes, my mouth!

With Solange's hand still firmly grasping my cock, I

swung one leg over her, straddled her hips, and lowered my head to her loins.

She still had her fingers spread. I probed my tongue between two of them, flicking the tip into the damp crevice she held so enticingly open. Her hips arched up off the mattress, urging me to penetrate deeper; the small cries of pleasure became a continuous low moan of delight, peaking occasionally when I licked the tumescent bud of her clitoris. I lashed my tongue up and down the entrance to her secret place, sinking it deeper and deeper into the hot, fleshy folds. Beyond my head, the muscles of her spread thighs twitched and trembled.

She removed her hand, and my mouth fastened over the whole hairy slit, sucking up the lips, tonguing the bud, exploring the ridged passage of her love canal.

The hand withdrew slowly, trailing along the tensed surface of my belly, teasing expert fingers through my pubic hair, finally clasping the creased sac bunched below the cock that its mate was milking. She fondled the sac, caressing the wrinkled skin as she manoeuvered the sensitive glands inside it. The hand massaging the skin of my quivering shaft over its rigid interior grasped me more firmly and accelerated the rhythm. I raised my head and gasped aloud; the exquisite agony constricting my loins threatened at any moment to explode into a spouting climax.

Solange writhed sinuously beneath me; her hips threshed wildly, jerking up faster and faster from the bed. When I lowered my lips to her cunt once more, she let go of me, placed a hand each side of my head and drew me gently away. I felt the hot tip of a wicked tongue on the underside of my tool. And then the whispered words: 'Paul, oh Paul! My love, my lover man. Come up, come up: be nearer to me now . . .'

I moved swiftly off her, turned around, and stretched out beside her prone body. Nerves at the bottom of her belly were trembling. I propped myself up on one elbow, leaned over and kissed her on the mouth. A hand crept out to grasp my stiff cock again, and I clapped my own hand over her heated mons, allowing two fingers to slide inside and roll the erect little shaft of her clitoris between them.

For a brief eternity we remained like that, scarcely moving, our mouths glued together, tongues gently thrusting, fingers subtly pressing, relaxing. Then suddenly I drew back my head. 'Solange,' I said hoarsely, 'you're so wonderful! I want you; I want you now!'

The wide eyes stared up at me, unblinking. Her lips were drawn slightly back from her teeth. 'Tell me,' she panted. 'Tell me, Paul. I want to hear you say it!'

I knew what she wanted, she needed. It arose, I thought, from the disparity between the natural self she was allowing herself to show me now and the tightly-reined, almost prudish image she was obliged to cultivate for her job. The tension this created in her had to be resolved. She needed to have her real personality confirmed.

'You little whore,' I said roughly. 'I'm going to fuck you!'

She was breathing very fast now, the tilted breasts quivering, their nipples stiff as a baby's thumbs. The eyes blinked once, then resumed their expressionless stare.

'Yes,' I pursued, 'I'm going to stuff it up you and

shag you until you scream for mercy! I'm going to fuck you rigid! Draw up those damned legs, bitch, and let me get at your cunt!'

Solange moaned. I moved down the bed, knelt between her thighs, seized her behind the knees, and shoved her legs up and back, so that she was doubled up, with the knees almost touching her tits.

I leaned on the thighs, forcing them even further back. From the top of her pubic bush to the puckered star of her anus, the whole thatched furrow of her underparts was now lewdly displayed. The lips I had manipulated gaped red amongst the dark, damp hair. 'Come on, bitch,' I grated. 'Open it up wider and let me in. Get a move on, you sexy little whore!'

The lean, flat plane of Solange's belly was rising and falling sporadically. Two hands stole down over it, grazed the furred hillock between her thighs, parting the spread lips wider still. The cropped head was thrust hard back into the pillows, the violet eyes now closed.

I stretched out, seized my pulsating cock in one hand, flexed my hips and lunged.

The rigid shaft squelched straight in, the whole length swallowed up to the hilt, balls splatting against the naked girl's arsehole.

She gave a loud cry, arching involuntarily off the bed to meet my thrust and embed me ever more deeply inside her.

I leaned over those obscenely spread thighs and supported myself on two hands placed one on either side of her waist. Solange had gripped her own ankles to keep the bent legs doubled up against her body. Using

Reckless Liaisons

long, slow strokes, I began shafting forcefully in and out of her.

She was panting now, fiercely contorting her pelvis to match my plunges, contracting the vaginal muscles to grip my intruding staff. I felt myself submerged in sensuous delight. The hot sliding clasp of that inner flesh eased along my tool concentrated all the nerves of my loins into a single bursting joy. I began withdrawing as far as the knob, then pistoning back in hard so that our pubic bones smacked together with each thrust.

Soon Solange released her ankles. Her legs scissored over my back and her arms wrapped tightly around me. Sharp nails raked my spine as she pulled me – still pumping away – ferociously down onto her. There was a channel of sweat between her pointed breasts.

Now we were a single unit, an oiled reciprocating machine, the matched parts of which moved silkily together in a well-tuned orgy of lust. Solange rolled wildly from side to side, carrying me with her, clasped to her breasts and belly as our flesh sucked and slapped. Her heels pummelled my quaking buttocks. Her breath jetted hotly against my ear; my face was lost in the perfume of her hair.

There was an obbligato to this orchestrated symphony of moving muscles and limbs – rising and falling with the thrashing of our hips, a continuous moan and groan moulded into a complex husky pattern each time it was forced from our two mouths by the torrid coupling of our bodies.

'Oh, God! Oh, *God*!' Solange cried, as the tension between my hips gathered to fever pitch. 'Fuck me, lover. Yes, give it to me. Do it to me, do!'

Somewhere deep within her, a distant shuddering had begun to shake her frame. Savagely, I penetrated, impaling her with increasing force and speed each time the shuddering gained in impetus and strength. There was an explosive trembling within me too. My distended cock pulsed again with an agony that was exquisite.

When finally the demonic jerks had reached a point where the girl's entire body was shaken like an aspen leaf, and the long-drawn trembling gasps of her palpitating release had climaxed in my ear, my own long-delayed orgasm seized my loins and propelled me remorselessly, irresistibly forward.

With one last spastic plunge, I homed in and spewed my tribute to her allure in fountained spurts far up into the muscled clasp of her quaking belly.

I don't remember falling asleep, but I remember waking once and finding that I was still on top of her, with her arms warmly around me and her legs still hooked firmly over my calves.

There was a second awakening too, but that is fixed more firmly in my memory. It must have been almost dawn, because I was aware of a lean figure bent over my hips . . . and there was a delicious hot sensation tingling my cock, with soft lips closing lasciviously over the tip.

PART TWO

Paris, September 1922

Dagmar, Nounou, Eve and the rest

Chapter Thirteen

The sculptor Tom Crawford arrived at the house in the Avenue Kléber driving a rakish, low-slung blue sports car with a chrome-rimmed, horse-shoe-shaped radiator and an outside exhaust. Silver on red enamel, the word *Bugatti* embellished the small oval nameplate at the top of the radiator. Crawford pulled up in the cobbled yard with a squeal of brakes, and the highly tuned motor spluttered into silence.

A Darracq tourer, two Laforge saloons, a resplendent Delahaye and a Citröen cloverleaf runabout were already parked between the entrance arch and the mansion's brightly-lit portico. Crawford swung a leg over the cutaway cockpit side of the Bugatti and stepped out onto the cobbles. Unusually for him, he was formally dressed in a dinner jacket with a starched shirt and — a concession to his artist's status — a floppy black bow-tie. He strode to the steps outside the portico.

Just before he reached them, a voice hailed him from the entrance and Bertrand Laforge, wearing black trousers and a white tuxedo jacket, ran up to join him. 'Good Lord,' the industrialist's son exclaimed, with an admiring look at the blue racer, 'where did you get hold of that bus? It's not *yours*, is it?'

Crawford shook his head. 'Wish it was! No, it belongs to a Yank, the Dolly Sisters' manager in fact. I was backstage at the Casino de Paris after the first house and the chap lent it to me for the evening.'

Laforge whistled. 'The *Dolly* Sisters! Music-hall stars, by God! Flying a bit high, aren't we? What's the score then — goings-on in the dressing room while the audience ogles the nudes?'

Crawford laid a finger alongside his nose. 'It is the fact that there are *two* sisters that makes it an extra screw of the turn,' he announced sepulchrally.

His friend laughed. 'Tom, you're impossible!' he said. They climbed the steps together and walked through open double doors into the checkerboard marble vestibule. Behind them a large limousine turned into the courtyard.

'What's this in aid of, Bertrand?' Crawford queried. 'My invitation just said cocktails, black tie and RSVP, but I suspect there may be something more to it than that. I hope so anyway.'

Laforge shrugged. 'You know Dagmar. When she goes to Mado Laverne's, it's to choose the mannequins, not the clothes! So there'll be pretty girls here, for sure, but whether they will be . . . shall we say accessible? . . . that's another matter. It should be fun finding out anyway. Paul Mackenzie and the other Knights of the Bottle will be here, I'm told.'

'Including Corinne?' the sculptor asked.

'Including Corinne.'

'Oh, well.'

A butler appeared and led the two men up the curving staircase to the first floor drawing room. They heard a babble of voices punctuated by shrill laughs and the bray of a saxophone from behind the beaten copper sheathing the double doors. The servant opened the doors and announced: 'Mistah Crowfoot et Monsieur Laforge . . .'

They walked into a wall of sound. There must have been at least fifty people in the lofty room. Beyond the close-packed jam of formally dressed men and chattering women in evening gowns, the saxophone player and a man with a banjo stood on either side of an upright piano which had been installed in front of the shuttered French windows. Two black men in white jackets manipulated chrome cocktail shakers behind the bar as if they were South American percussion instruments accompanying the musicians. The pianist was vamping an introduction to *Valencia*.

The Comtesse van den Bergh glided forward with outstretched arms to greet the new arrivals. She was wearing a floor-length, tube-like dress in primrose chiffon which emphasised her prominent bust and fleshy hips. 'My dears,' she crowed, 'how good of you to come! You arrive just in time – when the lack of *good-looking* men was beginning to be felt!'

'Oh, come on, Dagmar,' Crawford said, kissing her on both cheeks, 'you know very well that the only feeling fascinating you is a fondle of female flesh!' He laughed. 'A miss is as good as a male, eh?'

The Comtesse wagged an admonitory finger. 'Don't be coarse, sirrah! And don't be too sure either.' She glanced over her shoulder. 'Most of these fools are duty guests, people I owe. In half an hour eighty per cent of them will have left. Stay on, both of you, with the rest of my *friends*, and you may learn something to your advantage.' Scarlet lips widened in an impish grin. 'Mine too, of course!'

'What do you suppose she meant by that?' Bertrand Laforge asked, when their hostess had wafted herself away to greet new guests.

'You tell me,' said Crawford. 'As you were saying, it could be fun finding out.' He clapped Bertrand on the shoulder. 'Your guest is as good as mine!'

'I fancy that is about as many puns as I need for the moment,' Bertrand smiled. 'I see Paul Mackenzie over by the bar. I shall join him there.'

'And I see that Corinne is dangerously near,' Crawford replied. 'I shall try and charm that redhead away from Hans Bohl on the far side of the band.' He sauntered away, threading his tall figure elegantly through the noisy crowd.

Mackenzie was drinking something pale green from a conical cocktail glass frosted around the rim. He replied to Bertrand's greeting warmly enough, and contributed to the bantering exchange which followed it — but his eyes all the time were looking over his friend's shoulder. Eventually Bertrand turned around and saw a young woman sitting at the bar behind him. She was wearing a dark blue dress — a not-too-pretty girl with a bang over her forehead and plaits coiled over her ears. 'Something special?' Bertrand enquired.

Mackenzie shrugged. 'I wish I knew. So far as I was concerned, she was nothing but a tease — one of those bitches who leads you on and then, right at the last moment, suddenly remembers a prior engagement!'

'Don't I know!' Bertrand sympathised.

'I was simply wondering why Dagmar should have made such a point of telling me that she was interesting.'

'Presumably,' Bertrand said, 'you found her interesting. At first.'

'Forget the face,' Mackenzie advised. 'Just look at that *derriére*!'

His friend swung round again. The girl was sitting on a stool with her elbows planted on the bar counter, exchanging confidences with Corinne Dubois. Bertrand allowed his eyes to wander down the trim lines of her back . . . and, yes, the haunches spread over the seat of the stool were certainly well formed. Lower down, the heels of black patent ankle boots were hooked over the stool's lowest rung. 'Promising,' he agreed. 'But she's talking to Take-all-comers Corinne. Maybe Dagmar meant interesting to *her*?'

'We shall see,' Mackenzie said. 'I hope.'

The crowd was thinning. Dagmar van den Bergh stood in the doorway bidding a group of expensively dressed socialites goodbye. The saxophone player was struggling with *The Lily of Laguna*. An elderly diplomat wearing decorations sat on a davenport telling some scabrous story to a circle of giggling girls. Now that there was a space in the middle of the room, the Comtesse's German baroness, still frowning, gyrated slowly with her arms around a tall dark beauty whom Mackenzie recognised as Françoise Dupuis.

Soon there were no more than a dozen people left around the bar. Dagmar ushered out the diplomat and his admirers, and closed the doors. Françoise and the German were still dancing dreamily. The band switched to *Tu Ne Sais Pas Aimer* — You Don't Know How To Love.

'All right, people,' Dagmar called. 'Now the party can really begin. We're going to go into the morning room, on the other side of the landing, where you will get something a little more substantial to eat and drink. After that . . .' She smiled wickedly. 'Well, you will have to wait and see!'

She re-opened the doors. The musicians played a final chord, and the saxophonist and banjo player packed away their instruments. The barmen were already stowing bottles and glasses below the counter. The Comtesse led the way to a panelled room with heavy crimson drapes over the windows, leather armchairs, and a buffet table spread with a white cloth. From gilt frames around the walls, Van den Bergh ancestors who had once presided haughtily over the salon now surveyed lobster patties, *pâté de foie gras*, quails in aspic and a row of champagne bottles in an ice bath.

When the party was complete, Paul Mackenzie looked around the room. Apart from himself, Corinne, Bertrand, Crawford and Hans Bohl — the self-styled Knights of the Bottle — he saw Françoise, Janine d'Arcy, his hostess and her German friend, a couple he didn't know and — rather to his surprise — the Lebanese couturier, Ahmed Simbel. Twelve people in all.

Two buxom maids — country girls in black dresses and frilly white caps and aprons — dispensed food and drink as the guests settled themselves around the buffet. Champagne corks popped. The conversation became animated. There was a lot of laughter . . . and then

Dagmar van den Bergh rang a small brass bell that was beside her glass on the table. At once a heavy oak door which Paul imagined led to the servants' quarters opened wide. The maids staggered in, carrying between them a sedan chair which he remembered seeing in the vestibule when he arrived. The conversation died away. In the silence, Dagmar rang the bell again and announced: 'A specialised dessert for you, my dear friends! Shall we say . . . a *bombe surprise*?'

She nodded to the maids, who lowered the sedan chair and stepped out, front and back, from between the shafts. The roof of the sedan chair flipped open; the door swung back; the hinged sides dropped . . . and there was a gasp of astonishment from the assembled guests, followed at once by a burst of applause.

A naked man and woman were twined together inside the chair!

Sitting on the low bench seat, the man held the woman on his knees, lifting her up and then lowering her again onto what Paul could see was a very stout piece of equipment indeed.

He could also see — he had imagined himself beyond mere astonishment, but this proved him wrong — that the man was Victor Houbigant, the non-diplomat he had first met with Janine on his last visit to the house in the Avenue Kléber.

And the busty woman impaled on his veined and distended staff was Desirée — the nubile intruder Paul had encountered in his own bed under the name of Rosette!

'Bravo, Victor!' the Comtesse enthused. 'Now let's see a bit of *action* in there . . .'

Reckless Liaisons

Houbigant's strong hands were clasped firmly on either side of the young woman's waist. Her legs were lewdly spread, the feet planted on the floor outside his own. As she flexed and relaxed her knees to rise and fall, he assisted her now with these hands, accelerating the rhythm until her ripe breasts bobbed energetically up and down with every stroke. Between the parted thighs, the oiled and rigid shaft of the man's penis pistoned with small sucking sounds in and out of the fleshy aperture dilating and contracting among the tawny hairs furring the girl's loins.

Desirée-Rosette had her eyes closed. There was a beautific expression on her face. Her chestnut hair was pinned up and her hands grasped the sides of the sedan chair for greater leverage. Houbigant's features were set in an expression of concentration, his eyes — a little wildly, Paul Mackenzie thought — flicking from side to side under the fascinated gaze of the guests around the buffet.

'We had intended to have them on the table in traditional fashion,' Dagmar said, 'but we couldn't find a pie-dish — or cook a crust for that matter — big enough to hide a couple! Never mind,' she laughed, 'we did the best we could . . . and to make up for it, here is a second surprise.' She got up from the table, walked to one of the sets of drapes along the outside wall, and tugged a heavy, tasselled cord.

The curtains slid back to reveal a shuttered bow window. And on the window-seat were the two country girls who had carried in the sedan chair. Nobody had noticed them leave, but now they were clasped together in a torrid embrace that was anything but platonic.

Once again the guests exclaimed aloud.

One of the girls was dark, the other fair. Their mouths were glued together, cheeks hollowed and jaws working as they sucked and tongued one another with frenzied passion. The brunette had already unbuttoned her companion's dress, ripped open the neck to expose one shoulder and thrust aside the apron top to drag out a heavy, pear-shaped breast. As they watched, she cupped the fleshy mound in one hand, rolling the thick brown nipple between her finger and thumb. The blonde, still kissing, uttered a choked cry. Her two hands scrabbled at the dark girl's tightly sheathed bust.

The guests chattered excitedly, some with open enthusiasm, others less spontaneously, with sideways glances to see how their neighbours were taking the salacious displays. Tom Crawford was pouring champagne. 'Good old Daggers!' he cried, splashing the frothy wine from glass to glass. 'What a splendid wheeze! How ripping to know, my old dear, that you realise it takes, as they say, all sorts!'

The German Baroness — her name was Helga von Frodenburg — had risen from the table. Her tall, thin, rather sombre figure was clothed in a severely-cut *tailleur*, the skirt of which reached halfway down her calves. She wore black lace-up boots with Cuban heels. She strode to the sedan chair, tapping a leather-covered riding crop into the palm of her left hand.

'Come on, get out of there!' she ordered the coupling pair, in her heavily accented French. 'Have you forgotten that you are supposed to be giving a *show*?'

The redhead scrambled hastily off Houbigant's knee, sliding a surreptitious look at the Baroness as she straightened up. She ran to the white-clothed buffet and bent forward over it, supporting her weight on her elbows. Houbigant left the sedan chair more slowly – a compactly muscled man with a mat of dark hair on his chest. His penis, glistening and erect, speared out from the bush at the base of his belly, as threatening as a trooper's lance.

Helga von Frodenburg tapped her riding crop lightly against the redhead's tautly rounded buttocks. 'Lie flat, the way you were told. Spread those legs: we want to see what you've got!'

Desirée lowered her torso to the white linen cloth, straddling her shapely legs as far apart as she could. Her generous breasts were squashed between her chest and the table top. Beneath the tightly clenched button of her anus, pubic hair dark with moisture flanked the gaping red lips of her savaged cunt. The muscles of her buttocks tightened and quivered in anticipation as Houbigant approached.

The Baroness swung back her arm and thwacked his bottom hard with the crop. Her straight black brows were knitted in a formidable frown. 'Are you deaf?' she grated. 'Madame la Comtesse has already told you that she wants action. Do *I* have to repeat myself a second time?'

The man was looking at the floor, an expression that was comically defensive on his face. 'No, Madam,' he mumbled. 'I am very sorry.'

'You are very sorry *what*?' She struck three more blows, each harder than the last. 'Am I never to get any respect here?'

'I am very sorry, *Madam*!' exclaimed Houbigant,

who had flinched visibly with each stroke. The four red weals crisscrossed the hirsute planes of his flank.

'I should hope so! Now get in there and do the only thing you're good for.' Helga von Frodenburg leaned over the recumbent girl, seized the cheeks of her bottom and drew them even further apart, exposing still more obscenely the gashed furrow between them. The naked man positioned himself immediately behind, bent his knees slightly, and lunged forward with his cock held in one hand.

The distended, blood-engorged tip ploughed straight in between the open lips, sliding on until the whole wet length of Houbigant's rod was swallowed up in Desirée's belly. She gave a smothered cry and bucked her hips back against his thrusts as he began pumping forcefully in and out of her. The Baroness had withdrawn; he bent forward with his hands on the table on each side of the prone girl, settling into a fast and easy rhythm that soon had her gasping.

Helga stood behind him, punctuating her words with strokes from the riding crop. 'Come on, man! . . . *Thwack*! . . . Give it to her . . . *Thwack*! . . . I want to see that cock rammed in . . . *Thwack*! . . . One, two, three, four . . . *Thwack*! . . . One, two, three, four . . . *Thwack*! . . . Faster, faster!'

By this time there was nobody left around the buffet. The guests, all of whom had been drinking for quite a while, reacted to the lascivious spectacle in different ways.

Tom Crawford, whose preference ran always to buxom, simple girls without too much intellectual pretension, had installed himself on the window-seat

Reckless Liaisons

with one of the maids on each side of him. Both girls were now naked to the waist, and the blonde had whipped open the sculptor's fly and hauled out his thick, throbbing stem, which she was massaging experimentally. Her companion was holding up one heavy breast so that he could lean forward and suck the nipple. There was a sly expression, almost a smirk, on her face; Crawford's two hands were hidden beneath their respective skirts.

Corinne Dubois, wet-lipped and enthusiastic, had seized the hand of Pierre Giotto — the male half of the couple Paul Mackenzie had never met before — and dragged him to the abandoned sedan chair. Once she had drawn him inside the cramped space, they saw her lift up her skirt . . . and then the sides were raised, the door closed, and the roof was dragged back into position. The sedan chair rocked gently in the middle of the room.

Pierre's wife Nicole, a sultry brunette with a pouting mouth, known to everyone as Nounou, was trying — not very hard — to fight off the attentions of Bertrand and Hans Bohl. The two young men had already unfastened the top of her silk dress, exposed her small, neat breasts and plunged a hand each beneath the swirl of her flared skirt.

At the far end of the table, their eyes fixed in fascination on the contorted features of Desirée as she suffered the assault on her loins, Paul and Janine were so far only holding hands. The Lebanese dressmaker, Ahmed Simbel, on the other hand, had seized the young Françoise by the neck and pushed her to the end of the buffet, where he forced her as close as he could to the splayed hips of Desirée and the rigid staff of the man fucking her.

'Watch carefully,' Simbel said silkily, in his high tenor voice. 'This is what will be happening to you. Quite soon now. I want to be quite sure that you know what goes on, exactly what goes on . . . from behind. I want you to be able to imagine it visually, each quivering contraction of the belly as the prick shafts in. Each hot spurt as it throbs and kicks up inside you.'

'Oh, no!' the girl's voice was little more than a shrill whisper. 'No . . . please. Don't . . . I don't want—'

'*Watch it*, you sexy little cow,' Simbel said, forcing her head down so that she was on a level with Houbigant's thrusting hips and the violated genitals of the girl bent over the buffet. 'I shall have you like this first myself. If necessary the other women will hold you down. And after I've finished with you, every other man here will take his turn.'

'Oh, noooo!' the girl wailed. But her eyes, fixed on the penis and the opening it was ferociously invading, were bright with anticipation.

Helga von Frodenburg strode back to the labouring couple. 'Victor,' she snapped disparagingly. 'You're moving like a damned machine. I think we are entitled to a little artistry here – a change of rhythm, a little manipulation with the hands, maybe the mouth.' She smacked him twice, hard, with the palm of her hand. 'What do you think you're here for?'

'Madam, I'm sorry,' he gasped, the regular beat of his pounding hips suddenly ragged and sporadic. 'I'll try to do better, really I will. I apologise, Madam.'

'Then make amends in the usual way,' Helga said

sharply. She jumped up onto the table, knocking over an empty glass to send a plate of *petit-fours* spinning to the floor.

Those of the guests who were watching exclaimed in astonishment at this unexpected development. The woman stepped over Desirée, standing with a booted foot on each side of the ravished girl's waist. She bent down to grasp the hem of her skirt, manoeuvering the tight garment up her slim legs until it was bunched around her hips.

She was wearing no underclothes. Naked below the waist now, she allowed the spectators a view of laced leather boots, white skin and abundant dark pubic hair before she squatted down and sat on the prone girl's shoulders.

Victor Houbigant was already leaning forward as he continued to pump in and out between the distended buttocks of his partner. Helga shifted her pelvis forward, leaning back to support herself on her elbows. Her knees were drawn up to expose her naked crotch.

Freeing one hand, she tapped the man on the shoulder with her crop, and then seized his hair, dragging his head roughly down until his mouth was buried among the black hairs thatching her loins.

'You know what to do,' she said.

Chapter Fourteen

Tom Crawford was lying along the window-seat with his legs drawn up. One of the maidservants — the brunette — straddled his hips; the other squatted over his face. The two girls were kissing.

The sight, as unexpected in its way as the arrival of the sedan chair, of the prim German woman herself joining the couple at the buffet had galvanised the other members of the party into activity. Bertrand and Hans Bohl, who had stripped the sulky-looking Nounou of all her clothes without much in the way of protests from her, now laid the voluptuously nubile young woman on a leather-covered settee. They stood on either side of her, flexing their knees as she reached up her two hands, unbuttoned each fly, groped inside, and then dragged out their cocks. The two stiff stems quivered in pale contrast to the dark material of their evening dress trousers.

From inside the sedan chair, there was a crescendo of gasps interspersed with lustful groans. Ahmed Simbel pushed Francoise to the floor. He forced her to kneel, bending forward to support herself on her hands, and lifted her skirt until it was draped over her waist. Then he pulled down a froth of white underclothes to expose the girl's naked buttocks. Françoise squealed shrilly —

Reckless Liaisons

with pain? with pleasure? with surprise? — as he produced an unexpectedly long and thick penis and knelt behind her to ram it between the bare cheeks of her bottom.

The guest who seemed the most affected by the display of unbridled lust surrounding her was Janine d'Arcy. She had jumped up onto the table, the better to see everything that was going on, and now she reached behind her to unfasten the blue dress and crossed her arms to ease it up past her small breasts before pulling the garment over her head. She stood breathing hard, absently undoing the white bodice that still encased the top half of her body. Her eyes were wide and very bright.

Paul Mackenzie was entranced. He too had climbed onto the table and now he was kneeling in front of Janine. Neither of them had alluded to the dinner at Fouquet's and Paul's cruel disappointment on the stairway of the girl's apartment block, but he was beginning to realise that, as definitely as Françoise, Janine needed a specific stimulus before her subconscious permitted her inhibitions to be overruled. With Françoise — as he knew, as he could see now — it was the classic rape complex; she wanted to be forced into sex. Janine, it seemed, was more complex. She was clearly some kind of exhibitionist. She had a strong sexual urge, as Paul himself had discovered. But it couldn't be allowed free rein in the simple context of one man, one woman; for her passions to be unleashed fully, she had to feel herself part of a composite scene, a *spectacle*. Interesting, as Dagmar van den Bergh had hinted, indeed!

Reckless Liaisons

The Comtesse herself stood by the servants' entrance. She had stripped off the primrose gown — she wore nothing beneath it — and now, splendid in her nudity, her firm breasts supported by her two hands, gazed at the obscene couplings around her with an indulgent and satisfied smile. The evening was proceeding according to plan.

Still kneeling, Paul exulted. Only a filmy pair of French knickers edged with peach-coloured lace separated him from the female hips and bottom which had so attracted him in the Champs Elysées — and this time, it seemed, nothing could prevent him getting to close quarters, to *intimate* quarters, with the heavy masses of flesh he so ardently desired. He reached up, grasped the waistband of the knickers, and with one swift movement pulled them down to Janine's ankles. She made no protest, stepping out of them automatically and looking proudly around as if to say: Look at me: I'm naked and there's a man at my loins!

The hips in front of Paul were wide, heavy with muscle. Between them the solid mass of the girl's belly curved down to a dense triangle of brown hair. He wrapped his arms around her just below the thick waist, clasping her whole pelvis towards him as his hands clenched on the taut and luscious moons of her bottom. With an inarticulate cry of delight, he pushed his face into that pubic triangle and shot out his tongue to search for the damp crevice nestling within it.

Houbigant, who was still manfully shafting Desirée Schneider, abruptly tensed; the rhythm of his pounding strokes faltered; he lifted his head from between Helga's thighs. He opened his mouth to utter a strangled cry and slammed against her one last time as the hot sperm jetted up into her belly.

At once the Baroness changed position. Swiftly she climbed off the girl's back and sat down again in front of her — this time with Desirée's head between her thighs. She reached forward to grasp the luxuriant crop of dark red hair and shuffled herself forwards until she could raise her pelvis and place her pouting inner lips immediately below the recumbent girl's hungry mouth. Dagmar meanwhile had strolled to the end of the buffet, where she waited for the exhausted Houbigant to withdraw before she herself leaned over Desirée. Lazily, almost absentmindedly, she began stroking the swollen outer lips of the girl's cunt, sliding her fingers in among the warm wet folds, sinking deeper to penetrate the hot interior, tweaking the rubbery clitoris.

The gentle, sensuous massaging, such an insidious contrast to the battering she had received from Victor Houbigant, induced a strong reaction in the sexy redhead. She squirmed her hips against the edge of the buffet, offering her most secret parts to the invading caress, groaning with muffled ecstasy as she sucked and gobbled greedily between the Baroness's twitching thighs.

On the far side of the room, Nounou, grasping the two shafts projecting over her from either side of the settee, drew Bertrand and Hans down to her level, urging them to kneel beside her so that she could position them precisely, with the glans of each young man just touching her cheek. Slowly, then, she swivelled her head from side to side, sucking, nibbling, nipping with her small teeth each suffused and distended knob

Reckless Liaisons

in turn. At the same time four exploring hands roved her plump body, penetrating anus and vagina, fondling breasts and caressing nipples, tracing lazy arabesques over the flesh of waist and belly. Under their ministrations, Nounou's small rounded frame shook and writhed with delight.

On the window-seat, Tom Crawford and the maids, heaving and thrusting in complicated rhythms, were still in the same relative positions — he on his back with one of the girls impaled on his thick prick and the other offering herself to his sucking mouth. Now, however, all three were naked, with their clothes strewn over the floor.

Ahmed Simbel too had thrown off his clothes, his compact, chunky body dark against the whiteness of his partner's satin skin. Françoise was nevertheless dressed — or partly dressed. She was lying on her back in one of the leather armchairs, exactly as she had been in Paul Mackenzie's studio, with her legs drawn up and hooked over the arms, her skirt still bunched around her waist and her breasts nude between the edges of a gown that the couturier had wrenched apart. Nestling between her canted thighs, below the creased and contracted fold of her belly, pink lips gaped invitingly among the thickets of her pubic hair.

Dagmar van den Bergh watched approvingly as Simbel leaned over the chair, took his weight on his hands and lowered himself until his thick and stiffened member quivered just above those parted lips. The girl's wide eyes watched him expressionlessly . . . and then closed in a sudden contorted grimace when he lunged down and penetrated deeply with a single powerful thrust. Françoise groaned, rolling her dark head from side to side as he shafted in and out increasingly fast.

The Comtesse transferred her gaze from the chair to the far end of the buffet, where Janine d'Arcy stood still with her hands on her hips and Paul Mackenzie on his knees in front of her. There was a faraway expression on the girl's face; she oscillated her pelvis very slowly this way and that while the Englishman, his arms wrapped even more tightly around those magnificent hips and buttocks, buried his face and feasted among the springy hairs of her mons.

Apart from the black patent ankle boots, Janine was completely naked now, though her cavalier was still fully dressed. Smiling mistily, she changed her position, playing with one small pointed breast with one hand and running the fingers of the other through Paul's hair. The Comtesse, whose manipulation of Desirée's genitals had become increasingly energetic, returned the smile and then turned back to the armchair.

Ahmed Simbel had withdrawn his penis from his partner's body; now he was kneeling, legs spread wide, wide, on the arms of the chair, holding the glistening shaft in one brown hand. With the other, he slapped the girl's face once, twice. 'I said open that mouth!' he ordered roughly.

She stared up at him pleadingly. He slapped her again . . . and slowly, reluctantly, her mouth opened.

Simbel jerked forward and thrust his rigid cock between her trembling, parted lips.

There was a sudden concerted cry from two female voices. Brought to a fever-pitch of sexual awareness by the Comtesse's caress and the thrill of Helga von

Frodenburg's inner lips on each side of her tongue, Desirée Schneider suddenly shuddered, convulsed, and shouted out her long-held-back release as her muscles contracted, relaxed, and slammed her hips up and down on the table in a frenzied climax. The sight, and the feel of the girl's jerking head between her thighs, was enough to bring the Baroness to orgasm too. She threw back her own head and uttered a hoarse cry as her belly and loins convulsed in turn. Dagmar van den Bergh laughed and clapped her hands with delight.

In the middle of the room, the sedan chair tilted and fell over on its side.

Chapter Fifteen

Nobody quite knew how Dagmar van den Bergh had arranged it — she was in her subtle way an organising genius — but the party in the Avenue Kléber mansion had taken on a completely different aspect. The scene in the panelled morning room was the same, yet the action was now on a totally altered plane. What had been a series of individual enterprises was transformed into a single, corporate effort, a composite activity involving the hostess and all the guests at the same time. It was as though a string of music-hall or cabaret attractions had been metamorphosed overnight into a cohesive show, a spectacle with shape and plot and overall production.

The nude maidservants had cleared the table. More champagne had been drunk, a fresh supply of *petit-fours* passed around. And now the activity, and the attention, of the whole group was centred on the two ends of the long table and the exertions of the couple on each of them.

Paul Mackenzie, still with the 'interesting' Janine, was at one end; Françoise Dupuis and the couturier had been installed at the other. Mado Laverne's new mannequin was spread-eagled, lewdly splayed out on the table top and held down at the wrists and ankles by Hans Bohl, the Baroness, Bertrand and one of the servant girls. Simbel knelt between the girl's widely parted thighs. Paul too was kneeling. He stared down lasciviously at the young woman whose body had so fascinated him. She too was spread-eagled, the wide haunches and meaty buttocks flat on the table, but she lay there quietly of her own accord with nobody to hold her down, whereas Françoise strained against the hands imprisoning her. Janine had unpinned her hair and shaken loose the plaits. She moved her head slowly from side to side with her eyes half-closed and a sly smile animating her face: Look at me; I'm wicked, I'm wild; see how I debase myself before you all! Françoise looked wild too, but in quite a different way: her eyes were wide and staring and her lips trembled; if they hadn't known better, Dagmar and her friends might have thought her expression signified, Won't somebody help?

Everyone in the room was stark naked now. Pierre and Corinne had extricated themselves from the sedan chair and stood with the rest of the party around the sacrificial table — the Comtesse at one end, Desirée at the other, Crawford, Houbigant, Nounou and the remaining maidservant spread out between the two couples.

'Is everybody ready?' Dagmar called. 'Very well . . . Five, four, three, two, one, *start*!'

The two kneeling men, each with a remarkable cockstand, lowered themselves between the spread thighs of their respective partners, penetrated with swift, sure movements, and started at once to shaft in and out with measured, rhythmic strokes.

At the same time all the others, led by the Comtesse,

chanted in unison, and in time with the coupling pairs: '*One*, two, three, four . . . five, six, seven, eight . . . *Nine*, ten, eleven, twelve . . .'

Janine uttered a deep sigh, almost a growl, of pleasure as Paul ploughed into her. Her pelvis was already arched up, tilting the entrance to her vagina so that he could impale her more easily. Françoise squealed shrilly the moment she felt Simbel's thick staff once again parting the lips of her secret place. Her eyes screwed shut and the squeal turned into a shouted cry as the whole hard length of him was swallowed in her belly. But before he had completed half a dozen strokes, her hips were rising from the table to meet every thrust.

The chant continued: ' . . . thirteen, fourteen, fifteen, sixteen . . . *seventeen*, eighteen, nineteen, twenty . . .' One or two of the spectators were now clapping in time with the words. Several, excited by the obscene spectacle, and especially by the fact that it was, most daringly, in front of *an audience*, were crouched down so that they could study, inspect, and lust over at first hand the sight of penis and vagina in close and intimate contact. Nounou, whose breathing had considerably quickened, had taken Houbigant's limp cock in her hand and was hurriedly massaging it stiff again. The maid who was not occupied with Françoise dropped to her knees in front of Crawford. Corinne and Pierre, open-mouthed, fingered themselves avidly as they watched. They had, after all, missed the *hors-d'oeuvres*: they had been concealed within the sedan chair while the settee, the buffet, the armchair and the window seat were used to such telling effect.

' . . . *Thirty-three*, thirty-four, thirty-five, thirty-

Reckless Liaisons

six . . .' The copulation, and the shouts and claps urging it on, were accelerating now, increasing in speed and power as the protagonists panted and heaved. ' . . . Thirty-seven, thirty-eight, thirty-nine, forty . . .' To the watchers this was a competition, a scabrous use of sex to titillate and stimulate more sex. To the participants, though, it was an end in itself; it had become all-consuming, obsessional, separate from the charged atmosphere, the rhythmic chanting, the encouraging cries that were now manifesting themselves more and more as the frantic pace increased.

'Lying on the settee, I missed the beginning,' Nounou whispered to Victor Houbigant. 'Is it a race?'

'Not exactly. It's a competition.'

'To find out what? Who comes the quickest?'

'No.' He shook his head, catching his breath as her grip on his cock tightened and she started to milk him. 'It's . . . Aaaah! . . . The winner is the one who lasts *longest* – allowing that they mustn't miss a stroke, or pause, and they must keep to the rhythm we set.'

'What fun!' said Nounou, the Bright Young Thing. 'Let's you and I have a go when this lot have finished.'

Houbigant laughed. 'I think I've done all the hard work I'm capable of! But I'd be delighted, absolutely delighted to . . . *Oh*! *Ah*! . . . to provide the raw material for you to work on, the way you are . . . now!'

The panting groans of Simbel and Paul grew louder every moment. Françoise had wrapped her long legs around the couturier's back; her nails raked his swarthy shoulders; her lips were drawn back from her teeth and a continuous low keening purred in her throat. Paul's two hands were clenched on Janine's splendid buttocks, holding her fleshy pelvis firmly against him as he bucked and plunged. The expression on her face was ecstatic. Except for a short explosion of breath each time he battered into her, she was silent.

The count was in the high sixties when Simbel abruptly faltered in his sexual stride. His head jerked back. 'Oh, no,' he gasped, 'I can't . . . *No!* . . . It's no good, I . . .'

He groaned heavily, leaving the sentence unfinished. The muscles of his behind contracted. His belly convulsed . . . and with a last desperate surge, he spewed his hot sperm into the twitching belly of the dark girl beneath him.

There was a cheer from the watchers around the table, and the rhythmic clapping broke into spontaneous applause.

Ahmed Simbel collapsed across his partner, exhausted. And it was then that Françoise was transported into her own orgasm. Her eyes closed. Her mouth opened wide. A faint shuddering somewhere deep within her grew in intensity, translated itself into a series of spasmodic jerks, and finally seized her whole body with a galvanic shaking that thrashed her hips on the table top and nearly threw off the inert form of the Lebanese. Her sobbing cries of release rose above the excited encouragement of the spectators.

At the other end of the table, Paul and Janine had continued their marathon. Only the Comtesse was counting now. By the time the others transferred their attention back to the surviving competitors, she was wondering whether they were going to make three figures – an unusual feat, she considered. At least in these circumstances! 'Eighty-five, eighty-six, eighty-seven, eighty-eight,' she intoned, 'eighty-nine, ninety, ninety-one . . . oooooh!'

Paul no longer plunged. Abruptly, the machine had stopped working. The two lovers lay clasped tightly together, belly to trembling belly, mouth to mouth, in a mutual climax that shook them to the core even though the outward, visible signs were restricted to a sudden electric tension, an inexorable, orgasmic convulsion eventually released in a shared groan of ecstasy.

More applause.

When Paul stirred, raised himself, and helped Janine to sit up, he grinned at the Comtesse and asked: 'So we won? All right — what's the prize?'

Dagmar van den Bergh smiled back wickedly. 'For you,' she said, 'a very special, very *private* . . . consultation, upstairs, with Helga and myself.' She turned to Janine, who was stretching like a contented cat. 'And for you, my love, confirmed exhibitionist that you are, the chance to seduce dear Françoise — who deserves to sample the joys of our kind of love, even if she was the loser!'

Paul nodded. 'Very . . . interesting!' he said.

The two young women, still naked, sat facing one another in the centre of the long table.

Janine d'Arcy, retaining her cat-and-cream smile, had climbed up and knelt on the white linen cloth, sitting back on her heels and allowing her arms to fall by her sides as she waited to see what the Comtesse's instructions would be. She looked almost demure, with the loose brown hair tumbling over her shoulders, her small, pointed breasts tilted upwards, and the heavy, near-maternal swell of her hips curved out over her legs. The nipples tipping those breasts, however, were stiff and erect.

Persuading Françoise to get into position had been more difficult. At first she had refused, protesting loudly. But since everyone there was well aware of her particular turn-on, the other guests were vociferous in their insistence — heckling her perhaps more roughly than they would have done in the case of someone genuinely too shy or too frightened. There were cries of 'Come on, Frankie!' and 'Be a sport!' and 'It's part of the game: you have to obey the rules!'

Finally of course she had agreed, and was now sitting, a little stiffly, in a kind of side-saddle stance with her legs, bent at the knee, disposed on one side and her weight, supported by one hand, on the other. Her eyes were downcast, there was a defensive expression on her face, and her free hand and forearm were raised to shield her breasts — 'Which is a bit silly,' Tom Crawford whispered to Paul, 'when you consider that she's just been fucked rigid by our Levantine gymnast with the rest of us watching!'

The two of them were comfortably settled in an armchair, Crawford lying back against the cushions, Paul perched on the arm. The Comtesse was similarly ensconced, with the nude and nubile Nounou, an arm around Dagmar's neck, sitting in her lap. Corinne and the others sat, lay or stood in various positions around the room.

Janine sat up very straight, pushing out her chest, the forefinger and thumb of one hand spread to hold up a provocative breast. She smiled. 'Touch me, Françoise,' she said softly.

For a moment the slender, willowy mannequin continued to look down, the expression on her handsome, racehorse features inscrutable. 'Françoise?' Janine said again.

'*Françoise!*' the Comtesse said sharply. 'Do what you are told!'

This time there was a reaction. The arm was moved to expose Françoise's breasts. They were, as Paul had good reason to remember, almost non-existent – gentle swells of flesh that barely disturbed the flat plane of the girl's chest. But the areolas were large and dark, the nipples at their centre thick and prominent. Those nipples were now most definitely erect.

And whereas Janine's small, pointed breasts were at variance with the broad, womanly frame of her hips and bottom, the mild curves of Françoise's bust were all of a part with her lean, taut dress-model's body.

She was still leaning a little sideways, weight supported on that hand, the shoulder hunched against her cheek. But the free hand now stretched out, very slowly, towards the tilted mound of flesh that Janine held up. Spread fingers touched the flesh. At once an electric thrill quivered through Janine's upright body. She removed her own hand and allowed the breast to subside into the dark girl's palm.

'Absolutely extraordinary,' Paul murmured to Corinne, who was sitting on the floor below him in what the newly fashionable Yoga practitioners termed the Lotus position, with her legs crossed and her feet tucked beneath her. 'If only she used it more . . . Françoise has a touch that is quite simply magic. An instant ecstasy!'

Corinne smiled. 'I know,' she said. But despite the enquiring expression and the arched eyebrows creasing the young man's forehead, she would add nothing further.

On the table, Françoise was now kneeling, squatting on her heels like the young woman facing her. Each had outstretched hands, fondling the breasts of the other. Janine was breathing fast, her chest rising and falling rapidly. The expression on Françoise's face was shy, a trifle embarrassed; the muscles around her mouth were stiff and her smile forced.

Suddenly Janine moved, straightening up still on her knees so that she was upright, nearer to Françoise and a little above her. She seized the other girl's head in both hands, tangling her fingers in the hair, and bent her own head to kiss her fiercely on the mouth.

The explosion of breath stifled into a half-gasp, half-groan in Françoise's throat was heard all around the room.

Paul glanced again at Corinne. Maintaining the Lotus position, she had shuffled herself a little nearer the table, rocking back and forth as she watched. He realised that, whether she was aware of it or not, she was masturbating, rubbing the lips of her genitals against the thick pile of the Turkish carpet. On the far side of the table, Ahmed Simbel was sitting in the window-seat with Victor Houbigant. From where he was, Paul could not see clearly, but he was convinced that each of them had a hand, a moving hand, over the other's crotch. Certainly there was an increased awareness, a tension, a stiffening at his own loins as he watched the lesbian spectacle develop on the coffee table.

The girls were still kissing, with cheeks hollowed and tongues wrestling and lips chewing . . . but now each had spread her thighs a little and at each crotch alien fingers scrabbled and stroked and probed amongst the pubic hair. The sound of laboured breath — not all of it from the table — was loud in the panelled room.

Janine changed position once more. She took Françoise by the shoulders, swivelled her sideways, and pushed her down until she was lying flat on the table top. Kneeling still, she leaned over her, trailing fingers smoothing the flattish breasts, teasing nipples, burrowing deep into the thatch between trembling thighs. She lowered her head and they kissed again . . . and this time Françoise's electric hands played like butterflies around Janine's generous hips and loins.

'By Jove,' Tom Crawford muttered, 'the old things don't half go it!' He was standing now behind the blonde maidservant with his arms wrapped around her and her heavy pear-shaped breasts hanging over them. He flexed his knees, moved his hands down to part her thighs, and eased himself gently but forcefully into her warm, wet and receptive vagina from behind. The girl gave a gasp of delight and moved her big buttocks back against him, rolling her hips very slightly, the better to feel the hard shaft speared within her. There was movement too from the armchair in which Dagmar and Nounou were wrapped together. And the second servant, her fascinated gaze fixed on the couple lewdly entwined on the table, was absently moving her large hands over the naked buttocks of Pierre on one side of her and Helga von Frodenburg on the other.

Janine was lying alongside Françoise, a knee wedged between the slimmer girl's thighs. Forcefully manipulating the lean breasts, she sucked and nibbled, drawing the hardened points up into her mouth as her free hand dabbled amongst wet hairs and penetrated deeply between hot folds of private flesh. Her big hips trembled sporadically each time the magic fingers in their turn rotated a swell of belly, swooped across a waist, traced the line of lips half hidden still in the depths of her secret furrow. Françoise was mewling now with desire.

Janine sat up. 'Turn over,' she ordered, the voice suddenly authoritarian. 'Lie on you face and spread those legs!'

The girl obeyed at once, breath sobbing in her throat. She spread-eagled herself, pillowing her face on her hands, and waited with nerves quivering while Janine clambered between her legs.

She pulled apart the tight half-moons of the mannequin's bottom and attacked with raping fingers the hairy cleft between them, widening the labia, caressing the clitoris, penetrating the tightly puckered hole of the anus.

Françoise heaved and squirmed with delight, murmuring incoherent endearments into her folded hands.

Soon, however, Janine was changing the scene once more. 'Turn over again,' she commanded, 'and stay on your back.'

The moment her partner-victim had complied, she renewed her manipulation of breasts and pelvic region and then, when Françoise had been raised to a pitch of excitement that was near-orgasmic, she turned swiftly towards the young woman's feet, straddled her waist, and lay down on top of her with her face buried in the dark triangle of pubic hair. Françoise's face vanished beneath the heavy spread of her hips.

'Think of a number, any number,' Tom Crawford said to the fleshy girl grinding against his own hips. 'Did someone suggest sixty-nine?'

A curious conformity, a symmetry of action now overcame the girls on the table, despite the fact that they were rolling from side to side and grunting and groaning in their lustful embrace: their single composite figure, resembling in a fanciful way a photographic blow-up of some giant insect, comprised a pair of grasshopper legs, drawn up with knees bent, at either end; a bobbing head oscillating between each pair; four breasts evenly disposed, squashed between the two bodies; two mouths wedged between four buttocks; and twenty fingers actively engaged.

It was clear from the mutual gobbling noises that an orgasm was imminent. '*Very* interesting indeed,' Paul conceded for the second time.

It was almost three o'clock in the morning. Some time ago the party had moved back into the big salon. The naked guests were dancing now. A wind-up gramophone with an oversize horn blared out the Comtesse's current favourites. They had had the foxtrot *Lovable*, an exciting *Tiger Rag*, *Auf Wiedersehn, My Dear* (three times, specially for the Baroness), and the 'daring' tango, *La Cumparsita* (twice). The record on the turntable was a slow, rather dreamy

Reckless Liaisons

number called *Mysterious Eyes*.

Paul was dancing with Desirée-Rosette. The rules of the game were that any man seen by another guest to be dancing while erect — and denounced as such — was obliged then and there to lie down with his partner and use the offending member in the manner for which it was expressly designed. Paul in fact was not sure how long he could keep up a pretence of physical disinterest: the girl's splendid breasts were pressed hard to his bare chest, her tawny hair brushed his cheek, and her green eyes themselves were dancing with . . . what? Amusement? Excitement? Challenge? He wasn't sure. But he knew that, each time he swung into a turn, a satin-smooth thigh brushed provocatively against his swinging tool.

Already he could feel the familiar tingling at his loins. He looked around at his fellow guests. Bertrand was dancing with one of the busty maids; Houbigant with the other. Janine and Crawford pirouetted in the centre of the room. Corinne and Hans, Françoise with Pierre, Simbel and the roly-poly Nounou spun past one after the other. Only Dagmar and Helga, kissing avidly as they swayed together in the shadows near the bar, broke the heterosexual chain.

'You know of course,' Paul said to his own partner, 'that I have the most enormous bone to pick with you, old thing.' It was the first chance he had had to speak to her, at least semi-privately.

'A bone?' she echoed, smiling. 'Oh, really? What fun!'

'You know very well what I mean. Using sex to worm your way into someone's confidence, and then abusing that confidence to steal — and steal something that wasn't even theirs — do you call that a friendly thing to do?'

'Oh, that.' The girl shrugged. 'You weren't a friend, after all. I'd never set eyes on you before. I don't see how you can accuse me of abusing something that didn't exist. In any case, it's not as if they were *your own* designs.'

Faced with this example of feminine logic, Paul was for a moment at a loss for words. 'Hell, they were *confided* in me,' he began. 'You forced *me*, unknowingly, to betray a confidence. I say again: do you honestly call that a friendly thing to do?'

'I don't call it anything. It was just something I did.'

'For money, I suppose. I assume that wretched little man over there paid you?'

She smiled and made no reply. The record ground to a stop. Dagmar selected another from a pile, fitted it onto the turntable, re-wound the machine and lowered the needle. The choppy, frenetic rhythms of a Charleston filled the salon, galvanizing the other dancers into activity. Heels kicking, breasts bouncing and genitals flapping, they giggled their way across the floor. Paul and his partner were marooned in the middle of the tide.

'And that sedan chair charade tonight,' the young man pursued. 'You don't think that was a little cheap? The sort of thing one would pay an out-of-work chorus girl to do? I imagine you *were* paid for that too?'

'Oh, I'd do anything for money,' the girl said cheerfully. 'In any case, it wasn't me who copied the designs and actually showed them. How was I to know he'd do that? I thought he just wanted to look at them.

If you're so cross about it, you should take it up with Ahmed. Have you mentioned it to him?'

'Of course I haven't. I can't see you owning up to your part of it, and without that I've no proof.'

'Well, there you are then,' Desirée said.

'Come on, you two. Dance!' the Comtesse called.

Paul sighed and bit his lip. He danced.

Dagmar van den Bergh's bedroom had not been transformed into the severe modernist style of the lower floors: it retained both the opulence and the elegance given to it at the turn of the century, when the Belgian Comte van den Bergh first bought the mansion.

The bed, a wide four-poster with heavy crimson drapes and a tasselled canopy, stood on a carpeted dais raised six inches above the rest of the floor. A white bearskin lay on top of the red silk eiderdown. Richly coloured Persian rugs strewed the floor between the dais and a huge bird's-eye maple closet designed *en suite* with the bow-fronted commode and a dressing-table littered with expensive cut-glass bottles of perfume and oil. A single gilt-framed female nude by Fantin-Latour hung on the damask-covered walls.

Paul Mackenzie lay back in an easy chair covered in cinnamon velvet, waiting with eager anticipation for his 'prize'. He was, of course, still naked. On the far side of an arch flanked by miniature Corinthian pillars, Dagmar and the Baroness soaped one another in a huge scented bath sunk into the marble floor of a luxurious wash-room. Gramophone music still filtered up from the salon. They were back to *Valencia* now, and the laughter was becoming strident. The last thing Paul had seen, just before he was beckoned upstairs, was an excited group around the bar. Both Simbel and Tom Crawford had been surprised with erections and were duly paying their 'forfeits' with their partners on the counter-top while the rest of the dancers once more started their chanted countdown. In his own case, Paul had found that the conversation with Desirée-Rosette effectively stifled any desire he had begun to feel. Now, however, his eagerness to sample the forbidden fruits promised to him had already stimulated a formidable cockstand.

He sat up, suddenly alert. He could hear water gurgling. In the archway leading to the bathroom, the two women materialised out of the fragrant, steamy air. Helga von Frodenburg was settling a white terry-towel robe over the Comtesse's shoulders. 'Very well, young man,' the German said. 'On your feet, and you shall be permitted to dry Madame's exquisite body.'

Paul shot up out of the chair feeling slightly guilty, a little ridiculous, a schoolboy caught nodding off in class: of course he should have been standing up when they came in! 'Y-y-yes, Ma'am,' he stammered. 'At once. It will be a great pleasure.'

'I should hope so.' The Baroness looked with disfavour at the quivering rod jutting from his loins. 'I don't know what use we can find for *that*,' she said disparagingly. 'You will have to keep that very much to yourself.'

'Oh, I will,' Paul promised. 'Anything you say.' After his session with Janine, he was prepared to make any sexual sacrifice necessary if only he could stay with these experienced, ultra-sophisticated and undeniably *different* beauties!

Helga pushed her friend gently towards him and sank into the cinnamon chair. Dagmar shrugged more deeply into the robe and grinned. 'Go ahead,' she said to Paul.

He stepped up to her and put his hands on the loose towelling. The perfumed body inside was warm and soft. Gently, he moved the material over her damp frame, scooping it over the pliant waist, rubbing the back, feeling the soft mass of breasts and the muscular curves of hips and belly shift under his caressing pressure. Kneeling, he towelled the elegant columns of calf and thigh.

'Are you dry, *Liebchen*?' the Baroness asked.

'Fine. That feels lovely,' Dagmar replied.

'Move to the next phase of the operation then.'

The bathrobe was removed and handed to Paul. Dagmar clambered onto the bed and stretched out on the bearskin. The Baroness selected a cigarette from a tortoise-shell case, fitted it into a long ebony holder, and reached for a gold Cartier lighter. She lit the gold-tipped cigarette and blew out smoke. 'I say!' Paul exclaimed, startled into impropriety by the sweetish, fragrant aroma. 'Is that Hashish you're smoking?'

Helga smiled, shaking her head. 'A special blend of Turkish. You already had the Hashish in the *petit-fours*,' she replied enigmatically. 'Now I suggest you get on that bed and take your prize . . .'

Paul hesitated, glancing from one to the other. Both women were smiling encouragingly. He moved towards the four-poster. Helga leaned forward and smacked his rigid cock lightly with a flat hand. 'Only *this* is not to be . . . used. Understand?' He nodded and mounted the dais.

The Comtesse lay on her back. The glossy red hair fanned out on a silk pillow. The full breasts, only minimally dropped when she was upright, stood sentinel over the upper part of her torso, the skin of their swelling slopes slightly freckled. Beneath voluptuously sculptured sweeps of hips and belly, her elegant, tapered legs were spread.

Paul placed himself between her knees. He shuffled back a little way and then lowered himself face down until his head was poised above the tawny thatch separating the Comtesse's thighs. He reached up his arms until his hands could touch her breasts. Helga von Frodenburg pulled her chair closer to the bed and puffed hard on her cigarette.

The young man lowered his head. Dagmar released a long sigh of pleasure. Her two hands were resting on the upper swell of her abdomen. Now the first and second fingers of each hand walked down over her belly, through the tangle of pubic hair, and onto the cushioned pads sheltering the outer lips of her vulva. Lasciviously, she eased those pads apart, exposing the outer, and then the inner lips. Paul's mouth brushed her knuckles and his tongue flicked between her fingers.

The Comtesse tensed momentarily when the tip lapped the sensitive creases enfolding the entrance to her vagina, then relaxed with another sigh of delight as Paul's lips clamped over the opening and the tongue darted snake-like into the scalding interior. For a little longer she held the labia wide, but as soon as that invasive spear of flesh and muscle found her clitoris she took her hands away, seized Paul's, and clamped them over her swelling breasts.

Paul feasted on the sliding, fleshy folds, exploring with that wicked tongue each hollow and crevice and protuberance, penetrating the ridged muscles of the dark passage beyond. He sucked and gobbled and licked, even nudging the erect clitoris, rotating it against the pelvic bone, with the tip of his nose while his lips were occupied still lower down. His fingers, imprisoned beneath Dagmar's hands, kneaded and teased her breasts.

Crooning sweet nothings, the Comtesse resigned herself to the young Englishman's sensual manipulations. Her head moved easily this way and that on the pillow. Her eyes were closed. From time to time her hips rose almost imperceptibly, thrusting her loins more fiercely against Paul's marauding mouth.

After some minutes, she murmured huskily: 'You're very expert, abnormally sensitive, my Paul! You realise, of course, why she's allowing you to do this? It's . . . Oooh! . . . It's so that she can prove afterwards how much better she can do it herself! But I can tell you . . . *Aaaah*! *Yes, oh yes, do that again*! . . . I can tell you, Helga darling: you'll have to surpass yourself to equal this . . .'

Scowling, the Baroness stubbed out her cigarette. She climbed onto the bed behind Paul. 'Get up,' she snapped. 'Up on your knees. Don't stop what you're doing,' – she slapped him on the behind – 'but get that bottom up into the air. At once!'

He drew up his knees, struggling to obey while his mouth still slobbered at Dagmar's crotch. Her breasts were palpitating under his hands. 'What Helga really likes,' she teased, 'is to watch—'

She broke off with a choked cry as Paul's tongue reached an ultra-sensitive nerve within her.

He himself tensed as a hard hand reached beneath him and grasped his balls from behind. Another plunged past his hips to seize his cock, aching almost unbearably already and distended to bursting point. Kneeling beside his hunched and labouring figure, Helga von Frodenburg squeezed the glands within their hanging sac and began to pump the stiff shaft lanced out in front of it in a practised, insidious rhythm. 'Go on, give it to her!' she hissed. 'Suck her! Stick your tongue up that cunt; frig her until she spends! I want to see her face when she comes!'

Paul redoubled his efforts. His breath snorted in his nostrils. His tongue was swollen. The blood hammered behind his eyes.

The Baroness was kneeling behind him now. She leaned forwards, pressing herself along his back, her winey breath on his neck. Both her hands were beneath his belly, clutching the scrotum again, milking, milking, milking the exquisitely throbbing shaft of his cock. 'You too,' she urged. 'I'm going to toss you off! I want to feel that *schwanz* kick in my hand; I want to feel the warm spunk trickle between my fingers!'

The Comtesse was already writhing uncontrollably, mewling out half-formed words as Paul sucked ever more ferociously and her belly muscles gathered themselves for the convulsive shudders of release.

Then, sudden as a lightning shaft, the young man himself was shaken with irresistible spasms. The fingers wrapped around his cock tightened cruelly, and he groaned aloud, feeling the hot sperm gush from his jerking loins.

The Baroness laughed. 'And now my friend,' she cooed, '*you* shall sit in the chair and watch while *I* make her satisfy *me*!'

Chapter Sixteen

Two days after the all-night party in the Avenue Kléber, three riders left the stables in the north-eastern corner of the Bois de Boulogne and trotted their mounts gently southwards along the Allée de la Reine Marguerite, towards the clay pigeon shoot and the open-air theatre. Once they had crossed the Avenue de Longchamp, they left the main bridle-path and urged the horses into a canter along a sandy track winding between the closely packed trees.

They formed a handsome trio, two women and a man, each sitting well, each in perfect command of a spirited animal obeying every slightest pressure on the reins.

The man was neat and compact, a well-knit figure perhaps forty years old, with something military about his bearing. He was wearing immaculate twill riding breeches with cavalry boots, a plum-coloured velour jacket and a peaked huntman's cap. The smaller of the two women, still demurely riding side-saddle, was dressed in an elegantly tailored grey habit, buttoned boots, and a tall hat with a veil pulled down from the brim and fastened around her neck. Above the nipped-in waist of her jacket, a white silk stock rode a generous swell of breast.

Her companion was tall and strong-featured, with pale hair drawn back into a chignon beneath a curly brimmed hard hat. She wore a tweed hacking jacket with lemon-yellow jodhpurs . . . and, daringly for the Bois in that period, she was riding astride.

Paul Mackenzie saw them jog past the end of a ride while he was resting his horse by a water trough after a testing gallop around the two lakes near the Auteuil racecourse. He would not have given the trio a second glance — the Bois was always populated with good-looking horsemen and women, many of them from among the rich and famous — if he had not recognised at once that the taller of the two females was the dress designer Mado Laverne.

He was never quite sure why he decided on the spur of the moment to follow them — perhaps it was just that Mado was the kind of person to whom things happened, or who made things happen, and Paul was still at an age when adventure could be around any corner. At any rate, he remounted, trotted to the end of the ride and cantered along the bridle-path a couple of hundred yards behind them.

Riders passed in different directions, several of them doffing hats or bowing to Mado as they realised who she was. Through the trees, horse-drawn broughams and open touring cars were visible promenading their owners along the Avenue de l'Hippodrome. Eventually the *couturière* and her companions hitched their horses to a rail outside a *guingette* on the banks of the larger lake. They sat at a table beneath a striped parasol and ordered a bottle of champagne. It was only then, when the shorter woman lifted her veil and folded it back over her hat, that Paul recognised the couple with Mado. It was Pierre Giotto and his wife Nicole or Nounou — the newcomers he had met for the first time at Dagmar van den Bergh's party.

Interesting, he thought, reining in his mount. What was this extra-'modern' couple doing here in the Bois with the fashionable arbiter of taste, Mado Laverne? No more than sharing an exhilarating ride on a fine summer's day perhaps. But Paul was intrigued enough to devote a little more time to the question, and he dismounted and allowed his horse to graze while he sat down and leaned against a large oak in such a position that he could keep an eye on the drinkers. The conversation over the champagne was animated, and from the gestures and laughter accompanying it he was loath to believe it had anything to do with clothes or the fashion business. It was, however, when Pierre Giotto pushed back his chair and rose abruptly to his feet, leaving the two women still drinking, that Paul's curiosity was engaged to the full. Giotto called out something that the young Englishman was unable to catch, waved cheerfully, and hurried out to his horse. He mounted quickly and rode away in the direction of the Porte Dauphine.

Five minutes later, Mado and Nounou in turn left the guingette and sauntered back to their mounts. It was the designer, Paul noted, who paid for the champagne.

The two women walked with arms entwined. For a few hundred yards they led the horses. Then, remounted, they trotted past the headquarters of the Racing Club de France, crossed a busy avenue, and took a narrow path that breasted a rise and led deeper into the woods.

Paul followed — lagging much further behind now, since the track was unfrequented and any other rider consistently in sight would be bound to raise suspicions. So far, evidently deep in conversation, neither Mado nor her companion had so much as glanced over her shoulder. They slowed to a walk as the path narrowed again and the trees grew more densely.

Often, now, as the woodland ride curved sinuously between thickets and spinneys, plunging into leafy dells and looping around forest knolls, they were out of sight for minutes at a time. Once Paul thought he had lost them altogether: the path emerged into a wide clearing where tree-felling operations had been in process, and the scarred landscape, dotted with stacks of logs, was deserted for as far as he could see in every direction.

It was a faint whinny from one of the horses — accompanied, he fancied, by a hint of girlish laughter — which told him that he had already come too far. He hitched his own horse to the low-spreading branch of an elm and returned on foot.

At first, casting this way and that, he was unable to find the track taken by his quarry. Then, parting a screen of bushes, he bit back an exclamation of surprise. He was staring down a short grassy slope at a narrow arm of the lake entirely surrounded by close-packed trees. And the two women were so close that even a stifled gasp from the undergrowth would surely have alerted them to the fact that they were being watched.

Mado had taken a rug which covered her saddle and spread it on the ground. The two of them lay side by side, enjoying the golden beams of sunlight which slanted between branches to bathe their private glade in summer heat.

Paul lay face down in the undergrowth, scarcely daring to breathe. The hushed and drowsy calm suffusing the clearing blanketed the sounds of horses and of traffic in the busier parts of the Bois, reducing them to a distant murmur. He was agonisingly aware that an inadvertent cough, the snapping of a small twig, could erupt like a cannon shot. Bees were active somewhere behind him, and birds chirped in a clump of willow at the water's edge. He could hear, somewhere in the shade on the far side of the slope, quick, short rasps as the horses nibbled grass.

Mado sat up suddenly, unpinned her chignon, and shook loose a mane of brassy hair. Light lanced across the glade as a sunbeam reflected from the polished surface of a solid silver flask she drew from the side pocket of her jacket. The cap of the flask, reversed, could be used as a small tumbler or beaker. She unscrewed it and poured. 'Dear friend,' said she, 'this is the best stimulant of all after champagne: it will give you an appetite for dinner after the ride home. I fear however that it may be above the ritual room temperature, since it has been riding against my hip for the past two hours!'

'My temperature too would rise, Madame, were I to find myself in so favoured a position for such a length of time,' Nounou Giotto replied with a silvery laugh.

'Oh, come now!' — Paul was aware of memories stirring as the older woman chuckled throatily — 'What is this Madame nonsense? You know very well that I am Mado to my friends.' She held out the silver vessel.

The young man's pulses fluttered. Excitedly, he realised his instincts had been right: something *was* going on here — an established ritual, such as he himself played with the designer? Or an entirely new scenario of which he was perhaps witness to the first extemporised moves? From the dialogue so far, he was inclined to think, indeed to hope, it was the latter case. He fixed his gaze unwaveringly on the two women.

Nounou was a delightful sight. She had unbuttoned her jacket and the twin peaks of her breasts thrust up the stuff of her blouse enticingly on either side of her stock. Her dark hair was spread on the rug. She had raised one knee and the skirt of her riding habit had slid back to reveal a crescent of pink thigh above her stocking top.

Two swans glided into sight, circled the inlet, and then swam away beyond the bushes overhanging the water. A dragonfly hummed past, electric blue above their rippled wake.

Nounou was struggling to sit up, levering herself with one hand and holding out the other for Mado's proffered brandy. But the designer would have none of it. 'Wait!' she said. 'If we're going to be hedonists, let's at least go the whole way! Relax now, and let me give it to you . . .'

She stripped off her tweed jacket, folded it, and placed it on the rug. Then, easing the younger woman back until her shoulders rested on the bunched cloth, she cradled the dark head with one hand and raised the silver cup to Nounou's lips.

Nounou drank, smiled, lowered her head. Mado drank straight from the flask . . . for that hand, somehow, had remained trapped in the dark hair at the nape of the brunette's neck. She poured a second cup and Nounou drank again.

Mado was leaning over her. From the subtle shift of flesh beneath the pale twill shirt, Paul guessed that her small, high-set breasts were loose. He stared fascinated at the chiselled curve of her lips, the bright white line of even teeth. The tip of her tongue swept a moist gleam over the upper lip. What expression would the eyes have?

Nounou's pouting lips were almost pursed. Her dark eyes stared fixedly upwards and the fingers of one hand plucked absently at the hem of her skirt. She was breathing rather fast.

'Perhaps I shouldn't say this, as a friend of Pierre's,' Mado began, 'but I can't resist because the temptation is too strong. I have to tell you, my dear, that you really must have one of the most beautiful bodies in the whole of Paris.'

End of Prologue, thought Paul in his hiding place. This is the crunch moment, when we discover whether the curtain is going to fall down on the whole production, or whether Act One can go ahead as planned by at least one of the parties concerned.

Nounou had murmured something in a voice so low that he was unable to distinguish the words. 'I know about bodies, you see,' Mado continued. 'It's my business after all. Most of them I try to beautify. But there are always some so pretty in the first place that clothes can do no more than . . . well, tarnish them.

Reckless Liaisons

Bodies like yours, my dear, which are perfect in their own right.'

She was leaning further over now, the broad hips swelling into the jodhpur curves, the voice sunk to its lowest register. 'It's all proportion, you see,' Mado said, allowing her fingers to rest lightly on each feature as she mentioned it. 'No one element, no two or three elements, however perfect in themselves, but *totalities*, the global effect . . . the relationship of this plane to that curve . . . of this hipbone to that swell of abdomen . . . of a calf to a forearm, an ear to a chin, the peachbloom of skin here to the satin shine there.' Dramatic pause. 'You really do have the most marvellous breasts, my Nounou!'

That was it. The young Madame Giotto still had one knee raised. Now the other leg flexed . . . but out sideways, towards Mado, not upwards, subtly parting the thighs under the tight skirt. Paul's imagination was already in there, amongst the damp and throbbing dark.

Mado's hand was on the thigh which had shifted, so imperceptibly but so significantly, in her direction.

Paul saw the fingers tighten on the grey cloth of Nounou's skirt. A tiny shiver momentarily spasmed the upper half of her body. The hand which had been cradling her head now rested casually on a curve of breast. The head fell back on the rug, eyes closed, lips parted and glistening.

The brunette's face was hidden then as Mado leaned over more closely still and a cascade of gold hair tumbled almost to the rug. Paul thought her lips might have brushed Nounou's brow or paid a fleeting visit to the soft hollow where the pulse beat so rapidly in her

Reckless Liaisons

neck. He realised only for the first time — because they harmonised so perfectly with the rest of her attire — that skin-tight black kid gloves sheathed Mado's experienced hands.

He himself was now suffering from an increasingly uncomfortable tightness about the loins as he crouched among the stalks and stems and leaves of his hiding place. The tension mounted painfully when he observed with an indrawn breath the black fingers drawing aside an edge of unbuttoned blouse to expose a mound of flesh tipped by a thickened, rosy bud that was quickly sucked up into Mado's mouth.

Clearly, her seductive moves were encountering no resistance: Act One was undisputably on the way. A low, breathy cry, midway between a moan, a coo and a gurgle, rose above the humming of insects in the glade. Both Nounou's knees were drawn up now; the skirt had slipped down to her hips. A gloved hand, the black leather tightly wrinkled around the wrist, was busy among the white frills between her thighs.

The excited young Englishman would dearly have liked to move a hand between his own thighs, but he dare not make a single move for fear of discovery and the scandal that would entail.

Nounou's erect nipple and the weight of flesh beneath it subsided as Mado transferred her lips to the brunette's mouth. They were chewing each other fiercely, tongues thrusting within the hollowed cheeks. One of Nounou's arms hooked around Mado's neck. The hand of the other appeared suddenly between her spread buttocks, curving around to cup the anal region and base of the spine, pulling the heavy hips ferociously against her.

The drawn-up knees threshed, knocking together and then jerking wildly apart each time the supine brunette's pelvis arched up to meet the maurading glove savaging her loins.

It was not really, Paul reflected, anything like as splendid a body as Mado had made out. It was a roly-poly body, full of soft intersecting curves . . . but it was a body that could be sexy as hell, especially when provoked by a touch as subtle as the couturière's. Ignoring the pain at his crotch he feasted his eyes on the scene.

Five minutes later, when the frenzy of the entwined women seemed to have reached some kind of interim climax, Mado detached her mouth, half raised herself on her elbows, and lifted her head. Paul froze, his heart thumping loudly within his chest. The gaze of those slumbrous eyes was trained directly on the clump of bushes concealing him; it was almost as though, like one of the newfangled X-ray machines, the eyes could penetrate the screen of leaves and search him out.

My God! All the blood in his body appeared to drain down to the soles of his feet — she *had* seen him. 'Very well, Monsieur Mackenzie,' she said evenly. 'It is time you stopped lurking in the audience and came on stage.'

Paul was never quite sure of the order in which things happened after that: excitement, embarrassment and anticipation combined to blur his recollection of the few minutes after he had emerged sheepishly from the undergrowth, nervously brushing twigs from his clothes.

One thing was certain: Nounou Giotto, for the moment at any rate, was supremely unconscious of what was going on; champagne, brandy, the heady air in the Bois and the transports of forbidden sexual delight has transferred her to a different plane. She lay with arms outflung, rolling her head from side to side and moaning softly to herself.

No such intoxication blunted Mado Laverne's activity. Paul had often remarked how the contained fury within the statuesque blonde's outward composure resembled a firework about to explode. This again, he saw now, was another of those occasions when the blue touch paper was lit!

The witch's mouth smiled wickedly. 'Did you really believe I hadn't noticed you trailing after us through the forest?' she asked. 'Well, you've had your *voyeur's* thrill; now it's time for you to provide a little pleasure for me. Off with those trousers! At once! Quickly! Now!' She hooked strong fingers into his fly and burst open the buttoned front, ripping apart the waist fastening a moment later.

Suddenly released, the rigid and throbbing proof of Paul's lust sprang obscenely into view. 'That's better,' Mado approved. 'Now get down there and follow the path I've already traced for you . . .'

She erupted into a whirlwind of activity, shoving the moaning brunette's skirt up around her hips, dragging off the white undergarments, and then hastily unfastening her own jodhpurs and tearing them off. Buttocks flashing naked in the sunny glade, she ran around and kneeled down to straddle Nounou's head. She leaned forward to grab the splayed legs, lewdly suggestive in their silk stockings and button boots, pulling them back and up until the knees were doubled against the young woman's bared breasts. 'Go on. Get down there and start to work,' Mado ordered, pointing a commanding finger at Nounou's loins.

Paul stared for an instant at the entire shamelessly exposed area of those genitals – the tight wrinkled button of the anus, the dark wet mat of pubic hair, the sexual lips, shockingly pink in the bright light, already gaping to reveal the entrance to the secret and sombre passage beyond. Another rapid glance at Mado, and he shuffled forwards on his knees, leaned to support his weight on his hands, and then lowered his hips to spear his pulsating shaft deep into the scalding depths of the young woman's heaving belly.

Nounou cried aloud as the raping staff ploughed in and out of her secret place. Her lips were moving, working, the tongue slobbering avidly as Mado lowered her hips until the scythe of blonde pubic hair, darkened now with moisture, and the salaciously parted lips within it, closed over that greedy mouth.

For a short space of time, Paul's hips, moving in an easy, compulsive rhythm, ministered to one end of Nounou's supine, shivering form while Mado's pelvis, rotating gently in an equally dreamlike motion, attended to the other. Then the young man leaned forward between the imprisoned thighs of the woman he was violating; Mado leaned forward over the quivering breasts she had been tweaking. Their lips met in a lingering kiss.

'Welcome to the Bois, dear Paul,' Mado Laverne said softly.

Chapter Seventeen

Paul Mackenzie sat nursing a *bock* at a table outside the *Deux Magots* café in the Boulevard St Germain. It had been raining but the sun was out now, and moisture glistened on the cobbled *pavé* of the broad avenue. Horse-drawn drays and canvas-topped delivery carts rattled past among the honking taxicabs and motor cars and buses. It was not quite noon and the lunchtime traffic jam had yet to pile up.

The café was crowded with the usual mid-morning collection — artists from the Latin Quarter, expatriate Americans trying to *look* like artists from the Latin Quarter, office workers taking a break, and tourists eager to glimpse the fabled creatures from the high bohemia about whom they read so much. Who knows: there might be a Surrealist, a Cubist or even a genuine artist's model among the chattering shopgirls at the close-packed iron tables!

The *Deux Magots* regulars were not above pandering to the sightseers' thirst for notorieties. Flowing capes and beards and broad-brimmed hats abounded; smudged, kohl-fringed eyes stared out from the pale faces of young women in dirndl skirts who looked as though they had just got out of bed; several men wearing floppy bow ties sat with sketch pads, waiting to be offered a drink. More than half the clientele were at pains to give the impression that they were about to be discovered.

Paul had no sketch pad: he was halfway through a letter to a friend in London who was working with his father on the latest model of the Mackenzie sports car. He was sharing his table with Denis Dupuis, the brother of Françoise with the magic hands and an honorary member of the Knights of the Bottle. Dupuis was a tall, fair man of about thirty with bright blue eyes and a neat, pointed beard. Between sips of absinthe he was scanning the latest edition of *Figaro*.

'I say!' he exclaimed suddenly, looking up from the newspaper. 'This should jolly well interest your old guv'nor all right.' His heavily accented English was embroidered with misused slang as often as Tom Crawford's conversation was scattered with puns.

Paul looked up from his letter. 'What's that?' he asked.

'Why, a race-track in a royal park at Monza, near Milan! It says here,' Dupuis read aloud, ' "Italy, jealous of the autodrones of America and England, has caused to be constructed in this park two circuits which can at the same time be used, a short and a long, the latter measuring no less than ten thousand yards around." It says there are bankings on the corners and bridges carrying one lap over the other.' He put more sugar in the perforated spoon balanced over his glass and dripped water through it into his absinthe. The fiery liquor clouded afresh. Dupuis sipped, nodded in satisfaction, and continued: ' "The public shall be well catered for, because there are no less than five grandstands at various parts of the circuit, and two well-stocked buffets. Nor must the racers themselves be affrighted, for during each Grand Prix there shall be four separate ambulances stationed at all times. At the first race held, the Italian ace Bordino won at the insane speed of ninety-one point three miles per hour!" ' Dupuis guffawed. 'Trust the old jolly dagoes! It says here that foreign competitors shall be encouraged with starting money, and that the curves are very safe.'

He folded the paper back and handed it across the table. Paul took it and glanced at the half dozen photographs and sketch-map of the track printed below the headlined story. Spidery, torpedo-shaped racers careered around a banked curve in one picture. Another showed a grinning Bordino, with leather helmet unflapped and goggles pushed up, displaying an oil-smeared countenance from the centre of a laurel wreath. 'Yes, this should certainly interest the old man,' he agreed. 'He's actually working on a hotted-up bus for racing work. Could you let me have this when you've finished with it? I'd like to cut the article out and send it to him.'

'Keep it,' Denis Dupuis said grandly. 'I have a *poule* to lay.'

Paul laughed. 'You're worse than Tom — if only you knew it! But talking of curves . . .' He shook his head in disbelief and flipped imaginary drips of water from his fingertips. 'Old boy, you should have been with me earlier this morning. My word, what a build!'

'Interesting? So tell me, tell me!' Dupuis urged.

'I had a date with a fellow who wants to commission a

series of drawings showing the racing at Auteuil and Longchamp. Chap from an English mag called *Horse and Hound*. He was leaving at lunchtime, so I met him for breakfast at his hotel — quaint little place next to the St Sulpice church.'

'The Récamier? Yes,' Dupuis said, 'as it should happen, I know this hotel. The receptionist is — ah — shall we say *accessible*?'

'This wasn't the receptionist. It was a guest. I didn't really notice her until my chap had gone, but after that . . .' Paul whistled and shook his head again.

'So what was she like?'

'I wish I could do her justice. It wasn't that she was beautiful, you see, or even pretty. It was just that she had it. You know, that completely compelling, that . . . I don't know. I don't know. I tell you what,' Paul said suddenly, looking down at the letter he had been writing. 'Why don't I let you have a look at this? I was trying to put it into words anyway, giving what you might call the low-down to a fellow lecher in London.' He shuffled half a dozen pages covered with his small, neat handwriting and selected two. He drained his glass and handed the sheets across the table.

Dupuis raised his eyebrows, took another sip of absinthe, and read:

'She was sitting at a small table a little in front of me and to one side. An illuminated tank full of tropical fish was let into the wall beside the table, and there was a bowl of artificial flowers on a shelf above that. My boy, I'm telling you this was the tastiest breakfast dish I've had since my little

sister's nursemaid forgot to close the bathroom door when I was eight!

'She was about forty. German, I think: her French was accented and she had a surprisingly deep voice. She was wearing a green woolly and green trousers. Trousers, old chap — Oxford bags just like yours and mine! Can you imagine a sexy woman in trousers!

'If you can't, read on — because strangely enough the slacks somehow made the whole effect more sensual than ever.

'The lady's complexion was dark, her cropped hair was black and the straight brows blacker still. The peach make-up was very discreet, the chiselled mouth scarcely emphasised by a pale lip-salve. She was a big lady too, but, well, thick rather than plump, and certainly not fat. Seen from behind, her shoulders were like that of an American Football player. At once I was imagining the columns of muscle of her spine, beneath the woolly and over the buttocks. Well, you know me, Hector. Those buttocks, spread on the seat of the chair . . . and oh, the hips! Bulging out the trousers and the hem of the pullover. And her thighs!! They were not exactly heavy, nor were they slender, but, God, they were voluptuous. I visualised them without the trousers, the weight of her pressing them apart on the chair; I saw the black, hairy cleft between and could almost feel my cupped hand closed over it. I imagined those thighs naked on the chair, not joined together where the lower point of the pubic triangle starts,

but apart enough to leave room for the lips to appear. My lips too, I prayed as my coffee grew colder. I dare not even think of the soft belly.'

Denis Dupuis laid the top sheet of paper down on the table and picked up the second. 'The lady certainly seems to have stirred your fancy!' he observed. 'She had, of course, a low voice?'

'Naturally. Husky too — and full of promise. If only there hadn't been a rather well-built husband sitting opposite her.'

'Yes, I see what you mean.' Dupuis finished his absinthe, raised a hand to signal a white-aproned waiter, and made a circling movement with his forefinger to indicate that he wanted the round repeated. The waiter nodded, whisked away their empty glasses and threaded his way back between the crowded tables to the bar. 'I have to finish it,' Dupuis said, 'having got this far.' He started to read again:

'The loose woolly gave me the idea of low, loose breasts, but not exactly dropped. In any case, as you know, old chap, it's a long time since I felt any longing for the fashionable, fictional cones passing for tits in such illustrated magazines as La Vie Parisienne *or* The Humorist. *I'm with Caesar every time: no lean and hungry look for me; let me have about me women who are, if not fat, at least roly-poly (talking of which, remind me one day to tell you about Nounou). But back to the hotel lady.*

'Did she have false eyelashes? If so, they were

very skilled. If not . . . well, I almost fainted thinking of the pubic hair! I tell you, this was the real earth-mother type. You would have loved her. There were smudges beneath her brown eyes, as if she had been . . . I'll say gainfully employed . . . throughout the night. I imagined the musky scent of the flesh between breast and shoulder. One of her hands was lingering on those parted thighs as I left. I imagined the fingers . . . oh, my dear fellow, I've been imagining what the fingers did, or could do, all morning!'

'And that's all?' Dupuis sounded disappointed. He laid the second sheet down on the first. There were two inches of space at the foot of the page.

Paul smiled. 'I was going to write more, but a friend wanted to talk to me about racing cars in Italy.' He gathered the sheets together and added them to the rest of the letter.

'That was foolish of me,' his friend said. 'What was the husband like?'

'A military cove. Compact. Handsome of course. Name of Ritter. I heard the waitress call him Major. Her name, apparently, is Eve. Most suitable, I thought.'

The waiter materialised with a tray carrying their drinks. He whisked away a napkin draped over his forearm, swabbed the table top, set down glasses, sugar and water, and added a saucer to the three in front of each young man in a single fluid movement. The price of each drink would be multiplied by the number of saucers when the time came to pay the bill.

Paul had turned over a page of the newspaper. 'What

about this!' he said. 'A cablegram from the *Figaro* correspondent in New York states that a speech made by President Harding at the Arlington Memorial in Washington was heard by several thousand people, three thousand miles away in California, *at the same time as he made it*, through the use of wireless telegraphy!'

Dupuis was attending to his absinthe. 'Remarkable,' he said.

'Clearly this wireless, as they call it, is the coming thing,' Paul pursued enthusiastically. 'The guv'nor tells me that they're transmitting, or whatever they call it, in public from a place called Daventry. If you have the right kind of receiver, it seems that you can hear dance music through some kind of horn! And sometimes people talking in French, from the other side of the Channel!'

'Remarkable,' his friend said again. 'My own concerns do revolve around a distance that is a little shorter. Between Paris and Melun to be exact.'

'The Knights' summer picnic next Sunday, you mean? On the river in the forest?'

'Precisely. The boat is hired from Melun. But that is a slow train and it takes an age. Otherwise we take a fast train to Fontainebleau, but that means either we wait for the change or we have to pay a taxicab. The transport question is difficult.'

'I fancy Tom Crawford may have that in hand,' Paul said. 'He's a genius at borrowing other people's motorcars. In any case, I'll keep you informed.'

'That would be kind,' said Dupuis. 'And now I must part. My *poule* awaits.'

'As long as the *poule* is laying,' Paul quipped. 'But

remember Sunday: don't put all your eggs in one basket!'

Dupuis counted the saucers, put money on the table and left. The young Englishman returned to his letter writing.

The friend in England was Hector Champney, a boisterous hedonist whom Paul had known a long time. After a passion for Montgolfier hot air balloons, dating back to the days before the Great War, had burned out, Champney had turned his engineering talents towards the motor car; he had for a time worked with Paul in the design department of the Mackenzie motor works. He had been asked to chaperone Paul on his first visit to Paris back in 1912 and had good-naturedly supervised the youngster's initial amatory exploits.

So far as his own sex life was concerned, Hector Champney was in a class restricted to one. Energetic and able, he suffered from the naïve belief — perhaps peculiarly English — that the measure of a man's skill as a lover lay with the speed in which he achieved orgasm. Any beau spending more than two or three minutes consummating The Act, he fondly believed, must either be craven or clumsy. 'Believe it or not,' he had confided once to a lady love, 'but some coves take ages over this. Sex, I mean. Go on for minutes on end. A quarter of an hour, even! It's a fact; sister of a fellow in my house at school told me one summer vac. Must be the devil for their wives; poor dears would be quite worn out. There you are though: some folks never think of other people.'

At one time, during the balloon era, Champney had lived for a few months with Milady. But the bruising effects of this theory had sent her swiftly back to Paris and the Rue St André-des-Arts. They had remained firm friends, however, and the idiosyncratic Englishman never visited the capital without at least one sojourn at the One-Two-Five, 'Sometimes,' as he once shamefacedly confessed to a friend, 'for as long as twenty minutes!'

Paul smiled fondly, adding a couple of sentences to his letter and then sealing the envelope.

A shadow fell across the table. He looked up. Tom Crawford was standing just outside the striped awning that still dripped raindrops onto the pavement. 'I bring good news,' he announced.

'Come in out of the weather and sit down,' said Paul. 'What are you going to have?'

'Thanks. I am thirsty, as it happens. I'll have a *formidable*.'

'Splendid.' Paul turned to catch the waiter's eye and mimed the giant measure of beer defined by this term, and the huge glass in which it would be brought. 'What's the news?' he enquired.

The sculptor sat down and stretched his arms above his head. He yawned. 'For Sunday,' he said lazily. 'Spanish diplomat I know, chap who's attached to the Quai d'Orsay, promised to lend me a Hispano. She's a tourer, seats eight at a pinch. As Corinne and her mates are mounted — Hah! When *isn't* dear Corinne mounted! — that should see us right for the party, eh?'

Paul drained his glass. '*Formidable*!' he said.

The Hispano-Suiza *was* a formidable car! It was enormous. Beneath about nine feet of louvred, polished aluminium bonnet was a six-and-a-half litre, thirty-seven-horsepower engine of incomparable elegance, which was capable of pushing the two-ton vehicle up to almost a hundred miles per hour. The dove-grey touring body, slung between wide running-boards and elegantly flared wings was lined with black hide upholstery and solid silver fittings. The aristocratic radiator, virtually a Flamboyant Gothic creation, was topped by a silver mascot representing a stork in flight (an emblem described by the novelist Michael Arlen in *The Green Hat*, published earlier that year, as 'soaring over the crest of the great bonnet as though in proud flight over the heads of scores of phantom horses — that silver stork by which the gentle may be pleased to know that they have just escaped death beneath the wheels of a Hispano-Suiza motor, as supplied to His Most Catholic Majesty').

There were to be twelve people in the picnic party: the five men and Corinne who comprised the Knights of the Bottle, plus Nounou, Françoise, two of Corinne's girlfriends and a couple that Paul had not met.

'It's a shame,' Tom Crawford had said, 'but I absolutely veto Dagmar and her lady. She's a spiffing chum and a jolly sport, but we've six of each, six of the best as you might say, and I'm damned if I want all the fair sex carted off into the forest by those two harpies! The book may have been a grand success, but we don't want to be landed with *six* men in a boat!'

Crawford drove the Hispano, with Nounou and Paul beside him on the wide front seat; Françoise sat between her brother Denis and Bertrand Laforge on the rear seat. Occasional seats that folded down on either side of the recessed cocktail cabinet in the mahogany partition dividing the front of the car from the back were occupied by Hans Bohl and one of Corinne's friends called Sophie. The society writer herself was driving her other friend and the new couple to Melun.

It was a sunny day, with a slight breeze chasing high white clouds across the blue sky. They drove with the hood down, buttoned into a leather bag above the rear seat. A second windshield in a brass frame, pulled up from the partition, carried pivoting glass sidescreens to shelter the passengers in the rear from the wind.

There was gin, vermouth, sherry, brandy and calvados in the cocktail cabinet. Once the *pavé* of the Place d'Italie had been left behind, the thirty-two miles of dusty white road separating Melun from the capital passed — allowing for a couple of pleasantly shaded stops for refreshment — in little more than an hour. The great car sped silently between the huge summer cornfields, bright with poppies, of the Ile-de-France, scattering dogs and chickens in sleepy villages where the inhabitants were still celebrating Mass beneath the tall spires of grey churches.

The hired launch was moored alongside a quay at the far end of the Boulevard Victor Hugo, opposite an island in the Seine. Corinne and her passengers had already arrived; the car was parked and the three girls had started to prepare the picnic. The table in the tiny saloon was strewn with tomatoes, artichokes, green salad, fruit, long crisp loaves and hampers packed with sausages and *charcuterie*. On one of the bunks, the man who made up the quartet — a stiff-faced, rather military type – was unwrapping cheeses and arranging bottles in a wine cooler.

Led by Crawford, the eight passengers from the Hispano crowded down the narrow companionway. Greetings, laughter, a babble of good-natured banter. The launch rocked at its moorings as the stream raced past. Corinne extricated herself from Denis Dupuis's embrace and laid a hand on Paul's arm. 'Sweetheart,' she intoned, 'I don't think you've met my friends from Rothenburg-am-der-Tauber. They're in France for a couple of weeks and I know you'll get on like a house on fire. Darlings, this is Paul Mackenzie, the fashion genius. Paul – I'd like you to meet Helmut Ritter and his wife Eve.'

Mackenzie shook hands with the military type, murmured the usual inanities, and turned to the wife, who was sitting at the table. His hand reached out again . . . and stayed, immobilised in mid-air, as she swung around to face him. His mouth dropped open. He was staring at the woman from the Hotel Récamier whose sensual allure had so fascinated him a few days before.

Eve was peeling an apple. She smiled, holding out a sliced segment of the fruit. 'Would you like to try some?' she offered.

PART THREE

Paris, Fontainbleau, Deauville,
September 1922

Paul

Chapter Eighteen

Tom Crawford would doubtless claim that you could have knocked me down with a feather – although at six feet and something approaching one hundred and sixty pounds the feather would need to have been plucked from a fairly substantial bird.

I was more in the position of the seaman who, when asked in court if he had been surprised to see a tanker loom up in the London fog and ram his own vessel, had blurted out: 'Surproised, y'r Honour? You coulda buggered me through me oilskin!' (The magistrate instructed: 'That will go down in the record as "The witness stated that he was . . . ah . . . taken aback". ')

So, yes, astonished would not be too strong a term to describe my own reaction on discovering that the nubile Madame Ritter was to be one of my companions on the Fontainebleau picnic organised by the Knights of the Bottle. It would not however be a true or total description were it not to be complemented by words indicative of pleasure, anticipation and, it must be admitted, nascent lust.

There she sat, brimming with sexuality, holding out towards me the forbidden fruit!

For a moment our eyes locked. Her face was completely expressionless. 'Thank you,' I said, 'nothing would give me greater pleasure.' I smiled and took the slice of apple.

For a tenth of a second our fingers touched. The temporary contact of those two skins told me more than the features of a whole face.

Soon afterwards we cast off and the launch headed upstream towards the forest. The wheel, by common consent, was entrusted to Hans Bohl, who had spent several summer holidays sailing off Haarlem, in Holland, and could at least be relied upon to know which side to steer past other traffic on a narrow waterway.

Since it was a Sunday, and the weather was fine, the traffic was pretty dense to start with. There were a lot of skiffs south of Melun — weekend parties like ours with something to celebrate, chaps in blazers and straw boaters showing off to their girlfriends, some of the local peasantry, aping the toffs. Threading their way between them, launches and cruisers piled on as much speed as they could, churning up the water to send their wash surging against the pegged boards protecting the banks of riverside houses and cafés. We were held up more than once by sailing boats, amateur yachtsmen who'd come to grief because they had yet to get the hang of tacking in a confined space. There was a lot of laughter and shouting, most of it good-natured, and then the gramophone records and the wheezing accordions took over once more.

Soon, however, we'd outdistanced the local stuff and joined what was in fact an unadmitted and unofficial competition — practically a race, really — to grab the best, and the nearest, forest moorings. There were a lot of factors to take into account here, the position of the sun, the amount of shade, the possibilities of seclusion, the state of the ground, the ease of getting ashore, and at weekends the rivalry between those competing for the choicest spots was fierce.

Lush fields and hedgerows bright with flowers drifted by. The exhaust below the launch's cruiser stern burbled peacefully. We passed a carter leading a wain piled high with hay, a crocodile of small schoolgirls being taken for a walk along the towpath, a noisy *guinguette* where sweating countryfolk danced to the music of two fiddlers. By the time a bend in the river hid the eighteenth century Château de Vaux-le-Penil on its commanding hill, the reach we were traversing accommodated half a dozen motorboats and a single Bermuda-rigged yacht crewed by three efficient-looking bruisers in striped jerseys and white ducks.

I was sitting between Bertrand Laforge and one of Corinne's friends — I think her name was Sara — on the padded thwart, thinking of Eve Ritter's thighs as I made polite conversation. Tom Crawford was flirting with the other friend on the far side of the cockpit. Denis Dupuis and Eve's husband had joined Hans at the wheel. The others were still organising food in the cabin.

I had been amused by the very evident keep-off signals emitted all day by Nounou. Although we had sat next to each other in the Hispano, she hadn't addressed a single word to me directly. Maybe she was one of those ladies who 'didn't know what could have come over her', whose highly selective memories allowed them a virginally modest view of their own activities. Certainly we weren't going to acknowledge the fact that she had been accommodating my cock at one end and Mado's pussy at the other while the two of us played kissing games in the Bois above! I can't say it worried me much.

An undulating outline blue with distance now resolved itself into the approaching forest. We glided past a farm and the river curled around and ran suddenly beneath overhanging trees on the left bank. A mile further on, Hans headed for a narrow creek winding into the forest opposite a small island. The yacht, two hundred yards ahead of us, had been hoping to run in there too, but the helmsman miscalculated the freshening wind and their bows rammed the far bank of the river. By the time they extricated themselves, the launch had slid in below the trees and blocked the inlet. At first I thought the bruisers were going to remonstrate, but when they had digested the fact that there were twelve of us and only three of them, they thought better of it and sheered off.

Hans and his companions flung ropes and made fast, and we all scrambled ashore. It was a good choice, no doubt about that. Thick undergrowth grew right down to the water's edge beneath the trees on one side of the creek. On the other side there was a gently sloping grassy bank which formed part of a small clearing dappled with sunlight — a larger edition, in fact, of the glade in the Bois de Boulogne which Nounou was so eager to forget. At the back of this clearing the ground rose; beneath elm and beech and birch, the forest floor was strewn with huge boulders — remnants of a sandstone ridge which had collapsed aeons ago under the weight of a Tertiary limestone formation laid down when the whole of the Île-de-France region was a tropical inland sea. Between the boulders and the limestone bluff, itself thickly wooded, there was enough space, enough comfort and privacy and seclusion for a dozen seductions, a score of intrigues of the kind so admirably suited to a sunny summer afternoon after a splendid Sunday lunch!

Hans, our far-sighted and feeling fellow-drinker Hans, clearly knew what he was doing.

We sat around a wide cloth spread on the grass, with the contents of the hampers, the crocks of salad, the loaves and fruit and cheeses, divided amongst us. It was a ripping spot. After the second glass of wine – cooled in the creek – every single woman there looked as alluring as the Rokeby Venus, as promising as Manet's barmaid at the Folies Bergère – and as inscrutable as the Mona Lisa.

My eyes, nevertheless, were concentrated on Eve. Was there some way I could contrive to play Adam in this particular Garden of Eden? Was there a chance, however faint, that the Ritters were 'modern' in the same sense as Mado and Dagmar van den Bergh? Or was the damned husband determined to assert his conjugal rights?

He seemed a pleasant enough fellow . . . and indeed he spent more time being attentive to Corinne's friends than he did to his wife. Perhaps they had been married some time.

I drifted around a bit myself, while we were eating. Mustn't make it too obvious – in case it all ended with a negative response. I managed to get in some pretty telling dialogue with the Earth Mother, just the same.

Well, yes, perhaps another glass would do no harm . . . Such a delightful spot, don't you think? . . . May I recommend the *crême renversée*: Corinne made it herself . . . Just so long as it stays fine. You never know in this part of France . . .

Ouf! A fat chance of getting away with anything more intimate than that with ten grinning idiots crowding around within earshot of every word! Maybe it would be better to scrub today as a definite target, to — what do the Yanks say? — to take a rain check and limit one's hopes to the possibility of snaffling a future rendezvous, a drink at a café perhaps, in the launch on the way home?

No! The hell with it! I wasn't going to give up before the bell rang. The trouble was, even if I schemed in some way to put myself, as they say, next to the lady, I had no indication whatever in what way my advances would be received. Oh, sure, we made eye contact often enough. But however much admiration and desire I tried to pour into my gaze, hers remained maddeningly neutral. And somehow or other a renewal of the finger-to-finger story always escaped me, however much food and drink I passed her way.

For the moment I was obliged to tamp down my lust to a below-the-surface simmer, allowing my eyes to do what they could for me.

They did all right of course — but look what they had to work with! I went to the creek and hauled out a fresh bottle of wine, uncorking it and pouring myself a glass before I came back, to allow myself space to stare lecherously without it being too obvious.

She was sitting half-turned away from me, between

Hans and Denis, leaning across to carry on some conversation with Corinne as she spread butter on a long section of French bread. The husband was on the far side of the cloth, still talking to the girl called Sara.

Eve wore a loose olive-green jersey in knitted wool, with a cardigan of the same colour thrown over her big shoulders. She sat with her legs tucked under her, those marvellous hips emphasised rather than concealed by that season's fashion 'discovery' – a pleated knee-length divided skirt in some soft fawn material. Her breasts, like Corinne's, were unconfined by bust bodice or brassiére, and could from time to time be glimpsed moving beneath the shift she presumably wore under her jersey. The unctuous, gliding, to-and-fro rhythm of her hand, spreading butter along that length of loaf and then smoothing Roquefort cheese in with it, started such a heated train of thought in my mind that I was forced to return and sit down quickly lest my interest should manifest itself via the front of my flannels.

Another half hour was to pass before the scene changed. We lay around the wreckage of the meal, drinking more slowly now, exchanging badinage in a tipsy way, laughing a lot. One of the girls had fallen asleep. Tom disgraced himself with an atrocious series of puns. The sunbeams, obscured from time to time by those hurrying white clouds, swept slowly across the glade. Bertrand Laforge flapped a newspaper in a desultory fashion at a platoon of wasps buzzing over the remains of a wild boar *terrine*.

It was Hans, bless him, who saved my life. Possibly my sanity too. 'Knights of the Bottle!' he cried, springing suddenly to his feet. 'Kings, Queens and Bishops on the board too, for that matter. This is no time for frowsting in the shade; we should be breathing in this fine forest air and gambolling in the sun! Come — we will amuse ourselves, and help our health, with a little outdoor exercise!'

And he proposed some silly, childish game: a competition to find the most interesting, or the most perfect, fossil to be quarried from the boulders scattering the high ground behind the clearing. For the purposes of the hunt we were to be divided into three teams of four, each team comprising two couples and each couple pairing a man and a girl with no previous connections. The prize would be announced by Hans himself once the winners were decided.

The idea wasn't exactly showered with exclamations of delight, but Hans was persuasive — and the project was greeted more warmly once people realised it was no more than a variation of Hunt the Slipper: an excuse to find opportunities for snogging, the moment the herd had been left behind.

He would never admit it, of course, but I reckoned that Hans must have been covertly watching while I ground my teeth in frustration . . . and that he had drawn certain conclusions. Because when it came to dividing the party into teams, organised naturally by Hans, who should I find myself coupled with but — the lovely Eve!

I flashed the dear fellow a smile of gratitude, but he was studiously looking the other way.

Admittedly the second pair in the team was Helmut Ritter and Sara, but that may just have been to make it look better. Into each life, in any case, a little rain must fall.

If I couldn't contrive a separation from them, I wasn't worth making the effort for anyway.

'There's nothing but gasteropods low down,' I called. 'The lammelibranch fossils will be much easier to dig out, but they'll all be higher up in the series. More recent species, you see.'

I hadn't the faintest idea what a gasteropod was, and I wouldn't know a lammelibranch from a bugle, but I remembered the words from some long-ago school lecture on palaeontology and I was putting my money on the hope that she would know even less about it than I did. The aim was to separate her from the others and manoeuvre her to the top of a thirty-foot bluff which rose behind the boulders. 'Come on: I'll give you a hand up,' I offered.

Eve shook her head. 'I can manage, thanks. There's kind of a pathway between the saplings here.' Another opportunity for skin contact down the drain.

I puffed up the steep incline behind her. This turned out in fact to be a pretty good second-best. The 'divided skirt' she was wearing was no more really than a heavily pleated and voluminous pair of knee-length shorts with very loose legs. And this meant that, the higher she climbed, the better the view I had of her bare calves and the splendid columns of her thighs above disappearing into the draperies that concealed delights I didn't even dare imagine. By the time we arrived at the top of the bluff my heart was hammering, and not just from the climb.

The rest of the party were distributed here and there between the trees and the boulders below: Denis with Nounou, Tom with Françoise, Hans — cheating a bit here, but he was after all the organiser — with his fellow Knight, Corinne. I could see at least one pair of shapely female legs splayed out behind a rock. Only one other couple had braved the bluff (Bertrand and the girl who had been asleep, I thought), and they were a couple of hundred yards away. We had left Helmut and Sara poking around a sandstone outcrop nearer the boat.

We'd found a couple of chunks of flint, and used them to chip half a dozen pale fossils shaped like scollop shells off the corners of a limestone seam rising above and behind the original bluff. There was a time limit on the game and we'd already used up half of it. I decided it had to be now or never. 'Eve . . .' I began huskily.

She was looking up at the sky. 'It's clouding over,' she observed in that maddeningly calm and even voice. 'I wonder should we—'

And she broke off suddenly with a gasp as her ankle turned on a loose stone concealed beneath the bracken, throwing her forward and almost causing her to fall.

You know who nearly fell over his own feet, trying to grab her before she plunged into the undergrowth.

For a brief instant, a moment in and out of time, I held the whole glorious weight of her against me. And then she had disengaged herself, smiled politely, and said: 'Thank you. That was quick. I would surely have cut open my knee if it wasn't for you.'

I still had one of her arms in my fist, the flesh firm, smooth as a ripe peach, the blood — mine? Hers? — tremoring against my fingertips. 'Eve,' I croaked for the second time, 'there's something I have to say to you, something I must tell you.'

She turned to face me, the tiniest smudge of down on her upper lip emphasising the curve of her mouth as the smile widened. The dark eyes bored into mine. 'Monsieur Mackenzie,' she said, 'you don't have to tell me anything.'

I swallowed. 'I . . . don't?'

She shook her head, the cropped hair snaring a final gleam of sun before the clouds closed in again. 'You have been making sheep's eyes at me throughout luncheon. You tried to persuade me five times to have more of the same salad. You refilled my glass twice when it was already brimming. And at breakfast in the hotel the other day, you practically burned a hole in my back with your stares! Even a foreigner, and a German at that, could scarcely fail to come to the conclusion that you were, as the French say, *épris de moi*.' She laughed. 'I guess I should consider myself flattered.'

There was a story going around that year, about a woman who dreamed she had been abducted by a tall, dark stranger, who threw her across his saddle, rode off with her into the forest and tied her to a tree. When at last she summons up the courage to quaver: 'Oh, s-sir— w-w-what are you going to do to me?' The stranger shrugs. 'Lady,' he says, 'it's your dream . . .'

That's kind of the way I felt, on that bluff, on that Sunday afternoon. Except I couldn't work out whether I was in the position of the lady or the stranger.

'Eve,' I said, 'you are the most magnificent . . . you have the most splendid—'

And that is as far as I got, because suddenly it was

raining. It is no use my saying it *began* to rain: it was an instant deluge. A whipcrack of thunder, a puff of cool air, and the heavens opened. It was as if the floodgates of some celestial reservoir had been lifted: water pelted down in solid sheets, flattening the grasses, piercing leaves, bouncing high off the rocks. In less than twenty seconds we were soaked to the skin.

I could hear shouts and cries from below over the drumming of the downpour. 'This way!' I yelled. 'Quick! There's some kind of shelter in the rock.' And I seized Eve's hand and sprinted for the limestone shelf, where I'd noticed earlier a niche or hollow partly concealed by a tall clump of broom.

It was no more than fifty yards away, but getting there was like battling your way through a line of Atlantic breakers. I had never seen such rain. By the time we made it, we were both panting with exhaustion.

'Grüss Gott!' Eve exclaimed, shaking herself like a dog. 'Never have I been in a tempest like this! And so sudden. I am but *drenched!*' She plucked the jersey and cardigan away from herself. They were almost black with moisture, hugging the slopes of her breasts, outlining her nipples.

The hollow was in fact a shallow cave, the interior invisible to anyone except a person standing beside the broom clump. 'This is no time for prudery,' I said. 'You've got to get that stuff off you right away, and we'll take one end each and wring it as dry as we can. In the meantime you must put on this.' I stripped off the striped blazer I was wearing and shook it hard. Drops of water flew off it like a cloud. The material wasn't impermeable, but the garment was lined, and it hadn't soaked up the rain like knitted wool.

She was already dragging the jersey over her head. We squeezed it and the cardigan until we were out of breath, and then spread them over a rock shelf at the inner end of the cave. My shirt was next, sticking clammily to the skin of my bare chest and shoulders. The cloudburst, punctuated by an occasional thunderclap and a flash of lightening, roared down outside the cave mouth. 'It's heavy as hell,' I said lamely, 'but it's probably only a shower. It should be over soon.'

Eve was staring at me through the gloom. Her dark hair was plastered to her skull. Her make-up had run. Above her thick waist, a thin shift, almost transparent now, sculpted the swell of two low, heavier than I expected, breasts. I thought she was the sexiest thing I had ever seen in my life. Her skin shone like mother-of-pearl; the sodden cloth of her divided skirt clung to the padded cushions of her hips.

If it was no time for prudery, it was no time for words either. I moved towards her. Her eyes glimmered and I reached for her. We slammed together like the closing of a strongroom door.

Jesus, the clasp of that strong body against my own!

We were kissing, avidly, frenziedly, the breath snorting through our noses as our mouths sucked and chewed. Our two tongues performed a lascivious *pas-de-deux* in the twin caverns of our mouths. With my arms wrapped around her, I jerked the shift from the waistband of her skirt and clenched my hands on the strong, supple columns of muscle each side of her spine. The skin of her back was as cool and moist and pliant as I had known it would be. The weight of her pelvis was slung against me and my right knee was dividing her skirt more than the makers intended.

I heard a low growling noise deep in Eve's throat and felt her nails rake down my back. My body was shaking, my loins were on fire. I grabbed the shift and hauled it over her head, exulting in the sensation of those swollen breasts with their distended nipples rolling against the flat plane of my chest. The padded swell of her belly ground against the hard ridge of my cock.

Abruptly she freed her mouth and pushed me away. 'My God!' I panted. 'My *God!*'

She leaned swiftly down, big breasts hanging, to fumble at her waist and then drag up one of the legs of her divided skirt. Whatever it was that she wore under it was stepped out of on one side, manoeuvered across the crotch and then dragged down the other leg to be flung away. She was naked beneath the hip-hugging garment. She stepped towards me, smiling. 'And now, Mister English,' she said softly, 'let us see what *you* have to offer.' Her palms cupped the throbbing bulge agonising my loins as my own hands took the weight of those breasts. 'Oh, yes,' she said. 'How *very* instructive!' Her fingers manipulated my fly.

The buttons slid through the buttonholes and the fly gaped open under the pressure exerted by the stiffened shaft within. I felt the waistband of my flannels wrenched apart. And then the air cold on my heated cock as the fingers searched and found and tightened and pulled.

'Oh, my!' Eve breathed. 'My goodness me!'

I gasped something unintelligible. The distended skin of my pulsating cock-head felt tight enough to burst.

Her two hands squeezed and stroked, milking, sliding as the scrotum was lifted and fondled. My own hands dropped to the wet stuff around her hips, lifted it, and fastened on the taut flesh beneath. I raked my fingers up her thighs, glided them inwards across the sopping crotch of the divided skirt, and felt at last the yawning, slippery heat amongst damply springy hair that I had been imagining all day.

Eve grunted, pulling me savagely towards her. A moment later — and I don't know to this day whether I shoved, or whether I was guided, whether I tore aside the leg of the damned skirt or she did: I only remember the sound of a ripping seam — a moment later I was in there, the hard graze of coarse hair sliding down my staff as the head ploughed into the hot sucking depths of her belly. She clamped herself against me, thrusting fiercely with her hips. We kissed, arms clenched around bare flesh. I fisted my cock harder and harder, faster and faster into the tight, dark tunnel of her ample body.

I've been in bed with lots of women; I've spent many, many nights in the most easy, comfortable intimacy; I've made love in a leisurely way in armchairs, swimming pools, automobiles, elevators. But nothing I had ever done came near equalling the explosive excitement of that scrambled, half-clothed fuck, hard up against the damp rock wall of the cave in Fontainebleau Forest that stormy Sunday afternoon.

We came together, quite quickly I imagine, in a shattering climax that left us numbed and shaking while the thunder roared and the rain hissed down outside.

* * *

'I like men a lot – and I like a lot of men,' Eve whispered in reply to my question. Time had passed. We were wrapped in a close embrace: she was sitting on my knee on the shelf at the back of the cave. Rain still splashed down relentlessly outside.

'I couldn't understand why you took so long to move,' she said.

I cleared my throat. 'I didn't like to . . . presume,' I said.

'But you knew my name: I offered you an *apple*, for God's sake!' She grinned. 'I could hardly make it clearer than that, could I?'

'You were so unapproachable,' I said weakly. 'So distant. So . . . I mean there was no indication whatever.'

Eve smiled again. 'Well, that's all part of the game, isn't it?'

'Apart from which,' I said, 'you were after all married. And your damned husband was – is – right there.'

'Helmut and I have an arrangement. We're very fond of each other, but we each go our own way when we want to. No questions. No recriminations.'

'He's not . . .' I looked uneasily at the curtain of rain beyond the cave mouth. ' . . . he's not a voyeur? Not one of the ones who like to creep up and watch secretly?'

She laughed aloud. 'Good God, no! He's a Bavarian!'

The hips, still covered in sodden cloth, squirmed against my open fly. She touched my cheek. 'Interest, I feel, has not entirely been dissipated!'

She was right. With all that weight of woman-flesh rolling my cock suggestively from side to side, I was hardening again like crazy.

She unclasped her arms, slid off my knee and stood up. She wrestled with some flap fastening the waist, pushed the divided skirt down to her knees, and stepped out of it. She stood in front of me entirely nude – a curvaceous, heavy-fleshed Rubens nymph, a caverned Aphrodite on some ancient Greek oracle isle. In the faint light filtering into the cave, the dark mat of hair barring her milk-white loins underlined the fact that within those alabaster limbs slumbered a wet-lipped tiger of female desire.

I pushed myself off the ledge and fell on my knees in front of her. 'You!' I groaned. 'Oh, God, you Earth Mother, you female fury, you *woman*!' And I wrapped my arms around her hips, burying my face in the soft smooth warmth of her belly.

I felt fingers combing through my hair. Very slightly, Eve canted her hips towards me. Strands of coarse hair scraped my chin. I grasped the meaty globes of her buttocks, clenching my fingers and drawing her pelvis against me. She flexed those hips more forcefully . . . and among the damp hairs my mouth found flesh.

The fingers tightened across my scalp, pressing my head remorselessly against her loins. My mouth was among moist sliding lips . . . I opened it wide, wide to suck in the folds of flesh . . . a stiff warm bud of tissue grazed my gums . . . interior muscles contracted around my tongue.

For a long time I remained there on my knees, oblivious of the sharp rock fragments pressing into my slacks, sucking and lapping my mistress's most private place while she crooned some wordless chant above me and the backs of her thighs trembled against my hands.

Then, as abruptly as she had first kissed me and later separated herself from my knee, driven still by whatever personal demon governed her actions when her need was upon her, she withdrew yet again and flung herself back at the rock shelf. She leaned forward over it, taking her weight on her hands, and slightly spread her thighs. 'Paul!' she cried in a strangled voice. 'I'm cold inside; I want you to fill me and warm me and love me now!'

I was already on my feet. My wet flannels were around my ankles. The rear view of that strong white body bent over with big breasts hanging, the calves and thighs parted below the great round globes of buttocks, with that yawning opening centred in the furred cleft nestling between them, was a sight no man could resist.

I hobbled up with my plank-stiff cock ready in my hand.

Eve's breath hissed in through clenched teeth as I guided the engorged head to the twin pads of hairy flesh compressed between the cheeks of her bottom, and then into the wetly gaping lips which I had myself so lovingly prepared. I slid the whole hard throbbing length into the heat of her, and she uttered a low groan as the shaft slammed into her belly up to the hilt. 'Yes!' she cried wildly. 'Push it into me! Stick it up as far as you can! Pump me and fill me . . . oh, *God!*'

She bucked back ferociously against me as I withdrew and then plunged in again. I leaned over her, cupping the weight of the soft swinging breasts in my palms each time my hips splatted against her buttocks. If anything, I was even more excited than I had been the first time.

The small cave echoed with the choking groans of our shared lust as we established a frantic, pistoned rhythm that sent the blood hammering through our veins and threatened to stifle the breath in our labouring chests. The pace accelerated; the graph of our excitement mounted inexorably.

At that pressure, with the tension, the passion between us that high, the end was inevitable; we were powerless to prolong it; we were already caught up in the wave. But we shared it and it was wonderful.

At the very moment that I sensed the entire life force of my body gathering tumultuously at the centre of my loins, Eve uttered a shrill, keening cry as she was seized by her own relief, and straightened suddenly in front of me with her belly shuddering. The unexpected change of position almost spilled me out of her, but the stiff ridge of muscle on the inside of her vagina slid hard down the hypersensitive underside of my tremoring shaft at precisely the right instant and triggered a searing climax that sent the hot spurts of my joy squirting far up into the depths of my love. She collapsed backwards into my arms and we both slid shaking to the stony floor.

It was only later, when we were gathering together the remnants of wet clothing strewn across the floor of the cave, that we realised the storm had passed. Beyond the sheltering clump of broom there was a total silence broken only by the stealthy dripping of rainwater from the leaves of the trees.

By the time we got back to the boat, everyone else was aboard, the remains of the picnic had been packed away, Hans's prize — a magnum of 1912 Pol Roger — had been awarded and drunk, and the members of the party were already impatiently waiting to cast off and head for home.

'I'm sorry, I'm sorry. I'm afraid we got lost,' I said truthfully in answer to the chorus of questions.

Tom Crawford winked. 'You can trust old Paul,' he said coarsely and unforgivably, 'to provide the only ointment in the fly!'

Chapter Nineteen

It was in one of the rooms above the spiral staircase in Mado Laverne's private suite that I discovered I was going to Deauville for the weekend. I don't remember very clearly which room: the bottle of brandy on the table had about three fingers left in it, and I had untwisted the foil and uncorked it myself only a little over an hour before. And then of course we had lingered over lunch at Maxim's. Mado had signed the bill. On second thoughts, I think it must have been the bedroom: we were lying side by side and there wouldn't have been room on the davenport in the sitting room.

We were already into Phase Three . . . and resting. The floor was carpeted with discarded clothes and the thickened nipples on Mado's small breasts were stiff with desire. Apart from small black boots that buttoned just above the ankle she was quite naked. Her humble servant, on the other hand, still sported flannel bags — nothing else, just the trousers, and these had been dragged halfway down my thighs. But Mado was a sucker for what she called obscenity, and she found black boots on bare legs, a stiff cock sticking through — or sticking out above — savaged pants much sexier than totally bare bodies. 'Nudes,' she had said to me once, 'especially female nudes, are something for a painter to put on canvas.'

To make the point — to make both points now I come to think of it — there was a painting on the wall above and behind the bed which showed in commendable detail a big-breasted brunette sitting at a dressing-table and wearing a tight red corset with black knee-length stockings. And on the wall beside the dressing-table was a painting of the same young woman, naked. The man peering through a half-open door in the background was ogling the girl and not the picture. You do get the point? There was another I'd never mentioned to Mado. The girl looked familiar and the corset definitely stirred a memory. In fact I thought the model could have been Nellie Lebérigot, one of the lushest lovelies from Milady's house of shame and joy in the Rue St André-des-Arts.

Dammit, I was sure I remembered that corset: it had been almost a trademark with Nellie at the time. And the time was ten years ago, on my very first visit to Paris. A winter's night, a bright fire burning, Mackenzie a little the worse for drink, a trifle blurred at the edges and — yes! — the red corset (it was laced with black then) which never came off all night. Which was more than could be said for Mackenzie, if you'll excuse the Crawfordism.

Of *course* I remembered. Bertie Laforge had wanted to worm some engineering secret out of me, something to do with the cars my guv'nor manufactured. And to keep me sweet he had himself paid Nellie to act the part of a society lady who'd fallen for the boyish charm of the callow young foreigner. Nellie Lebérigot! Oh, well . . . Number Five, was it? Or Number Six? . . .

'It's the Prix de Rouen on Saturday,' Mado was saying.

I was still ten years away and it took me a while to swim back and let down a foot to feel solid ground again. She had to say it a second time.

'The Prix de Rouen?'

'At Deauville, silly. The biggest prize money of the season.'

'Oh, really?' I wasn't interested in that kind of racing. The only horsepower that thrilled me was connected with Monza and Brooklands rather than Deauville. Anyway, I never bet: I invariably lost, and I considered it a rotten trick to play on all the other punters who would have backed the nag I chose.

'I have—well, there's a little job you could do for me at Deauville,' Mado said.

Well, that was no surprise. I already told you: work and play went hand in hand at Madame Laverne's; it was rare to have one without the other. That was the relationship *I* had anyway. So I'd known there would be something. But Deauville *was* a surprise. I said: 'Anything I can do for you, Mado, is always a pleasure.' I laid a hand on her pubic mound. The hair was still wet. '*Anything*. What could I do to please you now?'

She giggled, squirming her hips slightly under my touch. 'Lots of things, Paul darling. But we'll come back to that. The job concerns a fabric design — a particularly lush, oriental design in the most marvellous colours.'

'But, Mado . . .' I frowned. 'I'm a *fashion artist*, not a designer. You know that.'

'Your work captures the *spirit* of fabrics and patterns perfectly. I'm not asking you to produce an original design: I want you to *copy* a design from a length of stuff and bring it back to me. From Deauville.'

'I don't understand,' I said.

She sighed. 'In Deauville,' she said, explaining to a backward child, 'there is a sample length of material printed with this particular design. I am asking you to get hold of the sample — keeping it for as short a time as possible — and copy the design as accurately as you can, with special attention to the colours, in watercolour or gouache. Then of course you deliver your copy to me.'

'Where shall you be?'

'I shall probably be in Deauville too. I like horse racing.'

'Why don't you just ask for the sample yourself?'

'I don't think the person who has it would want me to see the design.'

'Why would they let me have it, then?'

There was a touch of affection in her tolerant smile. 'They wouldn't, my Paul. That's the point. You have to steal it.'

I stared at her. '*Steal* it?'

'Not permanently. Only for a little while: just long enough to make the copy. Then you put it back, of course.'

'Mado,' I said, 'what the *hell* are you getting me into?'

'There would be a lot of work for you if you succeeded,' she urged. 'Some of it would be the same design again — only this time in the form of dresses.

Model dresses, half a Collection of them. A lot of fashion drawings, Paul.' You get the Laverne touch: the iron fist in the iron glove. My turn to sigh.

'Where does this "sample" come from?' I asked.

'Indo-China, actually.'

'Is the Orient becoming scrutable at last?'

'A princeling brought it,' she said. 'Phnomh Xuan Chih.'

'Bless you,' I said.

'*Pardon?*'

'I thought you sneezed.'

Her turn to stare. Two-all and one to play. 'He has palaces in Laos,' she said. 'And little yellow goddesses with expensive green eyes. And elephants and a Delaunay-Belleville limousine with lamps that are real gold instead of brass. The design — it's really beautiful — was by one of his daughters. He has forty-three.'

'And he comes to France to *sell* this design?'

'Oh, not for money. He feels the publicity of an important European exposure — highlighting a *haute couture* fashion collection, for instance — would be good for the image of his little principality. He wants a good match for this daughter, but until now he hasn't been able to compete on equal terms with the Rajahs.'

I was frowning again. It was getting to be a habit. I said: 'And your next Collection would be an ideal showcase? So why don't you just ask the dusky gentleman to let you have it? Why steal the design if he wants to give it away?'

'Because he's already given it. And I'm sure I could do a better job for him than the *racaille* who talked him into it. But I can't actually talk him *out* of it. You know: his word and all that. He went to Eton.'

'And just who, dear Mado, is the *racaille* who has actual physical possession of this incomparable design — and from whom, I imagine, I have to steal it? What dangerous threshold are you bribing me to cross?'

This time the smile was wicked. 'Ahmed Simbel,' she said.

I laughed. 'Of course! Who else! He steals a design of yours to cap his beastly little show; now you have an opportunity to turn the tables . . . with a much better show. You must have been reading about poetic justice. The biter bit, and all that.' She shrugged. The breasts rose and fell. The heat between her legs was scorching my palm. 'If you want to put it that way,' she said.

'What other way would you like me to put it?' I asked.

'I shall tell you very soon,' Mado said. She turned towards me and raised herself on one elbow. The fingers of her other hand trailed across my bare thigh. 'I haven't told you the nicest bit,' she said softly. 'About Deauville, I mean.'

'All right,' I said, 'surprise me again.'

'It's priceless. He stole my designs by paying some little tart to crawl into bed with you and pinch them when you weren't looking . . . and the only way you can steal his — well, *you'll* have to crawl into bed with some other little tart — the one who's keeping the sample for him — and whip them while *she's* not looking. You have to admit, Paul, that it's—'

'Priceless,' I said.

'Oh, don't be like that, darling.' The fingers walked across my groin and touched my quivering cock. 'You know you like to fuck. And you did say *anything* for me would be a pleasure.'

'I also like to be able to choose,' I said. 'This . . . lady . . . is, I suppose, in Deauville?'

'But of course.'

'Simbel too?'

'Naturally; he has horses running there. He's rented a big house. She is staying there too, but in a different wing. It's just that she happens to be in charge of all the designs he's stacked up for the Spring show.'

'What's she like, this woman I have to seduce, this battleaxe in charge of the King's treasure? Ugly, I suppose? Fat?'

'He's only a Prince, actually. She's all right.'

Mado was being deliberately vague. 'What does that mean?' I asked. 'Fair, dark, short, tall? Buxom? Skinny? How old is she?'

Mado remained evasive. 'You won't be run in for interfering with a minor,' she said. 'Anyway, my love,' – the fingers wrapped around my aching stem and tightened – 'You must admit, whatever she's like, that it's better than having to crawl into bed with *him*.'

I raised my hips slightly. The fingers were cool and strong. 'Perhaps,' I said, 'you'd better tell me the Deauville score. The whole plan.'

She told me the score. It took quite a while. I was still hard when she finished. My palm was wet and my middle finger had sunk between the warm lips which smiled so invitingly from between her legs. Soon afterwards I was smiling myself. She was leaning right over me now, with her head poised above my hips. I told you she was a sucker, didn't I? Well, it wasn't only for obscenity.

'I have to go to Deauville for the weekend,' I told Solange. 'Job of work.'

'But that's marvellous. I'll be there myself as it happens.' She smiled. 'We can sit on the beach, watch the horse-races, maybe even lose some money at the casino.'

'If there's time. The job may keep me . . . rather busy.'

'Oh, that's all right,' Solange said. 'I'll be working too. Sort of. Madame Laverne's going down for the horses, but she wants me around anyway. Something about a new fabric for Spring that she wants to discuss with me. But I shall have lots of free time.'

'Well, I hope I do too,' I said. And meant it.

Something told me that it might be prudent not to reveal that I knew Mado would be there. And certainly not to say what the job was. Ever since that delirious night at my place after I had shown her my work, I had been, as the Irish say, doing a line with Solange . . . in between other pursuits, of course. But we saw quite a bit of each other, when each of us felt like it and time allowed. If she liked, as she had told me, to play the field, that was fine with me — as long as I was allowed my field to graze in too. I don't know if she knew of or suspected my — shall I say loose? — relationship with Mado. I didn't know what *their* relationship, outside of business, was. And I certainly wasn't going to ask questions. Or tell secrets. Jealousy is an odd thing, especially with women. Many a happy couple, agreeing to lead a 'free' existence, have split up immediately the theory was put to the test, that is to say put into practice. My own practice — and for once I agreed with Tom Crawford — was to follow the adage 'Never tell them anything'.

We'd had a lot of fun, though, Solange and I. As I had noted before, behind the demure demeanour and the horn-rimmed spectacles worn in the showroom above the Rue des Capucines, a wildly adventurous spirit lurked. And as a contrast to the rigid constraints of her job, Solange was game for absolutely anything that could be considered naughty, or sexy, or 'fast', or provocative by the prudish. And not just in the bedroom either. We had made love in the most outrageous places: against a wall behind the Ritz, under the colonnades of the Rue de Rivoli at dawn, in a lift going up the Eiffel Tower, in a crowded pleasure boat steaming past Notre-Dame — once even, when the urge took us suddenly, on the staircase leading to my own apartment. When I first told her I would be going to Deauville, we were in the last coach of the last train of the day on the Métro, heading for Passy.

We sat on a seat against the rear partition. There were half a dozen other passengers in the coach — a drunk who'd fallen asleep, a girl who looked like a student, an elderly couple, two nondescript men. But most of them were down at the far end. And anyway the seat backs would be hiding our lower halves. Unless, of course, they got up and got off . . .

But that risk was part of the game. And part of the thrill for Solange. In any case, once they had registered, the doors would have closed and they would have been left gawping on the platform, sliding open-mouthed past our window as the train gathered speed.

It was a little cool for late summer, and I was wearing a lightweight buttoned raincoat. Solange's hand was thrust in between two of the buttons, my flies were undone, my cock was sliding wet under her milking caress. It would have been clear as a bell to anyone watching — if only from the rise and fall of the front of the raincoat — that I was being skilfully masturbated.

And equally clear from Solange's spread knees and the tight, short skirt pulled above them that this was a reciprocal affair. Even if my arm hadn't been moving and my hand out of sight between her thighs. She was wearing French knickers with wide, wide lace-edged legs, and my fingers dabbled enticingly in the warm depths of moist flesh beneath them as my knuckles lifted the damp silk away from her heated mons. She was squirming on the seat, uttering small mewling cries, pumping my throbbing staff with increasing speed.

She turned her head suddenly and stared straight at me. What a difference there is in the way people look at you! Françoise likes to seem scared, guilty even. In the glance from Mado Laverne's oddly pale eyes there is always a challenge, the quizzical anticipation of an answer to a question that has yet to be asked. The wide violet eyes of the slender young woman leaning against me brimmed always with a barely suppressed but delighted complicity.

'Paul,' she said quite loudly. 'Do you know what I am going to do?'

I was already breathing fast. 'Tell me,' I said huskily.

The fingers gripping my lubricated rod tightened;

they slid more rapidly up and down the shaft. 'I am going to toss you off,' Solange said steadily. 'Here on this seat in this train I am going to jerk your cock publicly faster and faster until you can't keep it in any longer and you come in my hand, spurting all over your clothes so that you will have to walk home with a dark telltale patch staining the front of your raincoat.'

I knew what she wanted, of course. This was part of *our* game — a different game from the one I played with Mado. I obliged, trying to stifle the gathering pressure in my loins. 'Toss me off then, you dirty little slut,' I croaked. 'I'm going to spread the lips of your cunt and finger your clitoris, on and on and on until you come so violently that you'll scream aloud and *wet* your sex-crazed little self.'

Solange groaned. 'Oh, yes,' she breathed. 'Make me. Make me come here with your hand on my . . . with your finger— Oh, your *finger!*'

I was getting pretty heated myself, staring with fascination at the rhythmic rise and fall, in and out, in and out of my lightweight, off-white mack . . . feeling the lewd grasp of that pumping hand on my cock, my naked slippery, iron-hard, aching cock so lasciviously milked in the sly dark between my gaping slacks and the heaving, rubberised cotton that hid her marauding hand. An exquisite agony tensed my loins, and I knew that she was going to do what she said: she was going to keep up that unbearable, that utterly wonderful squelching piston stroke until — Oh, God! — until I came in my clothes in her savage, jerking hand.

I leaned harder against her, throwing caution, as they say, to the winds. Her breath was hot against my cheek.

Reckless Liaisons

Her thighs slid apart so widely that I could see my own hand swallowed within the pale silk of those French knickers, the wrist glistening now, the fingers avidly parting the folds of flesh so greedily sucking their raping tips. There was a roaring in my ears, louder than the rumble of the train, as the sensations from all my nerves shot down to my loins. I was fantasising in an extravaganza of sex: my cock was tall as the Eiffel Tower, and as rigid, squeezed by giants' fingers; my hand, my wrist, my arm had been sucked into the great dark maw screaming between Solange's thighs, engulfed in the hot lubricious depths hundreds of yards up in her belly. I could hear the panting of my own breath.

She was jerking her pelvis rapidly back and forth, exaggerating the movements of the train. My hand beat wildly against her clitoris, rolling it fiercely from side to side in time with the accelerating rhythm pulling at the taut skin of my pulsating shaft.

The train rounded a corner, hurling us closer together.

That did it. The abrupt, unexpected movement, in a direction neither of us had foreseen, tightened the finger on the trigger.

Solange's quivering loins erupted into a shudder. The shudder transformed itself into a shake. The shake grew violent. The genital lips sucking at my hand dilated and then clamped over my fingers. Her head banged back against the partition and she gave a small sobbing cry that was halfway between a gasp and a yelp.

My own release was simultaneous. The tunnelling grasp working my cock slid frenziedly down to the base one final time . . . and my loins contracted, heaving into that minor death that we find so life-giving, to explode my staff into a squirting spasm that spewed the thick proof of my desire between my lover's fingers to widen shamefully the dark patch already moistening the front of my mack.

The train was shuddering too. Light streamed past the windows as it ground to a halt at the next station.

Trocadero. And I saw to my horror that the elderly couple were on their feet by the doors, waiting to get off. We had been too engrossed . . . but they must have witnessed the whole shattering climax as we rounded that last curve, groping hands, spreading stain, everything. The man's mouth had dropped open; the grey-haired woman's eyes were wide behind gold-rimmed spectacles. Her mouth was pursed severely. The doors slid open.

'Gaspard,' I heard her say as they stepped down to the platform, 'why do *you* never think of doing that on the last train home?'

Mado had booked me a hotel at Deauville, but we reckoned — in the circumstances — that it would be better if we didn't travel together. Even more so, from my point of view, since she would be going down with Solange. So they bowled westwards towards the coast in Mado's chauffeur-driven Laforge *coupé-de-ville*, and I took a train from the Gare St-Lazare.

Before I took a cab to the station, however, there was an entirely unexpected encounter that took my personal score to an astonishing forty-seven . . . no, wait! Looking at it logically it was forty-eight. Not counting Laurence, either. Here's what happened.

It was all because of the train really. Or because, selfishly, I had hopes that there might be no need of a train. It occurred to me, you see, that Dagmar van den Bergh might also be going to the races. And if she was, she would undoubtedly be driving down in the resplendent Rolls Royce Silver Ghost she had imported in 1912, which was still kept in showroom condition. Even if she was taking three lesbian lovers with her, it seemed to me, there would still be ample room for an old – an intimate – male friend to get lost in the luxuriously equipped *habitacle* of that vast limousine.

So before I started thinking about railway tickets and taxicabs, I walked from my place, up through the 16th *Arrondissement*, to the Avenue Kléber.

Madame la Comtesse was not at home. She had left three days ago to stay with friends who owned a château near Dieppe. From there she would be driving directly to Deauville.

Too bad, I said. Never mind. I should of course have called earlier.

That's when the unexpected took charge.

The servant who had answered the door when I rang was one of the two maids who had 'assisted', as the French say (which means taking part), in the – shall *we* say? – unorthodox party of Dagmar's which had ended with me in bed with the lady and her German friend. The footman who normally answered the door, it seemed, was off duty. I was turning away when the maid said: 'Monsieur will excuse me, but . . . if Monsieur has troubled to come all the way to the Avenue Kléber, only to receive a disappointment, I am sure that Madame would wish me, at the very least, to offer Monsieur some refreshment — a coffee, perhaps? A glass of wine? — on her behalf before Monsieur is obliged to take the onerous return route.'

To this day, I don't know what prompted me to hesitate. The woman was fleshy, almost heavily built, perhaps forty years old. She had large, loose lips, a neat cap of dark hair, and a generous bosom thrusting out the front of her starched apron. I should of course have said thanks-very-much-but-no, and left. But seeing my hesitation she added quickly: 'My colleague and I are sampling the new Veuve Clicquot. If Monsieur would care to join . . . ?'

'Well, that's very civil of you,' I said awkwardly. 'Perhaps . . . well, just a glass then.'

'It will be our pleasure, Monsieur.' Smiling, she held the door wide.

They were sitting in a morning-room that looked out on the small garden at the back of the big house, immediately beneath the salon with its balustraded balcony. The 'colleague' was of course the other maid. I accepted a glass of the champagne and sat down at a broad mahogany table. The room was dark, heavily carpeted, furnished with deep-buttoned brown leather armchairs and glass-fronted bookcases. Gilt-framed nineteenth century seascapes depicting sailing ships in distress hung from the picture rail. It didn't look much like a sitting-room set aside for the use of servants: that would have been in the basement. While the cat's away, I thought.

The other maid, the blonde, was sitting on the far side of the table. She was a little younger, equally well built, with large breasts loose beneath a black dress with a high neck and long sleeves. A frilly white cap with a black velvet band sat on her curly hair. She raised her glass; we drank.

The dark woman's name was Chantal; she came from the Vendée. Blonde Hortense was an Alsatian. We made stilted conversation. We talked about Paris in the summer, about the pleasures of the country, about horse-races and gambling at casinos. We lamented the passing of the famous night-time fair at Neuilly. It was all very formal, very third person: Monsieur this and Monsieur that . . . if Monsieur would care to, Monsieur would be most welcome. Hortense: a drop more in Monsieur's glass . . .

And yet the atmosphere in that room was charged, electric. I felt strangely embarrassed: the air was heavy with the unspoken, the unsaid. After all, these simple country women were employed by – lived with – one of the most notorious lesbians in Paris, an adulteress, a seducer of young girls, an organiser of extravagant orgies involving both sexes; and they were not only aware of this – they were sometimes part of it. I had myself seen them actively participating; although I had not as it happened been physically involved with either, I had seen them, watched them both naked. One of them had sucked off Tom Crawford; the other had helped to hold down Françoise Dupuis while she was (willingly) raped by Ahmed Simbel.

They knew that I knew this; they knew that I was aware they knew it.

It didn't make for comfortable conversation. It was absurd, on the one hand, to ignore the whole thing, to pretend, to go on talking as if nothing had happened.

And yet in the circumstances, in the context of our relationship when we *weren't* naked, in the absence of Dagmar . . . should the subject be introduced at all? And if so, how? It could so easily degenerate into something, well . . . vulgar, elbow-nudging, distasteful. Something to run from.

It was Chantal who did make it comfortable. Turning to her friend, she laid down her empty glass and said casually: 'Monsieur has a splendid cock.'

'Indeed,' Hortense agreed, equally casually. 'He acquitted himself well during Madame's last *spectacle*, don't you think?'

'Admirably. As well perhaps as that other Englisher, Monsieur Crowfoot.'

'Especially with that one of the big hips, Mademoiselle Janine.'

I was staring at them in a daze. Big hips. Janine. Very faintly in the afternoon air I detected a hint, the slightest tinge, of female sweat.

'Would you say,' Hortense asked conversationally, 'that Monsieur of the admittedly splendid cock,' — they were using the slang word *bitte*, which is like saying prick or tool in English — 'admirably though he used it, was in fact as well endowed as Monsieur Crowfoot?'

Chantal shrugged. The bosom moved beneath the starch. 'Impossible to say without a direct comparison.'

'Clearly,' Hortense said, 'that is *not* possible. At any rate, today. I am of the opinion, nevertheless, that my memory of the latter — closer, you may recall, than yours — would be sufficient to effect at least a temporary evaluation, enough to form an interim judgement.'

'You may be right,' Chantal admitted. 'What is certain is that Monsieur's weapon is stimulated to a particularly satisfying degree by the large hip.'

'True.' The blonde pursed her lips. 'Would you say that our hips — yours and mine — were as wide and as fleshy as those of Mademoiselle Janine?'

'That,' said Chantal, 'would be for Monsieur to decide. Were Monsieur to be so inclined.'

Monsieur in fact was still speechless. The brazen, explicit nature of the sudden, unexpected change of subject — cloaked still in the formal, impersonal 'butler's' French worthy of a Gallic Jeeves — had left me totally at a loss for words. But not at a loss of inclination. Already, as I was sure these two harpies suspected, the bizarreness of the encounter was hardening me up, though I was so far unsure how to take advantage of the situation.

I needn't have worried. I was in experienced hands.

'One can of course,' Hortense said, 'envisage a situation in which this of the cock and that of the hips could be examined impartially at the same time.'

'Indeed. At such a time,' said Chantal, 'each one of us, Monsieur included, could then advance a considered opinion on the subjects involved.'

'Were Monsieur to be so inclined.'

Suddenly they were both staring at me hard. The wide dark eyes of west-country Chantal, the blue eyes of the blonde Alsatian — unfathomable in each case. I was talking about the different way people look at you. Here there was something as inscrutable as Mado Laverne's oriental sample. The eyes were virtually expressionless, neither warm nor cold, hard nor soft, as impersonal as the forms of speech so decorously implying such outrageous behaviour, and yet brightened unquestionably with a tinge of humour. There was something else too in those secret depths, something I was familiar with but could not at that moment name.

The name, I was to learn soon enough, was lust.

They were looking expectant. Were they anticipating an answer? Of course: *was* Monsieur so inclined? I opened my mouth . . . but got no chance to speak.

They moved swiftly, expertly, smoothly for such big girls. In a single concerted action they rose, moved towards me, picked me up, carried me across the room and flung me down on a leather sofa. Chantal ripped open my fly before I could utter a word and yanked my flannels down to my ankles. My stiffening cock sprang free and she grasped it at once, cradling my balls in her other hand. Hortense stood on one leg by the sofa, her other knee pressed to my chest as she dragged her black dress off over her head. I stared up bemusedly as the pear-shaped breasts swung heavily down.

She bent over to whip off my necktie, unbutton my shirtfront. With a forefinger and thumb, Chantal was already massaging my staff into an even stiffer state. For a moment longer the fondling of my scrotum continued, and then more urgent priorities intruded: she reached behind her to untie the tapes of her apron and finger open the press-studs fastening the side of her dress.

I had noticed, at Dagmar's party, how the two maids appeared to have a particular flair for the swift undress: one moment they would be wedged into the window-seat with Tom Crawford, perhaps with a neckline immodestly bared but otherwise fully clothed; the next minute, without anyone apparently noticing, they would be stark naked, lasciviously entwined with an equally nude sculptor. I realised now that it was not so much a gift as a skill, probably rehearsed and perfected over months or even years. For in no time at all both of them *were* naked . . . and so was I.

So far I had not uttered a word. Such a whirlwind of activity, striking with no advance warning, had left me with no time for speech. In any case, by now I was breathing too fast for the words to get out.

They had me on the floor, one at each end of my prone body. Despite their very different origins, they were strikingly alike physically – meaty women with sturdy legs, billowing hips and thick waists. Their bellies were a little prominent, slightly loose, with a hint of creases at the base in Chantal's case. The breasts were heavy, pear-shaped as I had noticed, not too slack or dropped. Hortense's nipples were small and pink; the tips of Chantal's big breasts were thick and prominent, surrounded by wide brown circles of puckered skin. The big difference lay in the pubic hair – a simple tuft, a pale crescent vertically marking the outline of the cunt for the Alsatian blonde; a wide, dark, tangled thatch between the thighs of her friend, with a thin line of hairs that stretched up as far as the navel.

Chantal stood with a foot on either side of my hips. Bending forward, she seized my genitals in both hands, holding them stiffly steady as she lowered herself until she was squatting immediately above them. She sank down further still. The engorged tip of my cock nosed aside flesh, a fiery heat slid down the shaft, swallowing it whole, and I felt the weight of her bearing down my hips. She rotated her belly slowly, stirring herself with my wand. Then she began slowly moving up and down.

While this was happening, Hortense was playing mirror-image to her friend. She stood with a foot on either side of my head, squatted when Chantal squatted, lowered herself at the same time. A weight of flesh pressed down my face; damp hair scraped my lips; of its own volition, my tongue speared up into the glutinous hot tunnel of her sex. I was like a seesaw pivoted between these two rising and falling girls. My arms reached up and my hands flailed amongst a forest of breasts.

I've had a fair number of mates and I've played a lot of games, but nothing I ever did approached that steamy session in Dagmar's morning-room so far as the sheer exuberance of impersonal, unbridled lust is concerned.

I had never — how can I put it? — I had never, ever been surrounded, encompassed, hemmed-in by such an ungovernable quantity of actual, demanding, adventurously female, physical *woman* before!

We did everything that a trio can do; we fucked, we sucked, we stroked, we screwed. No part of our several bodies remained unstimulated or unused. At the end of an hour we were slippery with sweat, the slabs of flesh sliding sexily one over the other as we clasped and squirmed. The musky female scent was spiced with the onion odour of armpits.

It is not possible to go into detail: too much was happening at once, and in any case the relationship, the situation of one person, one thing, with regard to

Reckless Liaisons

another changed so swiftly that the entire torrid scene altered shape and colour as totally as the fragments of a kaleidoscope shaken at the end of a cardboard tube. One thing I do remember is the lack of words. I don't mean we slaved and slobbered away in silence: if grunts and groans and gasps and crooning noises be (if you will excuse the pun) the *lingua franca* of love, then we were shouting. But the first time actual speech was used – apart from the formalities before the clothes came off – was when I was shafting Hortense from behind and she was kneeling on the floor, her head resting on folded arms at the end of the leather sofa.

She was bucking the cheeks of her bottom fiercely back against my pelvis each time I smacked into her, the long stiff pole of my cock penetrating far up into her clasping tunnel of love. My arms were wrapped around her fleshy body, one hand fondling those bulbous breasts, the other clamped over her vaginal lips, where I could feel myself plowing in and out.

Suddenly Chantal positioned herself behind me, lying forward along my back exactly as I was draped over Hortense. Her two knees slotted into the backs of my knees, her hands reached around my thighs to hold my balls. She began slamming her hips against my buttocks in time with my own movements, driving me even harder, faster still into the impaled and quivering blonde. I felt her hot breath against my ear.

'Give it to her,' she whispered savagely. 'Pile it on. Shove it as far up that belly as you can. She loves to feel the hot spunk spurting in.'

Groaning, I gave it to her.

A little later, the hot stuff was spurting again. When

Hortense had recovered her breath, she too had found time to speak. 'We were talking of comparisons,' she said to Chantal. 'To be fair, we should now repeat the performance, with yourself at the end of the sofa, Monsieur entering from behind and myself along Monsieur's back. Only then can Monsieur analyse the respective merits of our hips and those of Mademoiselle Janine.'

'If Monsieur is so inclined,' Chantal said.

'Naturally. If Monsieur is so inclined,' Hortense agreed.

Against all the odds, Monsieur was.

They both saw me to the door when I left. 'If Monsieur would consent to remain and dine with us . . . ?' Chantal ventured, the thick nipples outlined against the black stuff of her dress. 'There is cold pheasant and perhaps three-quarters of a magnum of Château Margaux . . .'

'That is extremely kind of you,' I said. 'Alas, Monsieur has a railway train to catch and an income to be earned.' I smiled. 'Another time perhaps?'

'Monsieur can always be assured of . . . a warm welcome,' they said.

Chapter Twenty

Deauville was a network of wide avenues with imposing slate-roofed, white stucco villas set back amongst the pines and Scotch firs flourishing on the sandy soil. Striped bathing tents lined the beach and there were still a few wheeled machines that could be pushed into shallow water so that the more prudish ladies could open the door and walk straight down the steps into the sea without having to suffer the scrutiny of the vulgar as they minced across the strand. The casino looked like a huge wedding cake. There was an area of flat grassland near the racecourse that was going one day to become a small aerodrome; a diminutive clubhouse and a large canvas hangar – probably salvaged from a wartime field in 1918 – already stood behind a line of half a dozen spidery private planes.

The hotel Mado had booked me into was on the seafront. My room looked out over the promenade – elderly gents in Panama hats and alpaca jackets, groups of young sports in blazers and straw boaters ogling the strolling flappers with their short skirts and cloche hats, widows in deck chairs cocooned in steamer rugs . . . and below the lifebelts hooked to the railings, the swarming, screaming, gambolling life of the beach. To add a touch of class, pretty girls with parasols patrolled the front from time to time in open, horse-drawn *calèches*.

Madame Laverne and her chief *vendeuse* were installed in the Majestic, a turreted hotel with its own nine-hole golf course a little way out of town on the road to Trouville. Perhaps Mado wished to keep as much distance as possible between herself and the mansion rented by Ahmed Simbel, which was just behind the casino.

I hired a *calèche* myself to drive out to the Majestic for my first briefing. The briefing was extensive and very thorough. I took ten pages of notes. God knows where Mado quarried out all that intelligence on the layout and intimate habits of the Simbel entourage. Perhaps a lot more folks had climbed the spiral staircase than I imagined.

I caught sight of Solange in the writing room as I made my way down from Mado's suite. As my own mission — to which I looked forward not at all — must necessarily take place during the hours of darkness, I reckoned it would be safe to make an afternoon date. We agreed to meet on the beach at three o'clock.

It was sunny, but a bit blustery. Puffballs of white cloud scudded across the sky. The waves rolling in were small, but at least they curled over and broke into foam before they flooded up the sand. It was almost low tide and there were four or five lines of them.

Solange insisted that we hire one of the old-fashioned bathing machines. They were small and square, shaped like a telephone box with a pitched roof of asphalt. They were made of wood, with no windows but a door opening outwards on the side facing the sea, and they sat on a chassis with four very wide iron wheels – wide so they wouldn't sink into the sand. Why they were called machines, I don't know, because they had to be manoeuvered down to the waterline, either manually or drawn by a horse. When they were in place and the door was opened, a short wooden ladder could be let down and the occupants stepped into the water – usually about knee-depth.

I suppose they were about nine or ten feet high inside. And cramped – because the floor couldn't have been more than a yard and a half square, with a narrow bench seat spanning the back and a couple of hooks for clothes on the wall. Having crossed the beach to get there I could understand why women preferred them to the tents below the promenade. Because if the fashion world was producing elegant, chic clothes for morning, afternoon and evening, the beach-wear that year was God-awful. Women's bathing suits were made of some kind of cotton that clung but had no body to it. The colours, often edged with white, were drab, the garments round-necked, short-sleeved and half-skirted back and front. And if I say the material had no body, that wasn't the case with the females wearing it: they had too much, of the wrong kind. Once those shapeless, clinging bathing suits were wet, all breasts looked flabby and dropped; stomachs, webbed with creases, protruded; bottoms drooped and most knees looked skinny. I could absolutely understand why the wearers didn't want to be looked at. The men weren't much better off either. The average male costume, in the same limp material, sported legs that came halfway down the thigh and a top, often striped, with a round neckline and wide shoulder straps. If a fellow was at all well endowed, by the time he came out of the sea the sagging lower half of his suit looked as if there was a bullfrog squatting between his thighs.

It wasn't as gymnastic or acrobatic as that ridiculous nonsense of writhing out of one's clothes in public beneath a towelling beach robe or even a raincoat, but Solange and I came to pretty close quarters when we stripped. So much so that I had willy-nilly touched her up enough to provoke a fairly stout erection on myself. My willy in fact was anything but nilly.

She hauled her bathing suit up over her hips, thrust her arms into the rudimentary sleeves and flattened her pretty breasts. I had got mine up as far as my waist when she turned around and brushed her hip against the part of me leaning most avidly in her direction. 'Oh, my,' she exclaimed, 'what *do* we have here . . . and why?' She rubbed the back of her hand – deliberately this time – up and down the prominence, causing the compass needle to make a more pronounced swing in a northerly direction.

'Since you mention it,' I said, 'and since I am reliably informed that there is no time like the present . . .'

I took her by the hips, spun her around so that she was facing the door, with her back to me. And wrenched the costume down again, past arms and breasts, over the hips and bottom, and halfway to the knees.

' . . . and since clearly,' I continued, 'there is no place like a bathing machine . . . well, I conclude that the best thing for you to do, my love, is to lean forward – yes, right forward like that – with your hands supporting you, one on either side of the door, and see what fate has in store for you.' Solange had drawn in her breath sharply when I dragged down her costume. Now, with her weight on her hands, she spread her legs slightly and started a very slow, highly provocative rotation of the hips, crooning softly to herself as the whole hairy cleft between her trim buttocks moved slightly under my lascivious gaze. Among the dark hairs, a sliver of pink, already dewed with a pearl of moisture, gleamed palely.

My own bathing costume was now around my ankles. I took a pace forward – that is to say, in that confined space I moved maybe eight or nine inches (just enough, as it happens, to touch her with the throbbing tip of my stiffened shaft). And I seized her slender hips, pulling them back towards me as I lunged forward and slid my whole hot length into her welcoming pussy.

What bliss! What a joy! My nerves trembled with ecstasy as warm flesh clasped around my cock and we began that dazed and delirious mutual rocking that has no beginning and no end but only the timeless, easy pulse of reciprocal motion, meeting, parting, sliding, stopping, but always and endlessly mounting, climbing towards that point of no return that lies at the end of imagined time.

As the tension increased, we rocked faster. I thrust into her harder; she backed up more fiercely to meet my plunges. The space in the cabin was cramped, especially as her position brought her hips more than halfway to the back wall, but we were sublimely unaware of the geographical disadvantage. I began withdrawing almost the entire length of my glistening staff on each stroke, until only the very tip remained sucked by those entrancing lips. But now my own backside smacked each time against the wooden wall before I slammed forward again to let her have the whole hard shaft in a single forceful shove, neat as a sword stabbed into its scabbard.

Solange gasped aloud, her entire frame shaken each time I lunged into her quivering loins.

I'll never know whether it was the repeated impact of my buttocks against that wall, some wayward vibration that our exertions had started, or maybe even that skylarking youths — alerted perhaps by the stifled cries of our lust — actually pushed. Whatever it was, the bathing machine suddenly started to move.

At that point, not far from the low-water mark, the beach shelved slightly beneath the incoming tide. The wheels beneath our floor rolled over the sun-hardened sand, the machine gathered way, and we trundled a very small distance out to sea.

No special problem there . . . not until one of the front wheels struck a submerged stone, halting the machine abruptly in its tracks. The shock threw Solange forward. The door burst open, and she spilled out — plunging, naked from the knees upward, into four feet of sea water among a troupe of schoolgirls playing volleyball.

That sudden, whisked withdrawal was a shock for me too. An instant later, caught on the forward stroke and hobbled by the costume around my ankles, I flew out after her, an empurpled erection jetting skywards my milky tribute to her vanished charms.

Chapter Twenty-One

I had agreed with Mado that it would be best to allow a couple of days racing to go by before I made my attempt on the Lebanese couturier's oriental design. By this time he would have been well settled in at Deauville and – hopefully – less edgy and suspicious than usual. In the event it was a wise decision: he had placed a huge each-way bet on his own horse in the Prix de Rouen, and it had come in third. The night I had decided on, he was hosting a huge celebration party at the casino – but the lady guardian at whose virtue I was supposed to be aiming would not be there: expensive parties were for expensive, and therefore important, people: the hired help stayed home to look after the assets.

Even though the boss's part of the rented mansion would be empty, however, I remained a prey to the greatest misgivings. Mado might consider it priceless that the idea of a girl seducing me in order to steal something should be trumped by the conceit of my seducing a different girl for a similar reason, but in fact the situations were in no way parallel. Arguably, a man finding a sexy girl unexpectedly in his apartment, even in his bed, might spend a little time – as I had – exploring the possibilities. But a woman discovering a man under the same conditions would be much more likely to yell for the local constabulary. And the sexier he looked, the louder she'd yell.

Again, I could hardly walk up to the front door, ring the bell, and say, 'Excuse me — I've come to seduce the wardrobe mistress.'

In Paris, anyone could press the button to release the outer door and walk up the stairs to my studio without seeing, or being seen by, a soul. Even the old concierge was usually having a gossip somewhere instead of peering through the window of her office.

But here there were two sets of doors, a glassed-in porch, a butler, servants that came with the house and people on Simbel's own staff (Mado's brief was thorough). The only entry I could make without alerting the whole bang shoot was a burglarious one. Here again the briefing had been all-encompassing; nothing seemed to have been left out. But that didn't mean I was looking forward to the exercise.

So far as I was concerned, the only plus point was the fact that the place was rented — usually by the month; rarely, perhaps in the summer, for three months at a time. This meant, however many servants there were, that at least there would be no resident guard dogs patrolling the grounds, avid for a mouthful of intruder's meat.

Did I say the grounds? Stretching away behind the casino, they seemed to embrace half the municipality of Deauville — orchards, lawns, shrubberies, a sunken Dutch garden, rose walks, even a small lake. My approach would be through a walled kitchen garden and then, via an ancient cedar tree and a palm growing against the house, to a sloping roof from which a second-floor balcony could be reached. No more than fifteen feet of a narrow ledge separated the balustrade of this from another outside my quarry's room. Nothing that a twenty-year-old Olympic athlete trained from the age of seven couldn't do with one hand tied behind him.

I won't go into details. In any case, as so often happens with tasks that seem insurmountable, when it came down to it, the thing was surprisingly easy (my briefing, as I said, had been thorough). The only thing obstructing my entry was a spiny bush – possibly a gooseberry? – which tore the sleeve of my jacket as I stole through the kitchen garden. The only thing that was physically difficult to do was traverse that dashed ledge. Fifteen feet isn't a great distance if it's the width of a hallway or the space between the wheel and the stern of a motor launch. The story is different, however, when it's the length of a string-course – a three-inch-wide strip of projecting brickwork – separating two balconies at second-floor level. When it has to be crossed face to the wall, with no handholds, the weight on the balls of the feet and the stomach knotted cold with incipient vertigo. And of course when it's pitch dark and the moon's somewhere over Tasmania.

The drop was only about thirty feet, but the bed at the foot of the wall was planted with standard roses and yuccas with razor-sharp leaves: not the kind of bed to encourage a dreamless sleep.

The night seemed awfully long, and the profession of fashion artist – especially one working for Mado Laverne – particularly precarious as I inched along that narrow ledge. I was afraid the thumping of my heart would crack the stucco cladding the wall of the house.

The place was built in a shallow vee, with a square tower housing the entrance, stairways, etc, separating the two wings. The far wing – Simbel's – was dark; the one I was burgling appeared to be a hive of activity. I could hear voices, a piano tinkling somewhere below, a wireless set unexpectedly crackling with English from a broadcast on the far side of the channel. Light escaped between drawn curtains or through the slats of shutters closed over windows at my level and higher up. It was just after midnight.

The air was warm, but my forehead was beaded with cold perspiration by the time I had negotiated thirteen of those fifteen feet and flung myself desperately sideways to grab the consoling stone rim of the balcony balustrade. It seemed a long time, again, before I could summon up enough extra strength to haul myself up and over, then lower myself to the tiled floor.

The balcony was wide. So far as I could make out in the dim reflected light there were three iron chairs set around a table beneath a folded parasol at the far end. The French windows were dark; I had the impression that there were drawn curtains behind them. No light showed. I moved cautiously forward. According to my brief, the lady who was unknowingly to be my hostess never bothered to lock them, sometimes they were not even latched (with her talents, I reflected, Mado should set up a detective agency).

A couple of yards from the windows, my shin struck some kind of low stool I hadn't noticed. A sharp pain flamed up my leg to my knee. I gasped aloud. One of the stool's iron legs scraped loudly across the tiles.

Reckless Liaisons

I bit my lip, holding my breath. Here was one operative too damned clumsy to hold down a job with the Laverne Detective Agency!

No windows were flung open. Nobody shouted. There was music on the wireless now. Finally I stole the remaining distance to the French windows. They *were* unlocked too. And unlatched. Millimetre by millimetre I pressed down the handle. The door section swung inwards; the frame brushed against a heavy curtain, lifting it slightly. Noiselessly this time, I slipped through.

Bright light seared my eyeballs. I was squinting across a bedroom at a woman in a négligée who stood with her hand on a light switch. 'My goodness,' she drawled, 'still ninety shopping days to Christmas, and look what Santa brought me already . . .'

My mouth had opened with shock and surprise at the unexpected dazzle. It stayed open. Even when the eyes had adjusted to the brilliance.

The woman was perhaps forty years old. Maybe even forty-five. Her dark hair, longer than was fashionable, was coiled into a bun — a *chignon* — on the nape of her neck. She was wearing thick-lensed spectacles behind which eyes of myopic blue blinked. Her nose was large, her chin determined, the wide mouth separating them loose-lipped. Good old Mado, I thought. A real stunner. And, no, I wasn't going to be run in for interfering with a minor!

The open mouth was because after that first impression I looked further down.

She had the most beautiful, the most perfect body I had seen in my life.

I'm not exaggerating: forget the face; the rest was

exquisite. Even her neck was pure poetry. It flowed into shoulders as smooth and well-sculpted as those of your actual Greek goddess. And as for the breasts . . . well, what can I say? They were full without being heavy, not dropped in the slightest, set fairly wide apart and clearly both taut and resilient. Nobody could look at them without wanting to touch. Her waist was slender, her belly flat, the hips trim and compact and the thighs and calves tapering with just that amount of elegance that causes a man to hold his breath.

Eventually I had to let mine out and take in some more. What the *hell* was I going to say? Caught *in flagrante*, the moment I broke in! Excuses would be worse than useless. There could be no explanation. Brazen it out, I decided, and then play it by ear. The négligée, diaphanous enough for me to have made the observations recorded above, was my lead-in. What the hell! 'I see you've been waiting for me,' I said inanely, with a leer in its direction.

'All my life,' the woman said.

To put it mildly, this was not the reaction — or the reply — that I expected. Even uttered with heavy sarcasm, those words would scarcely be credible in the context of an unknown intruder surprised breaking into a woman's room at midnight. But they didn't sound sarcastic. Or even ironic. They were spoken in the kind of tone one party guest might use to another after a few drinks if there was a hint of attraction between them — the sort of half-mocking, half-humorous approach that used to be called raillery. I mean . . . well, it sounds absurd, but for a moment I almost believed she actually *meant* it.

I was still staring. The négligée was expensive, probably part of a set including a nightdress of the same material. If it was, the nightie was either on a hanger, in the wash or still in the bottom drawer, for it was clear the woman was naked underneath. The negligée was floor-length, frilled down the front, loose-sleeved and fashioned from some filmy, oyster-coloured voile that only partly concealed her superb body. The light came from a crystal chandelier in the centre of the ceiling, casting soft shadows beneath the curves of flesh veiled by that sexy garment, emphasising the firm jut of breasts, the subtle swell of belly, the cushioned hips. Dark circles tipping the breasts were clearly visible, together with a smoky haze of pubic hair triangled between her thighs.

'Well, say something,' my target urged. 'Even if it's only hello.'

I swallowed. 'I . . . don't know what to say,' I stammered.

'Presumably you're here for a reason? I mean you didn't just happen to take the wrong turning, leaving the square: you must have intended to come. But you don't look like a burglar — where's the black mask and the striped jersey, the holdall marked with the word "Swag"? I cannot believe, either, that you are a rapist after my virtue — not with a face like mine.'

I couldn't allow myself to pass up an opening like that.

'That's it,' I said quickly. 'It was the only way I could think of, the only possibility of seeing you alone. Paulette,' — Mado had told me her name — 'I've wanted desperately to meet you ever since I first saw you, sitting outside the café, on the . . . yes, on the beach in a bathing costume.'

'Bollocks!' she said in English. 'I haven't left this house since I arrived the day before yesterday. Anyway, I know perfectly well that I look like the back of a bus.'

She was looking at me very directly. I dragged my gaze away from the body and glanced at the face for the second time. It was true that she wasn't exactly what the Yanks call cover-girl material. But even with those strong, rather coarse features . . . I stared more closely. And then I got it.

I got two things, to be precise. Number One, she was fishing; even with a total stranger who could be a burglar she was fishing for a compliment; she was conscious of the discrepancy between face and body, she was agonisingly aware of it, and she wanted to be told she *didn't* look like the back of a bus. Number Two – why hadn't I seen this before? – Number Two was the combination of myopic eyes behind thick lenses, a full lower lip that glistened, and very slightly projecting front teeth, the two centre ones larger than the rest.

Of course! Paulette was no problem; she was a *type*. And a type I was familiar with. In my own private tally, since we're talking numbers, it would have been Number Seven, Number Eleven – or was it Twelve? – and could have been Number Twenty-Seven if a Dutch sea captain hadn't read the signs and got in first. Each of them proved a point *I'd* checked time and again with other chaps: short-sighted girls with bee-stung lower lips and projecting top teeth were invariably crazy for it . . . nymphos, in fact.

As an extra check, I lowered my gaze a few inches.

Yes — her nipples were outlined against the stuff of the négligée. Hard and thrusting.

For the first time since I was surprised by the light, I moved forward into the room. Turkish carpet, wide brass bedstead with silk sheets, dressing-table with wing mirrors, inlaid *art-nouveau* wardrobe and commode. And, visible through a half-open door, an anteroom stacked with bales of richly-coloured materials.

Right. I reckoned I knew my way now. That Mado Laverne! She must have known, or she would never have suggested this particular caper. Devious bitch!

'If I *had* seen you sitting at a café — or, even better, in a bathing costume,' I said to Paulette, 'I'd have been here yesterday.'

Behind the spectacles, the blue eyes brimmed with brightness; the mouth was half open, those teeth visible, the lower lip still glistening. 'You're beautiful,' I said. 'You're absolutely stunning.'

Momentarily, the lips pursed as she half hid a smile. But she wasn't going to ask any more questions; she was going to take it from here. I'd read the signs right and given the correct password. I was home and dry. Well, home anyway.

We had been moving closer together, as if drawn by a slow-motion magnet. She stopped about a foot away and stood looking up at me, the shoulders slightly hunched, the head tilted well back, the way women stand when they expect to be kissed within the next ten seconds.

My mistake. There was one more question. 'You're a good-looking boy,' she said huskily. 'You're not queer? You're not a pansy, are you?'

I shook my head. 'My name's not Laurence either.'

'*Pardon*?'

'A private joke. Excuse me. I should be happy, very happy indeed, to prove to you – to have the opportunity to prove to you – that I am no liar. Nothing, in fact, would give me greater pleasure,' I said, emboldened by the lack of any kind of rebuff.

The dusky négligée was beginning to rise and fall a little at breast level. 'Really?' she said.

'Really. I would hope,' I dared to add, 'that any doubts you might have concerning my relationship with the opposite sex could be speedily removed to your . . . er . . . satisfaction. I think, granted that permission was given, that I could do that.'

She was looking down now, her eyes focusing on a point between my hips. 'So I see,' she said.

That was when I reached out my arms, pulled her towards me and kissed her.

Some things turn sour on you, others go like anything right from the start. The former, often enough, are those to which you were specially looking forward – the ones where hopes ran high. My first encounter with Janine, for example. The others, conversely and perversely, are frequently the kind you were hating the very idea of. My night with Paulette was like that. After that frightening start, it turned into a wonderful dream.

I knew it was going to be all right from the very first instant that gorgeous, resilient body melted against me. I knew I had read the signs right the moment our tongues touched. Sexual chemistry is fired by a touch of magic, there's no doubt about it. And that night

Paulette played witch to my wizard.

At first I was quite happy to stand there, allowing that marvellous sensation of well-being spiced with anticipation and excitement to flood over me. Cool hands cupped the back of my head; my rigid cock pressed into a pliant curve of belly; the clinging weight of those breasts leaned firmly against my chest as my arms tightened around Paulette's slender waist.

We kissed slowly, passionately, for a long time, as if every possible combination of lips and tongue and teeth must be explored before the next step was taken, as if each successive thrill must be savoured to the full and not a fraction of sensation wasted. She was breathing very hard, and I realised that this was one of those women for whom every tiniest touch of a man's hand, any man's hand, was enough to set the blood singing.

Finally, almost of their own volition, my hands began to move, sending her smooth back arching against me, sculpting through that gauzy material the hollow curve of the waist, feeling at last the taut and fleshy curve of breasts. Through the swathes of voile, the stiffened nipples were hot against my palms.

I don't recall the unfastening of my jacket, or how it was pushed back over my shoulders and slid down my arms to the floor. She was unbuttoning my shirt, fingertips teasing my own hardened nipples. I was bare to the waist, my hands clasped over the delirious swell of Paulette's buttocks. Our genitals ground together through the stuff of our lower garments, though neither had yet been touched, as they say, by human hand. Were we still kissing?

Perhaps not, for suddenly, unbuckling the belt at my

Reckless Liaisons

waist, she said quite simply, a little breathlessly: 'I think I would like to lie down.'

On the bed, our lovemaking pursued its inexorable, subtly restrained but heartstopping course. Each of us was exquisitely aware, with each slow burning caress, of the further tingling delights to which it could, to which it must lead.

Now I let her lead. My fly was undone; I smoothed aside a swathe of négligée to expose a satin stretch of thigh. I felt exploring fingers reach inside and a shiver shot through my loins as my scrotum was touched; in turn I sensed a shudder of expectation as the heel of my hand rested on her mons.

Then . . . Ah, then! That was the time the intruding hand groped . . . and touched . . . and explored, and finally grasped the throbbing staff of my desire and pulled it *slowly* out into the open. I felt the cool air zephyr-smooth on the heated, distended skin. My palm swivelled and my fingers traced the double outline of sexual lips through the diaphanous négligée. Paulette's hips jerked and she uttered a low sound that was almost a groan. The fingers wrapped tightly around me and started the slow massage that always had the heart hammering and the pulses racing in my wrists. My own fingers started a leisurely promenade up and down, gently, gently stroking the delicate cushions of flesh that I could feel.

We kept the preliminaries, the foreplay, going a long time. What the hell, there was no taxi waiting for me outside; I had my own key and there was nobody to scold if I came home with the milk. We caressed, we sucked, we squeezed, we chewed. We licked and gobbled and tongued up to the very moment when the precipice yawned and one more movement would send us plunging over. And that's where Paulette's expertise – the result, no doubt, of long experience – was invaluable. As a finger pressed hard to the upper lip just below the nose can stifle a sneeze, her little pressure tricks – there were several of them – turned on the red light and lowered the tension in that last fraction of a second before the wave of orgasm broke and carried us away.

There was no question, when it came to the final stage, of a decision having to be taken, a definitive, overt move being made. It just happened.

I was supporting myself on one arm, half leaning over her. My trousers had vanished long ago. My free hand was cupped over her crotch, the middle finger deeply sunk into the hungry wet depths of her vagina. As the tip manoeuvered the hypersensitive button of flesh at its outer edge, causing her to arch up off the bed with small mews of delight, she milked the slippery, lubricated shaft of my cock with practised ease.

I had opened up the négligée so that the whole nude length of her body was stretched out below me; I was staring at the firmly swelling mounds of her breasts, reddened now around the nipples from the continuous sucking and the fondling manipulations of my hands. And then slowly I raised my eyes to meet her misty gaze (the spectacles too were long gone). The flesh of the eyes crinkled at the outer corners. She smiled – a wide, salacious curving of those loose lips that sucked with such agonising skill.

It was a smile of infinite complicity. She shifted her

legs slightly, canting her pelvis to reveal the darkly glistening opening amongst the thatch of moist pubic hair. I took my hand away, rolling over her to sink down between her thighs. She spread her legs wide, drawing up the knees . . . and all at once, with no conscious effort on my part or hers, I was inside her, the entire hard length of my lusting stem in the hot clasp of her inner flesh.

After that I was lost in a world of sensation. It was all sliding and honey-smooth, it was easy and glowing, dilation and contraction, with her thighs clamped around my waist and the heels crossed on the base of my spine as I lunged and withdrew in a dreamlike daze.

Her arms wrapped around my shoulders; I held her face between my two hands and kissed her frenziedly, sucking her tongue up between my teeth. I reached between our straining bodies to part the warm lips of her cunt and feel my wet stiffness shafting between them. Her nails raked my back and she groaned aloud.

Relentlessly, ineluctably, the excitement gripping us increased, the tension heightened, the sliding became a plunging, accelerated to a pounding, and at last reached that point of no return when the quickened breath stoked up such a powerful surge of nervous elation that there was nothing to do but let the floodgates open and go with it . . .

It seemed a long time later — I was still lying on top of her and my suddenly opened eyes fell on the anteroom door, which was still ajar — that I remembered what I was supposed to be here for.

I pushed the thought away, but Paulette, playing the telepathic witch again perhaps, picked it out of the air and whispered: 'And now, my Paul, delightful, *wonderful* though that was, perhaps you will tell me why you really broke into my bedroom in the middle of the night?'

I told her. The hell with it. She'd been absolutely topping; I wasn't going to do a Rosette on her, however priceless Mado might think it, and betray her confidence. I told her the whole sad story. 'I came to "borrow" something and then put it back – in a word temporarily to steal it,' I began. 'But if I'd known you first I'd have come anyway. Earlier in the evening.'

'You mean you wanted that stuff brought by the Indian prince or whatever he was?' she asked when I'd finished. 'But there's a whole bolt of it, yards and yards. It's not just an *échantillon*, a sample. You'd never have got away with it; you'd have had to cut a piece off. And I can do that for you.'

I stared at her. 'You mean you . . . ? But what about your boss? Won't he notice? I don't want to get you into any trouble—'

'The hell with him,' she interrupted. 'Even if he did notice, I'll have *no* idea what could *possibly* have happened. It must have been while I was in the garden.'

'You sound as if you don't like him very much.'

'He's a poisonous little man. He pays well, but he's a ghastly snob and he treats us, the employees, like shit.' She eased herself out from under me, wrapped the négligée around her, took a pair of scissors from the dressing-table, kissed me on the cheek and went into the anteroom.

Five minutes later she was back with a strip of cloth. The pattern was certainly striking. Stunning, even. The oriental motifs were worked in a combination of gold and crimson, with occasional accents of peacock blue and a background of extraordinary, luminous dark green. I could visualise it at once in a whole range of the kind of clothes Mado created. Fortunately the repeat was quite small, and it worked from side to side as well as from top to bottom. Two or three hours work in a good light should allow me to make a copy accurate enough to satisfy Mado – and, more importantly, the silk screen experts and printers who would transform it into dress materials.

Paulette rolled up the strip tightly and stuffed it into the pocket of my jacket. Bright light from the chandelier still bathed the room. She switched on a low-powered pink bedside lamp and killed the overhead dazzle.

'You're sure he hasn't measured the bolt inch by inch?' I said awkwardly. 'I mean, I'd hate you to—'

'Don't even think about it,' Paulette cut in. 'Just be sure to burn the strip once you've got what you need.'

'It's very generous . . . I mean . . . I don't know how to thank you,' I said lamely.

'I'll show you,' Paulette said. She piled pillows against the head of the bed and settled herself against them. The négligée was wrapped tightly around her, but the belt was not tied. A deep vee separated the edges above the waist and two slopes of warm breast – one with a crescent of darker flesh visible – swelled within it. I was still naked.

She patted the bedcover beside her. 'You'll have to leave before daylight,' she said. 'But that's not for at least a couple of hours. Come and tell me more about yourself.'

Most nymphos are frigid in the clinical, medical sense of the term. That is to say they're hot as hell for sex — but they never come, they're incapable of reaching orgasm, which is why they're always crazy for more, hoping, I guess, that next time may be The One. Paulette was nympho all right, but the rest of the definition didn't fit at all: she came all over the shop, and still wanted more.

Maybe it was just enthusiasm in her case.

All I know is that my autobiography never got off the ground. Instead we re-set the board and began for the second time the moves in our private bodily chess game. Only this time the cautious advances of bishops and knights were dispensed with, the castles had already been stormed, and my king made a bee-line for her queen.

I don't know, in the long run, whether you could say there was a check involved. But it was certainly mate.

EPILOGUE

Paris, October 1922

Paul

I was at what Tom Crawford would no doubt call a loose end. There was no-one, that is to say, who was sharing my bed or my *bitte*.

Solange had been offered a marvellous job with American *Vogue* and – with regrets on both sides – had left for the pleasures of New York. Francoise was fighting off eager suitors every time she showed Mado Laverne's creations in the *salon* above the Rue des Capucines. Mado herself was working day and night on her new Collection. She had advanced the date of the show by ten days, so that she could be certain of beating Ahmed Simbel to the post with a whole series of designs based on the oriental sample I had obtained for her – just as the crooked Lebanese had beaten her with the designs Rosette stole from my studio. Now it would be Simbel's turn to gnash teeth and re-design an entire show.

So far as my other recent conquests were concerned, Eve was back in Germany, Janine was going to marry – a lion-tamer, I imagined – and before I left Deauville I had seen Paulette with Crawford, Bertrand Laforge, Hans Bohl and half a dozen other mashers... apparently violently in love with each of them.

I sat with Bertrand in the Deux Magots, drinking a

fine à l'eau and bewailing my carnal fate. Outside the steamy windows, rain bounced high off the sidewalk and swashed in waves from the wheels of passing buses and taxis. 'Cheer up,' Bertrand said, clapping me on the shoulder. 'There'll be another party at Dagmar's soon.'

I nodded gloomily. 'I know — but it's not the same.'

Soon afterwards, Bertrand left to take an oil-man from Houston, Texas, for a demonstration run in one of his father's limousines.

It was late afternoon. I had delivered the final gouaches illustrating the Laverne Collection to the *Gazette du Bon Ton* and *Modes et Manières d'Aujourd'hui*. The evening stretched emptily ahead.

I looked around the café. Most of the tables were empty too. The shopgirl contingent and the secretaries and typists from offices were still at work. The only possibility was a young woman with a very short blonde Eton crop, who was sitting alone at a table in the far corner. She was smoking a cigarette in a long ebony holder. From time to time she picked up a pencil to make a notation on a sheaf of typescript lying beside her coffee cup. She could have been a student, or even a teacher correcting papers.

I looked more closely. I could see, beneath the table, that she had pretty legs. There was a wet mackintosh draped over the back of her chair, so it looked as if she might be staying a while. She wore a black jersey with a high neck, and — Yes, by Jove! I could see now that she leaned back to a blow a plume of smoke into the air — she was sporting a magnificent pair of breasts. I don't just mean well-shaped; I'm not talking about firmness. These were both of those things. But they were *huge*.

When she leaned forward again they were practically resting on the table.

I sipped my drink, pondering. Had I been mistaken, thinking I saw a repressed smile when she noticed that I was looking at her with undisguised admiration? Easy, Mackenzie: don't rush things. Clearly, it would be fatal to attempt to make any kind of contact now, to interrupt whatever fool thing it was that she was doing. Wait until the precise moment that she gathered the papers together and prepared to leave: that would be the time to strike. But it would have to be speedy. And I would need to be adroit.

Perhaps, if the timing was perfect, a small, contrived lurch against her table on the way to the bar?

Oh, *excuse* me . . . My God, how clumsy can one be? . . . Mademoiselle, I'm so *sorry*: look, I've knocked your papers . . . Do let me pick them up for you. Forgive me, that was unpardonably gauche . . . At least permit me to offer you an apéritif . . .

It might work. If I could carry it off convincingly. While I waited, stealing a glance at her from time to time, I checked off my personal scorecard once more.

Not counting you-know-who, Desirée-Rosette, I remembered, had been Number Forty-One. Mado was already on the list and I don't count professionals, however desirable. That left Françoise of the magic touch in the forty-second spot. Number Forty-Three, when finally I got next to her at Dagmar's party, was the hippy, cockteasing Janine. My lovely, adventurous, super-sexy, now lost Solange was at forty-four.

I hadn't actually made love to Dagmar van den Bergh's lesbian friend, although she had, so to speak, helped me with the Comtesse herself — but Dagmar and I had first been in the same bed together years ago. So that left the strangely prudish Nounou, with Mado's assistance in the Bois de Boulogne, at forty-five. And Mother Eve in our Fontainebleau Eden at forty-six.

Dagmar's warmly welcoming maidservants in the Avenue Kléber, and lastly Paulette in Deauville, brought the card up to date.

Forty-nine exactly.

Tom Crawford was standing by my table. He was holding an English newspaper. 'Drinking alone, old man?' he asked. 'With a spiffing blonde piece equipped with the most monumental charlies sitting all by herself over in the corner?'

'It had not escaped my attention,' I said. 'Arrangements are . . . under way.' I stole another look. This time the girl definitely glanced up. Message received and understood? I hoped so.

'That's my boy,' said Tom. 'Knew I could rely on one of the Knights.' He held up the paper. 'Have you seen the news?'

'The news?'

'The news from New Zealand, where else? The Test Match. England are 416 for 6. What about that!'

'Oh,' I said. 'Cricket.' I flicked one more glance at Mademoiselle.

'Actually, I was hoping to make the half-century myself before close of play.'

More Erotic Fiction from Headline:

Lustful Liaisons

Erotic adventures in the capital city of love!

Anonymous

PARIS 1912 – a city alive with the pursuit of pleasure, from the promenade of the Folies Bergère to the high-class brothels of the Left Bank. Everywhere business is booming in the oldest trade of all – the trade of love!

But now there is a new and flourishing activity to absorb the efforts of go-ahead men-about-town: the business of manufacturing motor cars. Men like Robert and Bertrand Laforge are pioneers in this field but their new automobile has a design defect that can only be rectified by some cunning industrial espionage. Which is where the new trade marries with the old, for the most reliable way of discovering information is to enlist the help of a lovely and compliant woman. A woman, for example, like the voluptuous Nellie Lebérigot whose soft creamy flesh and generous nature are guaranteed to uncover a man's most closely guarded secrets...

More titillating reading from Headline:
AMOROUS LIAISONS
LOVE ITALIAN STYLE
ECSTASY ITALIAN STYLE
EROTICON DREAMS
EROTICON DESIRES

FICTION/EROTICA　0 7472 3710 7

Headline Delta Erotic Survey

In order to provide the kind of books you like to read - and to qualify for a free erotic novel of the Editor's choice - we would appreciate it if you would complete the following survey and send your answers, together with any further comments, to:

    Headline Book Publishing
    FREEPOST 9 (WD 4984)
    London
    W1E 7BE

1. Are you male or female?
2. Age? Under 20 / 20 to 30 / 30 to 40 / 40 to 50 / 50 to 60 / 60 to 70 / over
3. At what age did you leave full-time education?
4. Where do you live? (Main geographical area)
5. Are you a regular erotic book buyer / a regular book buyer in general / both?
6. How much approximately do you spend a year on erotic books / on books in general?
7. How did you come by this book?
7a. If you bought it, did you purchase from: a national bookchain / a high street store / a newsagent / a motorway station / an airport / a railway station / other........
8. Do you find erotic books easy / hard to come by?
8a. Do you find Headline Delta erotic books easy / hard to come by?
9. Which are the best / worst erotic books you have ever read?
9a. Which are the best / worst Headline Delta erotic books you have ever read?
10. Within the erotic genre there are many periods, subjects and literary styles. Which of the following do you prefer:
10a. (period) historical / Victorian / C20th / contemporary / future?
10b. (subject) nuns / whores & whorehouses / Continental frolics / s&m / vampires / modern realism / escapist fantasy / science fiction?

10c. (styles) hardboiled / humorous / hardcore / ironic / romantic / realistic?

10d. Are there any other ingredients that particularly appeal to you?

11. We try to create a cover appearance that is suitable for each title. Do you consider them to be successful?

12. Would you prefer them to be less explicit / more explicit?

13. We would be interested to hear of your other reading habits. What other types of books do you read?

14. Who are your favourite authors?

15. Which newspapers do you read?

16. Which magazines?

17. Do you have any other comments or suggestions to make?

If you would like to receive a free erotic novel of the Editor's choice (available only to UK residents), together with an up-to-date listing of Headline Delta titles, please supply your name and address:

Name..

Address...

....

....

A selection of Erotica from Headline

FONDLE ALL OVER	Nadia Adamant	£4.99 ☐
LUST ON THE LOOSE	Noel Amos	£4.99 ☐
GROUPIES	Johnny Angelo	£4.99 ☐
PASSION IN PARADISE	Anonymous	£4.99 ☐
THE ULTIMATE EROS COLLECTION	Anonymous	£6.99 ☐
EXPOSED	Felice Ash	£4.99 ☐
SIN AND MRS SAXON	Lesley Asquith	£4.99 ☐
HIGH JINKS HALL	Erica Boleyn	£4.99 ☐
TWO WEEKS IN MAY	Maria Caprio	£4.99 ☐
THE PHALLUS OF OSIRIS	Valentina Cilescu	£4.99 ☐
NUDE RISING	Faye Rossignol	£4.99 ☐
AMOUR AMOUR	Marie-Claire Villefranche	£4.99 ☐

All Headline books are available at your local bookshop or newsagent, or can be ordered direct from the publisher. Just tick the titles you want and fill in the form below. Prices and availability subject to change without notice.

Headline Book Publishing PLC, Cash Sales Department, Bookpoint, 39 Milton Park, Abingdon, OXON, OX14 4TD, UK. If you have a credit card you may order by telephone – 0235 831700.

Please enclose a cheque or postal order made payable to Bookpoint Ltd to the value of the cover price and allow the following for postage and packing:
UK & BFPO: £1.00 for the first book, 50p for the second book and 30p for each additional book ordered up to a maximum charge of £3.00.
OVERSEAS & EIRE: £2.00 for the first book, £1.00 for the second book and 50p for each additional book.

Name ....

Address ....

....

....

If you would prefer to pay by credit card, please complete:
Please debit my Visa/Access/Diner's Card/American Express (delete as applicable) card no:

Signature .... Expiry Date ....